Lost Sheep

A novel by

Bettie Anne Doebler

PublishAmerica
Baltimore

© 2007 by Bettie Anne Doebler.

All rights reserved. No part of this book may be reproduced, stored in a retrieval system or transmitted in any form or by any means without the prior written permission of the publishers, except by a reviewer who may quote brief passages in a review to be printed in a newspaper, magazine or journal.

First printing

All characters in this book are fictitious, and any resemblance to real persons, living or dead, is coincidental.

ISBN: 1-4241-9826-7
PUBLISHED BY PUBLISHAMERICA, LLLP
www.publishamerica.com
Baltimore

Printed in the United States of America

Acknowledgments

Special thanks go to Thelma Richard for her labor of friendship in editing my manuscript and correcting its inconsistencies. Needless to say, whatever errors that remain are my responsibility. I should also like to thank my friend Barbara Levy for reading and commenting upon several sections.

On a broader level I should like to thank my dear son Mark, his wife Kimberley, and my granddaughter Hanna for giving me the support of family life during the time of writing the novel.

My appreciation goes to all the libraries, galleries, and museums that I have had the privilege of working in during my academic career, but especially the Bodleian Library in Oxford. The gateway to the human past provided by such places give to us a sense of connection that is more invaluable than ever in this rapidly changing world.

Prologue

Once upon a time in Oxford during the last outbreak of the foot and mouth disease…

Fiona Deveraux clambered down from Cityline Bus 39, lifting first, then rolling, a small black overnight bag on the cobblestone crossing near the bus stop. The suitcase was indistinguishable, she thought, if anyone had been looking, from all the other bags that students seemed to be rolling all over the cobblestones of Oxford, part of the weekend traffic. But she was no longer a student. She had come from Cardiff, Wales, on the delayed morning train, and she was exhausted. The trains were a mess these days, frequent delays and cancellations, not to mention nervous railmen checking the line for defects while the trains waited at the entrance to heavily traveled cities like Exeter and even Oxford.

It had taken her three extra hours this time to come to Oxford from Wales. But being here for her, a former student, was almost joy—more than a pleasant change and worth the journey. She was grateful to her friend Victoria, one of the lesser librarians at Oxford's Bodleian Library, for having invited her to housesit over the bank holiday. She and Vicky had been students together at Magdalen College just a few years before.

Vicky would be on her way this afternoon to her cottage in Brittany for the short Easter weekend. At least they would each have Monday as well as Good Friday for vacation. That would give Fiona a day to get home and prepare for the next week even after she had completed her business in the library. Fiona, who had three years ago achieved a solid second in classics in her final examination, had been graduated from Magdalen College with its beautiful tower, but now she was teaching English and Latin to sixth formers at a school in Wales. One year she had sung on May Day from the tower to the crowd that always gathered at dawn, and like most Oxford graduates, she would have been happy to have any job that allowed her to remain in Oxford. She looked around her at Walton Street. It was not far now down the Kingston Road to where she was staying. She pulled the black bag a little faster. She loved the very cobblestones still, but she was glad that the Walton Street sidewalk was mostly smooth concrete.

Warm from the exercise, Fiona brushed her hair back from her face, reminding herself of what the job possibilities had been when she finished her degree. She had known early that the competition, even for a young teacher with a "second," was keen. She would have needed at least one graduate degree in addition to her baccalaureate to obtain any position in the sixth form in Oxford schools, much less what she desired at a higher level. Fi hoped eventually to return for a master's, but so far she had not been able to afford it. Sometimes she thought her tastes for expensive clothes and food made it seem an unlikely event. She glanced longingly into an expensive shop she was passing but did not let herself linger. She had too much trouble saving, and so far fellowships and grants were still scarce, even under the Labor government, which seemed to her to be treating education much as the Tories had.

Fiona had been fortunate to obtain full support for her undergraduate degree. Probably that was because of her excellent A-levels and the recommendations from her favorite English teacher in her last two years of school. But now she seemed stuck. Her bitch of a mother living in Paris was not coming across. She herself had been an exotic dancer in Paris when she became pregnant all those years ago, and she had floated among lovers for years, sometimes enjoying cushy apartments and designer clothes but never having any real money. You'd think she would have figured out something better at her age. Fiona did not intend herself to be dependent on men for the rest of her life. Not that she had ever been as beautiful or as sexually attractive as her dark and sensual mother. An Irish blonde, or what some called "black Irish," that was what her mother was; somewhere in her gene pool swam one of those Spaniards from the age of exploration who had been shipwrecked on Irish shores. Dark black hair, fair skin, and blue, blue eyes.

Fiona, too, had dark hair, but her eyes were also dark, like those of her father. Now at least she was making her own way and did not want to return to University until she had more of a financial cushion. She supposed she would have to put up with being in Wales, away from the real centers of learning and culture that she associated with Oxford and London. At least she could visit Oxford, she told herself as she bumped her bag along the cobblestones that emerged just outside the Radcliffe Infirmary.

It had not been all roses when she was a student here. She remembered that young man Ian, who was so beautiful and posh and had invited her to the May Ball. Even after a concerted search of all the second-hand shops, she had not been able to find any gown that would be worthy of the invitation. Perhaps her standards had been too high; she was so impressed by Ian, who had taken her to tea once at his mother's. She had just passed the window to the charity shop that contributed so much to the mentally ill: the Mind Shop. The year she had been invited to the Ball she had almost bought a lime satin strapless number there that was long and simple and elegant, but it had been too tight. Not only did she fear fainting from the constriction about her midriff, but also the way it pushed her boobs up over the top had made her fear that men at the dance would be eying her in embarrassing ways.

The young men, she knew, those like that bastard Evan, who had slept with her once and told it all over his college, would be all over her, and she preferred to save that for Ian. The experience with Evan had made her feel inferior—she had to face that, and her feeling for Ian had not gone far when she canceled the date for the Ball.

Finally—it had not been a long walk, but her eagerness to arrive made it seem a slow process—she turned the corner from Kingston into St. Margaret's Road, where her friend Vicky owned her small house. She was not used to walking so far on cobblestones and cement. In Wales her walks were usually in the country, and already her feet felt sore. As she moved towards the door, it opened and Vicky's deep voice greeted her.

"Fiona, darling, you've come at last. I was going to have to dash for my train, or I wouldn't make the last ferry." She had draped her ample form in a green tartan cape for the journey. And Fiona saw that she already had her own suitcase outside the door. "I wanted to show you the thermostat and also the button on the furnace if you want more heat during the day." A taxi was drawing up to the space in front of the house, and Vicky waved to the driver.

Vicky gestured toward the hall closet. "It's in here—the furnace box, I mean. I am not here during the day from ten to five, so it is set to go off for a number of hours. But if you are here, I don't want you to be cold." Almost as she spoke, she had kissed Fiona warmly on both cheeks, slightly bumping her nose, drawn her into the house, taken her bag into the drawing room, and now walked briskly back to the front door.

Though openly admiring such energy, Fiona demurred. "Best to be on your way, Vicky, your cab is waiting. I'll manage. I've been here before, you know. Your house is familiar. I wish it were mine." She surprised herself at the bleakness of her tone. "Thanks for the chance to be here."

Vicky smiled broadly as she was walking out. Her house was a beloved extension of herself. Seconds later she left, calling over her shoulder, "Remember now, don't let it get too cold for you. And for heaven's sake, don't grade papers or work in the library all the time on that paper you are writing for the teacher's journal You need a break from those hormone-driven monsters, those girls you have to pour Latin into—or Greek, or whatever uncongenial bits of knowledge."

"Go; we'll talk later." Fiona walked out behind Vicky and waved as her friend got into the taxi.

Fiona knew she needed a break; that's what holidays were for, though she always had other things that needed to be done. Like this time. The speed with which minutes later she put away the few clothes she had brought into the newly built-in blonde cupboards in Vicky's room suggested otherwise. Even that she was hurrying towards pleasure with the speed of light, trying to put all work behind her. A few minutes later, when she left a trail of silken undergarments behind on the bedroom floor and climbed into a long hot bath with the fragrance of Vicky's lavender salts coming out in the steam that rose from the tub—even that suggested she was going to follow her friend's advice immediately and get a head start on a weekend of leisure and other pleasures.

But an hour later when she checked her purse for the keys and let herself out of the shiny red door in a smartly cut suit from the Jaeger shop in Oxford, a Louis Vuitton purse with long straps over her shoulder, she knew she looked more as if she were going for an interview than towards the pursuit of pleasure. The purse was her most recent extravagance, still on her Barclay's charge card. Fiona reminded herself that she was determined to return to the house on tree-shaded St. Margaret's that evening with the means to pay for it, and more.

Much more. Made possible by a fifteenth-century book of hours she would have with her, a manuscript book with illustrations, originally commissioned by Catherine of Cleves. Not a reproduction like the ones ordered from the gift shop at Christmas, but the Bodleian Collection's own book. It was not large—

she had looked at it the last time she was here, but it was precious. Desired by book collectors who were not particular about where their gorgeous finds came from.

She walked along St. Margaret's narrow sidewalk as she thought about the object of her task with all its beauty and age. Especially the incredible craft with which it had been done. Books had surely gone downhill since then. When she was still a student she had gone often to the Duke Humfrey's room there at the top of the Old Bodleian, where all the rare books were available, though often the librarians had to go into the rabbit warren below the library to retrieve them. Still there were many in the room itself, on shelves even over the desks where scholars worked. She loved the musty smell of old leather that bound such books above the desks where she was reading and taking notes. Mostly dons from Oxford and some from America were hunched over the old wood of desks reading and taking notes, and she noticed that as the year wore on, many of the Americans disappeared. She never knew whether they finished their work and went home or whether the dark overcast winter light drove them down to the lighter, more airy, graduate reading room. Occasionally she glimpsed a familiar face in the lower room where she worked most often because she loved looking out the large windows at Oxford, its spires so visible there on the third level. In the upper reading room on the third level readers could only work in more recent books.

But she frequently escaped to the dim room at the top of the building with its brilliant ceiling of painted crests. It was the coat of arms of Oxford in rich colors, embossed with the motto about lux and the mind. And she herself loved to treat herself to romantic time travel in the Caxton texts printed in the late fifteenth century or even sixteenth-century or early seventeenth-century English volumes. Once she had shocked a librarian by asking if she could take a sixteenth-century book home for the night. Of course, it was not permitted. And Duke Humfrey's was where she had met James, the American, almost six years ago now. Towards the end of her last year she had discovered the manuscripts—some even earlier than the Catherine of Cleves—that gave her a greater sense of the hand of the writer or the early owners of the precious books.

Fiona walked along the end of St. Margaret's Road, then turned right onto Woodstock Road, going towards St. Giles and then Broad Street. The old lime trees were a brilliant spring green, and she felt a surge of happiness. After all, she might go another more attractive way, cutting through Church Walk and North Parade so that she could walk more deeply into the University along

Banbury Road, perhaps leaving that briefly to pass by the brilliant multi-colored stone of Keble College and its Victorian façade. She had almost an obsessive attachment to Oxford architecture.

But now she must hurry. Time for rambles afterwards. She wanted to get to the library before afternoon. She had thought as an undergraduate that the security at the Bodleian was not tight, though she heard scholars in the women's cloakroom complain about how insulting it was to show your library card or to have someone else look in your bag as you went out. It seemed such a casual practice to her. And certainly she did not take it personally. The blue-uniformed guards did not actually search.

The whole process had been more of a safety precaution in the beginning, she knew from a graduate student who had worked at the British Library. It was the damned IRA again (they said) and its bomb threats that had brought about searches among the scholars' bags. After all, the only people allowed in the Bodleian had special permissions. They were screened by interviews and required letters of recommendations.

The students were clearly bona fide; the older scholars brought letters of recommendation, and they all took an oath from ancient times, by which they swore not to start fires in the library to keep themselves warm nor to harm any book in any way. The tradition of respect for the institution was so strong that she knew most students could not imagine stealing any books. That did not keep dons, who were allowed to check them out in special circumstances, from holding them out for months in their digs, and Vicky had told her that there were many missing volumes. But somehow she could not imagine many English friends of hers who would not think conscious book theft a major crime.

It was not until she became involved with James, the older American professor she met in Duke Humfrey's, that she eventually became aware that some of the books were prize targets for theft. How he had managed to draw her into his criminal associations was not entirely clear to her even now. But he had eventually involved her, seducing her with a few expensive gifts and stories of his adventures, and now the vicarious pleasure of owning such treasures was the greatest excitement in her life. Perhaps she had been more than a little in love with him. Those Saturday afternoons at the Memorial Hotel.

Though he was so much older, his sexual experience and a kind of tenderness she had not expected made him romantic to her. He had almost convinced her that the rare books in special collections were better off in the hands of the collectors who lusted after them rather than with indifferent librarians and dull scholars. Even when she realized that James had in some measure used her for his own purposes, she could not find it in her heart to regret her actions. Especially after what happened to him.

Perhaps forty minutes after leaving Vicky's she had walked happily into the library, in spite of the tightness of her smart red high wedgies. She spent about an hour at a desk in Duke Humfrey's, poring over the manuscript catalogue for the Bodleian, and then reached up on the shelf above her to lift off a book. She breathed a sign of relief. It was there, where she had located it the last time she was in the library. She was especially glad that she did not have to put in a call slip for it that might lead them to her, though she knew where the library assistants kept the slips. With a quick breathless look around, she slipped the book into the waistband of her skirt under the loose red jumper and zipped up her Jaeger jacket over it.

Then she walked out coolly past the enquiry and request desk, prepared to smile at the assistant if she caught his eye. "Did you leave your library card?" asked the short dark man at the request desk.

"Not this time," she answered, waving it at him as she walked by. The assistant Adam Perkins was not there, and the older man at the desk at the entrance to Art's End barely looked at her as she passed, going down the stairs on her left to drop by the cloakroom for women readers. Pushing open the heavy door, she sat down on the small couch and pretended to look for something in her purse until two other women had left. She looked carefully at the stalls to be sure that they were empty before she examined herself in the mirror over the basin. She was looking for telltale signs, possible bulges about her waist, but nothing underneath the mohair jumper showed. Thank heavens for the fluffy surface. And of course the Jaeger jacket also helped with camouflage. She could not help noticing how becoming the red of her jumper was with the gray suit and her dark eyes, making her pallor almost ivory.

Fiona washed her hands with soap very carefully. No telling whose hands had been on that manuscript book in five hundred and more years. She always washed her hands after being in the library. She tried to be scrupulous about cleanliness even if she left a trail of clothes and small jars of cosmetics wherever she went. She wondered if the bacteria that lived on fleas that in turn lived on rats that carried the bubonic plague would still be contagious after all this time. She shuddered when she thought about modern plagues, the AIDS that racked Africa. She determined not to pick up any stray bugs from old books. She had read somewhere that bubonic plague still existed in northern Arizona, carried by small animals of that faraway state. Who knew where one might pick it up? Her doctor, who had done some charitable work in India, said there were still instances of the plague or even epidemics there.

On her thick sexy retro wedgies she clumped down the old wooden stairs to the ground floor, not having seen anyone since she left Duke Humfrey's except for the two shadowy women in the cloakroom. At the small desk at the end of the Gift Shop, a Bodleian guard gave a cursory glance to her slim notepad. She waited for him to ask to look in her purse, but he did not. Perhaps it seemed to him the purse had no room for concealing stolen books or manuscripts. On all sides of the entrance were Bodleian gifts, crowded in somewhat helter-skelter fashion into the small space. They included many different tourist items, notebooks that bore Shakespeare's reproduced signature, cards with reproductions of Bodleian manuscript illustrations on them, T-shirts and tote bags, two or three beautiful silk scarves.

When she thought about it, it was no wonder that the guards showed little suspicion. No English girl brought up in this tradition where books were so precious would risk what she had. Anglo-Saxon attitudes were too different from whatever notions of survival her Paris dancer mother had taught her. Get what you can while you can. As for her father, according to her mother when she was in her cups, he was an Arab merchant who had gained his wealth in dubious ways. Even the American, who had not had the excuse of coming up the hard way, had shown her a kind of selfish drive for pleasure that was light years from that of the traditional English intellectual.

Perhaps the major genetic pieces in the chessboard of her background were not the reason at all for behavior that she knew perfectly well would be reprehensible to her college and her university. Maybe it had more to do with the Catholic School in Paris, where the nuns had seemed both tough and amoral, their attitudes fostering in the girls a strong sense of survival. She had lost her virginity going home one day. That had nothing to do with the school, of course, only with the lifestyle of her mother. That day she had stopped by the bar on the corner where her mother sat semi-conscious and maudlin over the loss of her latest lover. When, sick with disgust, she had left her mother there, the lover himself had followed her from across the street as she came out of the bar. He had gone back to the apartment with her, to slink away afterwards and never to return. Though she hardly remembered the quick and brutal sex, she still carried an image of him as she watched him walk away, hands in his pockets, his dark hair shining over the sheen of his leather coat. Completely casual, as if he had merely eaten an apple. That attitude, hard and greedy, perhaps lay in the background of what she thought of as her new criminality.

Or more likely, she sometimes thought, when it surprised her to think what she was doing, the cause of her willingness to move beyond English values was her desire for all the nice things she saw her English and American counterparts enjoying in Magdalen College. They had opened her eyes at last. If no one was going to give her those things, she was smart enough to take them.

Usually Fiona did not bother to analyze her motives. She just knew what she wanted and went out to get it. She was like the young men she knew in that way of being direct. But when she was seventeen she had had some counseling at school, brought about by her English teacher, who thought she was worth saving within the educational system. An English psychologist who saw her once a week had given her, after much listening, his theory about her rebellious attitude towards the rules of society and her actively hostile view of most people. After that she was a little more reflective. She admitted to herself that he had advised her well about getting along better at school, and the result had ultimately been her time at Oxford, surely her best time. But she would not think about that now. She must keep her own fine intelligence separate from her feelings.

She needed money to live the way she wanted to. That is what it came down to. She was determined to get it. After she obtained the financial stability, she told herself, she would lead a better life. Do it for yourself, that's what all the pop psych said anyway. Even Kilroy said it every morning on that silly talk show on the BBC: "Take care of yourself," as if self were the most important thing in life. As she made her way through the cluttered aisle of the shop, Fiona felt a flush of triumph. Excitement rose in her throat.

She was getting away with it for the third time. No one had even questioned her about the other two, one a rare book, the other a manuscript. She had taken the rare book, an early seventeenth-century quarto of *Twelfth Night,* from the exhibit in the Undergraduate Reading room in the Radcliffe. Anything of Shakespeare's was so incredibly valuable. She could not believe the English had let all those folios be sold to the Folger Shakespeare Library in America. She had gone then quickly to meet James at the hotel, and he had taken the quarto to the courier. In fact, as far as she knew, there had been no notice taken by the Radcliffe or the Bodleian. Lifting the manuscript was simpler. After James was dead, she had done that simply because she needed money and a woman courier had asked her to stand in for James. One rare book she had taken for the American professor, one manuscript for money and excitement, and this one because she needed money to get through a summer when she wasn't paid.

* * *

"Miss," the low English voice of the guard came at her from the side as she made her way through the crowded gift shop of the Bodleian Library, "May I have a word? Would you step over here, please?" The uniformed guard gestured to her to come down to the other end, nearer the entrance to the library.

Fiona's heart began to beat more rapidly, and her throat was dry.

"May I see your purse, please? Sorry, miss. The man on the desk forgot to check it. I'm here to monitor procedures."

"I noticed that. I just thought things had changed." She smiled, willing him to smile back. At the same time, she glanced quickly at the door to the outside. It was too difficult to make a dash for it. There were at least five people in queue at the cash register between her and the door. She followed the guard meekly, adrenalin pumping. "I suppose you have to supervise these things." Fiona fluttered her eyelashes.

"Oh, yes," he said politely, seemingly impervious to her eyelashes. He did not even look at her directly but began to open her purse. He checked it casually and quickly now that he had made his point. After all, this was his job. "Thank you for your cooperation." He returned the black rectangle to her. For a moment she felt a wave of anger. After all, the purse was too small to hold a book.

As she walked out into the damp, cool air, she flushed with relief, almost joy. She walked briskly away from the Bodleian Library, to her left through the arch towards the Clarendon Building, and then left again towards the gate into Broad Street, over the pebbles past the Sheldonian Threatre and the stone heads of some of the Roman emperors that were mounted at intervals on the fence. God, those pebbles came right through thick-soled red shoes. And why would there be Roman emperors outside the Sheldonian? She wondered briefly who had put them there. She needed to book one of those tours that Americans take when they visit Oxford.

The hair on the back of her neck bristled as she became conscious of a man in a dark gray suit with a bright blue shirt and purple tie. He had come up behind her on the right, and she began to realize that he was following her, about three steps behind. He was still there as she crossed the street to Blackwell's Book Shop. Could the guard have alerted him? There were four or five of the Blackwell shops on the street, each of which had a different speciality; but she was headed to the original store across from the Clarendon Building, and that now had a small café run by an Italian company on the second floor.

She needed a cigarette and a cup of coffee before she started the walk back to Vicky's house. It was a good walk to St. Margaret's Road, either of the two routes, up the Woodstock Road with its large shade trees or the narrower Walton St.-Kingston Road way. In the late nineteenth century, the houses along Kingston Road had belonged to the supervisors at the old car factory, in contrast to the more genteel ownership by dons and college officials of the sprawling Victorian homes on the Woodstock Road. Fiona often preferred to walk the longer route up Woodstock Road and imagine she was the daughter in one of those privileged houses with their grassy front yards and huge overarching trees. But today she probably would go whatever way was fastest to the haven of Vicky's house.

She made her way slowly through the front room of Blackwell's, stopping deliberately to look at the table where some of the old winners of the Mann-Booker Prixe were displayed. He was still behind, the bloke with the blue tie, looking at the display on another table. Then she snaked around into the ground-floor room on the left, where the public lift was located; but when she entered the door, he edged in after her, moving to the back of the lift as she punched the button for the coffee shop floor.

When she emerged on the first floor, Fiona decided not to stop at the counter to order her coffee. Hooking her purse on the back of a chair, she sat down at a small table in the café. The man behind her pulled over a nearby chair to her table and sat down, reaching in his shirt pocket for a package of French cigarettes.

"I beg your pardon," she said, hoping there was ice in her voice, but she felt the anxiety beating in her chest.

"I am Ackman," he said.

"I don't care who you are—" she began, starting to say she didn't care if he was Saddam Hussein.

"The ferry is packed this time of year," he said quickly.

She knew then he must be the courier and flushed with relief. "I did not expect you until tomorrow. The Brittany Ferry, you mean?" Double checking the signals; she knew that was important.

"Oh yes, the *Duke of Normandy* especially," he completed the agreed-upon code.

"I am glad you could get here this afternoon," she said. "I'll be happy to get rid of the frame I have finished for you—that is, if you would like to pick it up. Do you have transport?" They could take a taxi to her house if he did not have a car.

"Yes, I am eager to see it, the frame, I mean. I have my car parked nearby outside at a metre. Why not let me give you a ride home? You can hand it to me then, and I can pay you for the job."

She had agreed upon the fiction of the framing task earlier with the man on the phone who had made the arrangements, the contact from the administration of the ring of thieves. She had already used that technique once with the woman and the manuscript. She should try something else next time. She almost had forgotten that she was going to stop with this one. But the framing story worked. It was a good cover. It sounded innocent, and she looked the part with her Jaeger suit and good color sense, as if she might be a framer or decorator. Certainly if the man Ackman had trusted her with a prized painting, anyone listening would assume they knew each other, that they had taken care of the formalities earlier of getting acquainted, even if she had seemed cold when he first sat down.

"Quite." She smiled, thinking of the money the manuscript would bring and what it might buy for her with the commission. Luck or better. "Let's not have coffee here, after all. Let's go to my house instead and seal the exchange with a glass of wine." She spoke out of elation, and then she thought that probably a framer would not have said that.

Ackman nodded, apparently not noticing that there was anything odd in his having a drink with his framer. He also gave her an appraising glance, his eyes lingering a moment on the leg extending from the slit in her skirt as she sat in the low chair. The two rose, almost together, just as a waitress approached. "Sorry, we realized we have to be somewhere by six," said Ackman in his soft voice as he took her elbow. She was irritated. He sounded as if he were apologizing to the girl, who after all was not a proper waitress, since people served themselves at the counter. She was merely a kind of busboy, and she might remember the stranger.

When they arrived at the stairs, he just managed to brush Fiona's breast as he gestured to her to go first. She looked down at the gray worcester of her jacket and wondered if it were intentional. She glanced at him out of the corner of her eye. Always sex rearing its head between a man and a woman. Then it crossed her mind that he might be checking for the book, perhaps realizing that she might have it on her person.

They drove onto Broad Street in his car, a small red Peugeot. "Did you do this—this kind of delivery, I mean—with that American who took the Shakespeare some years ago? The one that was killed?"

"It is better if we don't share too much information." He tightened his lips, watching the road where students tended to cross in the middle. "Besides, I have to concentrate on driving in this mad town."

"I heard that it was his wife who killed him, anyway. But okay, you're right."

About this time, he narrowly averted running down a bicycle as a motor scooter passed them on the wrong side. "Fucking students," he said softly, a slight accent coming through his near-perfect English.

Second language, it occurred to her. She had thought of going herself to one of those jobs where you teach English as a second language in Japan. The salary was good, but she did not want to live abroad. She ignored him then, thinking her own thoughts about the future as they drove down the Woodstock Road. They had put so many speed humps on Kingston that this was clearly the best way by car or taxi. Gray stone colleges on her right as they headed toward St. Giles. She hated obscene language. A mild swearing was all right, even masculine and attractive, but she never could understand why her generation seemed to favor obscenities.

Curious that she felt this way, a recent student herself. Maybe Classics majors were more sensitive to language than young people in other fields. She wanted to live a more elegant life, not one dragged even further down by ugliness. Perhaps that was why she was sympathetic with those who would enhance their own rare collections, even with stolen books and art objects. She would like to have a beautiful house with a few manuscripts herself, and English and Chinese porcelains carefully placed on surfaces. She wished vaguely that she could be on that end of the arrangement. Perhaps later she could have a few drawings or minor paintings. She wanted refined and crafted things around her, but she was beginning to think that still the only way into that was marriage.

The book was beginning to cut into her stomach as she sat belted into the low car. She hoped the seat belt was not damaging the manuscript book. It was not, she reassured herself; the stiff cover had been designed to protect the brilliantly hand-painted vellum that was the canvas for careful painting and delicate lettering by some monk hundreds of years ago. How had they treated the sheep's skin—or was it lamb's—to make it into the soft pliable vellum? That was something she needed to look up before her next job. A flicker of sadness passed across her mind as she saw last night's BBC image of piles of dead sheep put to death in the foot and mouth epidemic. Sheep always at the mercy of power, she thought. But back to her own life.

The small room at the Memorial Hotel where the American had first shown her a stolen manuscript rose in her mind then. It was mixed up in her head with the sex they had later and the fresh lilac scent of the linen. He had been surprisingly gentle and powerful at the same time. Later she was sad when she heard that he was dead. He probably had thought she was inexperienced. But he was inexperienced himself at theft. He must have done something wrong. She would not think about that now that she had to complete this deal with Ackman.

He slowed down suddenly as he was nearing the number of Vicky's house on St. Margaret's. No place to park here usually. Hardly room for residents. But small miracle, a place had opened just in front where visitors were allowed. Fiona took it as a sign of the success of this lucrative career. She was meant to be a master thief, suave and sophisticated like Cary Grant, whom she had once seen as a cat burgler in an old movie at the college, a master jewel thief. He, too, had come from modest beginnings.

Suddenly an image of herself flashed into her mind against a gold background like those Irish reproductions of the Madonna and Child with which she had grown up. They were paintings that her mother, a lapsed Catholic nostalgic for her childhood, had brought from Ireland to Paris. Only, in her waking dream, Fiona had no blue mantle but rather a draped blue silk dress she had once glimpsed in *Vogue*. It must be the excitement that was creating such vivid mental images. Money, that was what she needed, she thought again. Greed was surely not the sin it was reputed to be—nothing like what the nuns had said with their dreary stories of horrible consequences. Or what was that tale by Chaucer that ended with all the thieves dead? No, greed was sexy and exciting. For her at least.

Then Ackman pulled over into the parking place, bumping the kerb with the front left tire. She bit her lip not to cry out. *Another incompetent male*, she thought, but she did not want to make an enemy by being critical. In Oxford everyone parked as close as possible to the sidewalk because the streets were narrow. One needed to know how to do it smoothly, like everything else.

"Ackman," she said aloud as they approached the door, "come into the house my friend has lent me for the weekend." She laughed. "You are my first guest."

"You are fortunate to have such friends," he frowned.

"We were in college together," she responded. "It was my happiest time."

"I can't imagine enjoying school," he laughed bitterly.

Fiona did not answer as they moved into the hall.

"I hope your friend is not here," he said.

"No, she's on holiday. We can relax. Sit down on the couch. I'll be only a few minutes." She walked toward the small powder room off the hall. Really, the man was absurd with his cloak and dagger mannerisms, though oddly handsome with his dark eyes. Also tall and muscular. But no one who lived on this street would dress in such a bright shirt and tie. Then she reminded herself that she had seen the prime minister on telly this morning with similar garb.

Perhaps it was something about the manuscript theft that made them both feel like wearing their best clothes. Whatever the morality, she did not feel like an ordinary criminal. The manuscripts were too old and too beautiful and out of her hands too quickly. She felt more like some Nietzschian individual from the future who was allowed a different morality from the common herd. She was not one of the sheep that dotted Britain, many to be killed now that the disease had taken such hold. She would think about it later. Now was the time to be decisive, to hand over the prize, get the money, and enjoy the weekend in her favorite place. She might even finish her paper for the teachers.

She turned on a soft lamp in the lounge and put down the manuscript on the table. "Here it is. I'll be just a minute more—I'll get the wine." She went into the small kitchen and grabbed the bottle of champagne out of the fridge that she had planned to leave as a housegift for Vicky. She could buy another, she thought, feeling reckless. She reached into the cupboard on the side of the sink and pulled out two crystal flutes. This would be a small celebration after all.

The manuscript had been fine when she lifted it out of her skirt. Now she needed to get her money and share a drink. She felt much better without what had felt like a board in her skirt. It had survived six hundred years and many more miles across Europe, but she was glad not to have damaged that survival.

She entered the lounge, where Ackman was carefully examining the book. "It looks perfect, though I don't get why anyone would pay £150,000 for it."

"It is very rare, I understand." He looked suddenly quite attractive to her as he handled the book in his long dark hands.

"Yeah." He put it down on the couch and moved toward the champagne. "You get ten per cent of the profit for taking it—why do I only get five?"

"How about some help?" she handed him the opener, not wanting to argue, though she thought her part required more specialized knowledge and risk and should receive higher pay. Vicky's corkscrew was rusty. She would get her another for the gift instead of the wine itself. There were nice pewter ones now on the market.

"I don't need that with this bottle," he said, expertly easing out the cork. She blushed, realizing that he would know she was unfamiliar with champagne bottles.

"I really did not expect you until tomorrow," she changed the subject. "Tomorrow was the day."

He gazed at her without answering, eyes hard. "You have done this three times with the same cut?" He poured the champagne in two glasses, then reached into his inner pocket for a large white envelope.

"Money," she said happily and smiled as she stretched out her hand for the envelope.

Ackman held it out to her with mock solemnity. "We should drink our wine before the bubbles go."

Fiona laughed softly: "I feel now as if the bubbles will never go. But yes, I have done it three times. And never even been questioned."

Ackman nodded, and she noticed him looking at her legs. She thought she knew what he was thinking. "Let's not drink now," he said. "Let's do something more interesting."

He looked very attractive in that bright blue shirt. All those years in college with young men mostly in T-shirts had made her a sucker for shirts with collars and ties. And in Wales she had no time to date. Even Oxford examination outfits with those funny looking robes had once turned her on. He was moving now across the room. Before she could react, he walked up to her, put his arms around her, and pressed her back up against the wall. She felt her excitement mounting as he brought his right hand up her side and then over to her breast.

Only a minute later or less, Fiona lost the warmth enveloping her as she felt his thumb against her windpipe. There was no time to struggle, and she was swallowed up in blackness as she tried to breathe. It was as if she were suddenly weak and helpless all over, and she felt herself sliding, falling to the floor, her leg twisting behind her, a swirling dizziness as her head fell forward.

For once, once upon a time had an unhappy ending as the tall dark man walked out of the house onto St. Margaret's Road and climbed into the red Peugeot.

PART I

Chapter One

Ellen closed her eyes as the plane raced through the dark night sky across the American continent and towards the North Atlantic and England. Her last trip to England three years ago was marked by what the police had thought was murder, although they wound up listing it as "suspicious death." Ellen Adams had been devastated. Ironic that she should be grief-stricken at the death of a husband who had already abandoned her.

But another seeming mystery was why he had appeared at that time in England—or rather Cornwall—where she was taking a few days' spring holiday. She had been staying in Bosinney after a month of research at the Bodleian Library in Oxford, on leave for a semester from the college in Pennsylvania where she taught writing and literature. He was obviously looking for her—he had told her enough to understand partially, but now she would never know the full story because he was dead.

Ellen shifted in her seat, her legs already cramped from the crowding in tourist. Thank heaven she could stretch out towards the space in front of the vacant middle seat. After the death, admittedly when she was less in shock, she had thought *yes*, grimly smiling, *he had spoiled the trip*, as he often had in the years they were married. But this time she wasn't angry. The odd thing was that his death had changed much of her attitude towards him. Her anger over his ultimate betrayal, on top of various earlier ones, had turned to overwhelming sadness, making all the best times they had spent together somehow the norm of their marriage. Psychologists would call that denial, but she thought it was really the truth about what death did to the survivors. There was some sort of transformation of the image of their past. Though now and then James' adultery still seemed to her unforgiveable.

That was what happened with the dead. A kindly grace of the psyche. Although obviously that increased the grief in the world. Ellen looked to her left in the plane at the dark woman sitting there. She would probably think, if she knew what the woman nearby was thinking, that she was being morbid. Sometimes she wondered how aware other people were of death. Surely it intercepted life enough to make it an object of thought, but even the function of memory was profoundly influenced by it. This softening of the bad memories. Perhaps this was a less literal form of resurrection. She could not help remembering how Ibsen thought we needed to live by such illusions.

And three years later, after her life had changed so drastically, everything had gone slightly wrong from the beginning of this trip, in spite of her hopes for the future. Ellen knew she had needed this holiday in England as much as she had ever needed any break. Certainly any one since she had become a widow at forty-six.

This time the necessity was to get away from home. She lived with her grown daughter and her family, happily most of the time; but sometimes all that youth with the frequency of its crises made her feel old and useless. They usually respected each other's way of life and had worked out a way of living together. But sometimes, in spite of the fact that she was only in her late forties, her daughter saw her as an aging mom, now almost middle-aged with the longer span of life, and her two granddaughters related to her as a sweet but school-teacherish old thing who had been alive when Elvis was. Her son-in-law viewed her, she sometimes thought, as someone who needed more to do in her own life. Two strong people, that's what they were, and they sometimes clashed. So, from time to time, she needed to get away.

All these perspectives are more or less true, she admitted, but her own point of view was that she had to know she had her own identity, unrelated to increasing age or even to her considerable desire to control the world. *Who am I anyway?* Once she had been a loving wife, a responsible mother, a good teacher-scholar; but most of that was gone, although she still taught and did some research. What was left?

Oh, she looked all right for forty-nine. She had kept her copper hair, with the aid of modern technology, of course—not that it was quite the same shade it had been thirty years ago. Or even three. It had been her most identifying feature. She had a fantasy image of herself sometimes as just a flame on a stick—well, not exactly a stick now. She was also heavier than she had ever been. Still, she hoped she looked and acted like the new middle-aged woman, still attractive, still alive. She tried to wear bright accessories with the inevitable black.

But lately she wondered if she were not ready to become the little old lady of the rocking chair. America did not allow that descent into old age at the upcoming fiftieth, probably not even at the sixtieth. And she couldn't even afford to retire fully, in spite of the benefits inherited from James. Besides, she needed some new direction. She worried over many things, and her inner world was more fragile, it sometimes occurred to her, than her outer. She had always been a worrier like her own mother, and worry had put deep lines in her forehead and around her mouth.

Her mother had told her from her own experience, "The only way to avoid looking like a prune is to stop worrying and do something. Brush your teeth, comb your hair, and think of others." She had tried that, but then she just worried about others. And in terms of herself she still worried about something she could only view as a deep psychological problem.

It was the feeling she sometimes experienced of disappearing, becoming something like a Greek shade. Invisible, perhaps, or shadowy. Once in awhile, when she was walking in the mall and four or five teenagers came directly towards her as if they could walk through her, she had the uneasy sense that she was indeed invisible. The only consolation was that she had to step aside to avoid them. When she traveled, however, she felt more like herself, except for the vague feeling of guilt over James's death that reasserted itself the closer she was to Britain.

Here she was on the Virgin 749 at last, all the travel arrangements made, and now just thirty minutes out of LA they were calling for a doctor over the loudspeaker. Shades of that frightening movie about the pilotless airplane. She sat up. First thing to go wrong. She had not wanted to see the film about what could go wrong in the sky, knowing it would set her imagination off in bizarre directions when she traveled by plane. But she had not been able to avoid the preview, and even that had taken hold of her imagination. Then the announcement came.

"Who do you suppose it is?" she turned to the woman in the window seat. "Not the pilot, I hope? Of course, I hope no one is really ill."

The exotic, dark-haired woman looked at her across the empty seat between them. Ellen had noticed her first in the waiting room with her big sad eyes, and she knew the woman had seen her, too, her own brightly tinted hair set off by the blue suit she wore on trips so that she would be clearly visible to motorists in England. Once or twice crossing she street she had looked the wrong way and almost been smashed. Her feeling about crossing British streets was neurotic, she knew. It reminded her of the old Roadrunner comedies, in which the Disney bird would look carefully both ways before crossing the highway and then walk out to be run over by a huge truck. *Only there it would be a lorry*, Ellen corrected herself.

When the two women had found themselves with a vacant seat between them, they had shared their delight over the space, rare phenomenon these days when airlines tried to cram every available seat. Her companion had introduced herself as Jean, now from Bermuda, though she had been visiting her daughter in Los Angeles.

Jean laughed at her question. "I doubt it's the pilot, but who knows? I think the attendant said it was one of the staff."

It had turned out to be a young woman with an appendicitis attack, not the pilot or co-pilot. Ellen felt for her, knowing how scary it would be to have that fierce pain so far from real help, and her sympathy doubled when there was another sudden illness. Before they made the emergency stop at O'Hare, another person had fainted with a threatened heart attack. Ellen hadn't been able to talk herself out of feeling that this was some sort of bad omen for the trip, even though she told herself that everything turning out all right was a sign of positive things to come. Both had been taken off by a Chicago ambulance, the paramedics coming directly onto the plane. It was all over in a few moments, and she knew how relieved the ill people must have felt, along with the others on the flight. It was almost as if she heard the collective sigh of relief. Help had come. It had turned out all right. The two had been transported immediately to an excellent hospital.

Still she had known from the beginning, even when warned of dangers, that she wanted to travel, whatever the risks. Once she had told her daughter, "If an accident happens on the way somewhere, I want you to know that I am doing what I want. I want to die in the midst of doing something I love to do."

When she was at home, she sometimes wondered about who she was now without James; but often when she traveled, strangers would mirror back to her a personality she could live with. Aging, of course, but "cool," as one granddaughter said of those she admired. These days fifty was the shank of life. Plenty of time to do something different, even to know different people. It was three long years since James had died in that terrible way, and she had gradually settled into some form of acceptance.

After all, the year before had given her a chance to get used to not having him around, not having anyone really close to talk to. She had partially retired from her teaching job at the college; she taught fulltime one semester and had the next off—it was a sweet deal in that it allowed for travel. Her old friend in Colorado had alerted her to this possibility. Life was too long to spend it all discontented with the way one mode of life had worked out. To remind herself of the many different possibilities in the world, she had traveled alone in several places, occasionally Europe, but mostly in England.

What the British police had first called murder had brought the end of the dying marriage and of the usual pattern of her teaching life. She sighed. No wonder she did not feel like herself. It was like that awful expression, being cut off at the knees. But she had a major weakness as a world traveler. Like most Americans and many English she spoke only a smattering of French, Italian, and Spanish. She read them all fluently, but the only foreign language she could actually speak was Latin. That was the big irony. Latin was not a spoken language, but when she started learning it in high school, she and her best friend had learned to speak it as a secret language. And she had done that later—just speaking Latin to herself as she went through graduate school.

Sometimes she imagined she was speaking to St. Augustine. But out in the real world she only managed to feel at home among English-speaking people. She looked across at Jean—she probably spoke several languages. She herself was politically incorrect, perhaps, and was insecure when she was not in control of the language of the country in which she traveled. At least among academics such an attitude was common. And she noticed that in England now even most of the English spoke French at least enough to rattle off several sentences—often, she judged from the laughter, some mildly amusing witticism. Now when everyone traveled so often, the old English refusal to speak other languages was changing. Not to mention all the new international businessmen, who often spoke several languages. It helped, she supposed, that more and more Europeans knew English.

But for her the language was what drew her back to England, again and again. She needed, especially when she was alone, to talk to people in some depth, and also in England she went to all those dramatic performances that brought back to her the more vivid life of her past. An image of her husband laughing at a Shakespearean pun floated to the top of her mind. What did it matter that BBC English or that of the Royal Shakespeare Company was no longer quite the standard it used to be? She talked to most people she met, sometimes to their surprise. Often she noticed the strangers she chatted with looking at her curiously. She suspected they thought her a garrulous woman, or at best someone who had lived alone too long. But mostly people responded warmly to her efforts, and she had amazingly intense conversations in odd places—in the theatre, at art gallery cafés, even in restaurants or on planes, sometimes in front of a painting. Jake, the taxi driver she met last time, had told her, "You're a nice lady. Just talk to people, and they'll respond."

And when they almost inevitably did, she would feel more alive, even if the person she was talking to were considerably younger. Because to tell the truth, she often felt herself as young as ever, imprisoned in an older body. She even occasionally fantasized that, when she really conversed with people, they had a similar experience of her, seeing beneath the surface that vibrant person she had once been in her *real* life, as she continued to think of the time before her husband's death. Perhaps she was just a little nutty now. She wanted to act as she did before her semi-retirement, when she was smack in the middle of the stream. *I still am*, she reminded herself. *It is just a different stream.*

"Yes, I am a writer now, though I still teach and do a little research," she said to the woman next to her, making an effort to come across as a person who was still doing things. "I often gather material when I travel, especially when I want to do a setting that is different from my own home town in Pennsylvania—or even from the city in the desert where I have been visiting recently. I am happy because I have a good excuse to travel and even sometimes to be a little curious about how other people live."

"My husband is in international banking," said Jean, "and he says almost the same thing. He is in charge of the bank's large loans and often has to make some major judgments about risks. That is how he justifies all the questions he must ask—but basically I think he is really interested in cultural differences that distinguish people from each other. And countries," she added. "I am originally from Brazil. My father was a diplomat there for many years." She almost seemed to be talking to herself then, Ellen thought. "I miss him still."

"I miss my parents, too. I think I didn't know how much I loved them until they were gone." Ellen responded in that direct way possible only when talking to strangers, almost sure that you will never see them again.

Her seat companion was dark and angular, also about fifty, Ellen judged, dressed in a severe, smart suit. It was not new, but it was good fabric, black with bold lines, though she was not familiar enough with expensive clothes to recognize the designer. Still she had always loved beautiful materials, especially. The heavy gold pin on the lapel was also striking, in the shape of a medieval letter. An M, she thought, but that seemed odd when the woman's name was Jean. Probably the husband was doing well in banking, though bankers were notorious for not being paid as well as executives in other businesses.

The two women went back to reading their novels then. They chatted occasionally, but Ellen sensed that they both wanted time alone. She knew that she coveted the privacy she felt when traveling, and she honored that of others. Except for a brief chat when breakfast came, it was not until they were going through the passport control line and then the line at the luggage carousel at the end of the journey that the two women spoke in a sustained way to each other.

"Goodbye," said Jean. "I hope your trip will give you lots of writing material. Don't think the beginning means that other aspects will be less than you hope. Here are my two bags." She took them off the carousel, struggling a little with the larger one. Immediately Ellen thought that she would remember that encouragement and try to cling to it. "Please take my card and call me if you come to Bermuda. And remember I'll be at the Strand Palace until our flat is ready."

Ellen took the small card just as she glimpsed her own two suitcases coming near on the carousel. She reached over and pulled them both off, and the four bags were side by side. She paused, taking the card to put in her purse before loading her trolley and fumbling for a moment for her own card. No luck, she could not find it this time. "I have your card. Mine has disappeared," she smiled at Jean. "I hope everything is just what you like in your flat that the bank people are lending you. And have a wonderful time being with your husband in London. There are so many things to do when he has time—make him take off some time."

Ellen sighed then, thinking of all the hours she and James had spent in the British Library when they might have been exploring London. Now when she did it alone, she sometimes pretended he could hear her comments.

"Goodbye." She moved the two bags that were left after Jean had settled the other two on her trolley. She grasped her own trolley handle and moved with the two suitcases, the rolling bag and the smaller black leather overnight case, toward the exit that led past customs, passing on from the airplane journey to the pleasure of being at last in one of her favorite places. "Yes, I am a partially retired professor," she had told the laconic man in the blue suit at the passport desk. And then he actually wrote down the name of her book on love and death. Before she knew it, she had found the familiar path to the taxi stand and was on her way. Two nights she would be at her small hotel in Bloomsbury, just time to catch up on sleep and see one play, then on to Cornwall for a writing, walking vacation.

But first, her usual conversation with the taxi driver. Some American academics she knew said they didn't like to talk to them because they were all such conservatives, at least politically; but she always enjoyed getting their views—even though she herself leaned toward the left. Maybe she just liked the young Prime Minister. "And what do you think of Blair?" she began. He was bright and lively, though easily satirized. And anyway she had found that in every foreign country taxi drivers were friendlier to strangers than most people, even patient when she did not know the language. "*Un peu. Un poquito,*" she muttered to herself, then stopped. No, she was in England this time and would only have to broaden a few a's. "Tomahto. Yes."

"And how has the weather been this winter? "she proceeded after the driver's brief comment on Tony Blair, the favorite topic of Englishmen. After they had moved through the usual "cold and rainy, no summer last year," they were on to politics and how badly the government was handling the latest crisis. A recent outbreak of foot and mouth disease. There were piles of dead sheep pictured on tellie every evening, part of the effort to control infection. Mostly it seemed to be sheep this time. Ellen hardly listened; it was all so grim, though it sounded slight after the BSE and people who had died mad from eating beef. Besides, she was half asleep after losing almost a night in the time change.

Before she knew it, they had moved past the dull outer edge of London and were passing by Buckingham Palace and down the tree-filled mall through St. James Park. The familiar drive into central London was especially beautiful this time of year. Even the lack of sun did not hold back the crocuses; and, as always, the brilliant green of new spring leaves was budding on the trees. The sun even shone through briefly, and she saw people scattered here and there in the park: walking, jogging, pushing prams, as they called baby carriages here. *I love it*, she thought, almost bursting forth with "If winter comes, can spring be far behind...." Just in time, she stopped. Even a friendly taxi driver would think she was a little mature for such enthusiasm. One friend had told her, however, that her unquenchable romanticism allowed her to recover from dark days. Perhaps.

"Here, love, this is it," said the cab driver, his Yorkshire accent strong as he pulled up to the front of the small hotel on Bloom Street.

She looked out at the old Georgian house that had been turned into a small hotel, in spite of renovation still a little shabby, and felt as if she were home at last. No glitter, no glaring signs, no glamorous entrances. Another home. She had been here often enough to feel possessive. All those English books she had read as a child and later studied. "Yes, home at last," she couldn't resist saying, though she knew he wouldn't understand that she felt the ghosts now. The shadows of Virginia Woolf and Leonard, Clive Bell, Vanessa. Later T. S. Eliot. The only place that beat Bloomsbury for her was St. Paul's, where Donne's cathedral had stood before it burned. She had not been to the Globe yet, but that would join her sacred places.

"That'll be forty pounds." He was all business now. Someday she would have to take the train from Heathrow. She had once traveled on that Oxford coach from Gatwick because it was even farther and more expensive than Heathrow, but it was so much easier after losing a night's sleep to come by taxi. And Oxford was farther than London. The cab driver took her heavy rolling bag and the small overnight to the top of the three steps of the hotel and rang the bell. Ellen handed him the forty pounds and another eight. "Thanks for the good conversation," she smiled at him.

"Have a good time and thanks," he said. "Americans are generous," he called over his shoulder as he climbed in the black taxi. One of her American friends had lectured her about adjusting her tipping.

Just as he pulled away she noticed that the small bag was different from her own. "Hey!" she tried to call him back, but the taxi had pulled away too quickly. She would have to call the cab company when she got to her room. The door opened, and the desk clerk picked up her luggage. "Come in, Madam," he said. "Reservations?"

She moved toward the desk and the problem of registration, taking out her passport. A second thing gone wrong. Maybe it was just life. Minutes later she was in her room, longing for a nap, but first she needed to call about the bag and unpack what she needed until Wednesday when she would be off for Cornwall. She should have asked the desk clerk to do it. She picked up the phone. She needed to do it now. "Hello, could you get me the number of the black cab company—the usual one, I think?" But when she dialled, no one answered. It was too early anyway, but she wanted them to call the driver about her bag. Already, she was worried. After all, the book—the crucial book, not really a book, but a manuscript that she had found in some of James's old things—was in that bag.

She called the desk and explained the missing bag. The concierge said that he would check on it, even though he did not know the number of the taxi she had arrived in. "I will call you about four o'clock," he promised. "And by the way, if it does not turn up, I will give you the number for Left Luggage at Heathrow."

* * *

"Go back to Cornwall, that northern coastal town where you were before. The place itself will help you. Some people think beauty heals, you know," her daughter had said when Ellen began to make plans for her journey. It was hard for her to get used to the reversal by which Ruth treated her, as if she were looking after her these days.

"It's not time yet," Ellen had responded, remembering James as she saw the image of his dark strange body once again turning and breaking free of the stone in the stream that came through the rocks.

She had been standing near the running creek in Cornwall that was part of the circle walk they had planned for her. It had been created from water pushing through a boulder that guarded the Cornish shore from the Atlantic Ocean. Now, after thousands of years, a waterfall ran down into a fast running stream cutting through the small valley. Something about the shoulder had seemed familiar there in the hollow that was Rocky Valley, where, as an early morning walker, she had imagined she was entirely alone. Even now, three years later, she could feel the blood draining from her own face as the body turned again and she thought she was seeing her husband's familiar face.

"Three years is long enough," said Ruth gently. "It's the time it takes to earn a PhD, if you don't have to teach during the process!" She tried to make a joke in terms Ellen would like.

She knew that Ruth was trying to say that three years was too long to mourn a husband you had already been breaking away from. Ruth did not know how the murder had in a curious way brought them back together even if it had been such a radical physical break. It was odd how death of any kind could change your perspective, even cause you to miss people you had thought you did not want to see anymore.

What Ruth did not even hint at was that Ellen was forty-nine now and virtually retired. If she were ever going to move on and build a new life, it must happen soon. Otherwise she would wind up being one of those widows who, after the death of their husbands, existed halfway between the living and the dead, always idealizing the dead husband until he was an entirely artificial construction. Certainly she had rejected James long before his death. After all, they had been in the process of a divorce.

Ruth didn't have to tell her that. She had read enough about getting stuck in grief. There are many ways to lose someone. She must admit she had this tendency to live in the past. To live in it so deeply that the present was a kind of shadowy dream. She had not been able to move on, even when friends had tried to introduce her to lonely men or even to groups that might catch her interest. Sometimes she thought that if she could only begin a new career—but she felt her hand slip away from anything that began to interest her. She was barely hanging on to life, as if she were gripping the edge of a cliff and felt her fingers slipping. Sometimes she dreamed that very dream.

Especially, she reminded herself, *because the so-called "suspicious death" (that had not really been a murder) has never been solved. Death by blunt instrument and drowning. Stunned by the blow, then drowned.* She blamed herself for that inconclusiveness. At least partially, however slovenly or inept the Cornwall police had been. No, that was not entirely fair, and the inspector who had come from Scotland Yard had taken an interest—even, she felt, somewhat of an interest in her. Oh, he was perfectly proper, but she had seen him watching her. Still, after all, it came to nothing in terms of solving the mystery.

I should have dug deeper. I was irresponsible to let them persuade me to go home, she accused herself yet again. Inevitably, the case had been closed as quickly as possible after she left. Even after all this time, she wanted to talk to the inspector again. She had some new things to tell him. It wasn't really James's death that was the mystery to her. Her missing overnight bag, in fact, contained something from James's belongings at home that had a bearing on it. The manuscript was marked with a Bodleian number.

* * *

Ellen tried to call Left Luggage, but the line was busy. She opened the black rolling bag on the rack in the corner of the dim room, but the sight of all those knit clothes that needed to be hung in the small wardrobe, even if she could only wear two or three outfits before she left Wednesday, overwhelmed her. She had to rest first. She lay down then on the bilious green bedspread. Prints and patterns were always different in England—to her American eyes usually twenty years out of date. After she rested a half hour, she would get back to the concierge and call Left Luggage again.

But first she would look in the small case the driver had mistaken for hers for some identification. She tried to keep herself from being as upset as she really was. Who had her bag? One major thing had already gone wrong. The bag had the manuscript in it. *That was largely why I came—to return it to Scotland Yard,* was her last thought as a drowsiness moved over her, closing her heavy eyelids, and she fell into the pit of jet-lagged sleep.

Chapter Two

At four that afternoon, after consulting with the hotel concierge, Ellen called the taxi company to discover that no bag had been turned in by a driver. *If only I had taken down his name!* Then she called the Left Luggage again at Heathrow. "Has anyone returned a black leather overnight case—probably someone on the #007 flight from LA yesterday?"

"No, Madam, no one has turned in any bag that was taken by mistake."

"Would you call me either at the Bloom Hotel in London or at the The Willow Hotel in Bosinney if anyone should bring one in? I shall be in London until Wednesday morning."

"Of course," said the very courteous English voice. "Give me the numbers, area code first, please, and your name again. If one comes in tonight on the midnight from LA, we'll deliver it to your hotel by eight in the morning."

She knew that was a long shot.

It had all come to nothing. When Ellen left at ten-thirty two days later, there had been no further call, and the suitcase belonging to God-knows-who sat reproachfully on the floor beside her rolling bag. It was black leather, like hers, but a different shape. No pockets on the outside, either. When she opened it, she found no sign of identification, only a sweater, Scottish label, good lambswool, belonging to a man, and two white shirts. There was also a single page letter on Crane stationery, but no envelope, no address. That brand had always been good quality paper, but whether that signified anything about the owner she did not know. She felt she shouldn't read it when she saw there was no address Maybe she would weaken later if no one made contact, but for now she would respect the privacy of the writer. She had been reared to believe that it was almost a crime to pry into the mail of others. All she saw was the greeting: "Darling Jean Marie." The name triggered her memory of the woman named Jean on the plane, and she vaguely recalled Jean removing two bags, one similar to this, from the luggage carousel.

After some waffling, Ellen decided to keep the bag until she heard something about her own. It would probably be a simple trade. If it turned out not to be, she would take it to the airport later. She would have to make do with what she had packed in the larger bag. That would not be difficult, as she had put mainly spare items in her own overnight case.

On Wednesday morning, Ellen checked out of the hotel and headed for Paddington Station and the train to Bodmin Parkway, the stop in Cornwall that was nearest her Bosinney hotel. She was careful this time to collect her things from the taxi. Suddenly she felt a slight lifting of her spirits to be leaving London, much as she loved the place. Perhaps this last problem could be resolved as simply as the illnesses on the plane. Last night when she walked back from the National Theatre across Waterloo Bridge, she had been happy thinking about the play she had seen at the Cottlesloe until she ran into some wild teenagers who were somewhat the worse for beer. Not that they accosted her. On the contrary, she always felt safe in London. But "pissed" as they were (as they say in England), they were, indeed, pissing loudly—and yelling to each other to call attention to it—on a chain mail fence in front of a building site in the Strand. It was near where she was walking, and somehow it spoiled her evening. Civilization gone to pot. London seemed as dirty and disordered as the rest of the world, and she was glad to be heading for Cornwall. *Maybe I am getting old, after all,* Ellen mused. As a young woman she might have seen their behavior as "animal high spirits," as Fielding says in *Tom Jones.*

Anyway, she was on her way to the country now—northern Cornwall, her own favorite section, where along the main road to the south of her hotel lay Tintagel, then its contiguous suburb Bosinney and then, just a short distance over a hill, Boscastle. On the north, almost at the back door of the The Willow Hotel, began the Coast Walk and its mighty boulders, overlooking the sea stretching from Tintagel to where it flowed somewhat inland at Boscastle, creating a peaceful harbor. During this year of the foot and mouth disease, the whole Coast Walk would be posted, and Ellen would be forced to go along the road between Tintagel and Bosinney when she took her walks.

She had hiked once through a stile at Boscastle along the creek and then up to the ridge where, just below the top, was Boscastle Minster, a Norman stone church that lay surrounded by gray gravestones marching to the top of the ridge. In some ways a gloomy sight, but this time of year in the midst of a thousand wild yellow daffodils—Nature always asserting life in the midst of death. She remembered Cornwall as pristine and pastoral—at least it was before the discovery of the body the last time she had been there. She hoped she had not romanticized it too much, this land of Arthur and Guinevere that still seemed a mingling of the mythic and archaic with the present. Failed marriages were no big deal today, and adultery was a commonplace story, not a tragedy.

Even the tourist information seemed doubtful that the ruins of the castle in Tintagel (just west of Bosinney) had been originally the ruins of Camelot, but it had clearly belonged to ancient kings of Britain, perhaps to King Mark and Iseult of the White Hands Another tragedy of love. But in those days people had not chosen their mates freely. She admitted to herself that in 1998, when she first visited, Cornwall was not entirely Edenic; but by 2001 she felt it was a thoroughly charming mixture of Celtic mystery and hokey tourism. She sat on the train, happily settled after the struggle to stow her luggage, concentrating on recovery of the English rolling hills and pastoral scene that moved rapidly out the slightly spotty window.

In the fields the sheep were grazing. Millions. Thousands still, anyway. She had forgotten the exact figures she had once heard. They undoubtedly changed from day to day, but on some coach tour she had taken, the driver had told the tourists how many more sheep than people there were in Britain. She felt a pang as she noticed the headlines on the back page of the newspaper the man across the way held up in front of him: "**Foot and Mouth Worsens**." What was this strange animal disease that threatened Eden? What would happen to the peaceful unknowing sheep on these green hillsides? Was there no health in them? It must have happened in America too, where it was called the *hoof and mouth disease.*

After all, it was almost lambing time. The only paper she had read since coming to London had mentioned both quarantine and slaughter of infected animals and possibly others, though the government seemed to be resisting vaccine. Something about it making the product impure. Oh well, many agricultural experts were flying in today from all over the world. Surely they would mount a plan before anything too terrible happened.

She had better get to the bar car before they lost it at some stop—was it Truro? She couldn't remember. But she felt starved—for a salmon sandwich and coffee. Jet lag always caused her to be devastatingly sleepy in early afternoon. Food helped. She loved the cut sandwiches here, especially tuna with cucumber and tarragon mayonnaise, but she knew the train would not have one that sophisticated. She had eaten that at the Barbican on the last trip when she had skipped Cornwall. She would settle for salmon and cucumber.

Moving down the aisle, she swayed as the train gathered speed. After all, Cornwall was way across the country from London in the Southwest. Still it only took four hours to get there. The smallness of this country was a real convenience after traveling in the States. Yet many Brits did not seem to have been to Cornwall, in spite of the greater encouragement of the tourist industry. Some even argued that Cornwall was another country, and she noticed that in Oxford, where she heard the morning weather news, they concentrated on the east of England and ignored the Southwest. But she had met many English and Welsh the last time she visited the hotel who returned each year to the loveliness of Cornwall. She could almost imagine for a moment the misty morning walks she had taken there—almost like time travel into the past, into mystery and magic, a legendary time in England and in Christianity. At least before the rude shock when the worst of the present had intruded with the advent of James.

* * *

Two hours later the train pulled in to Bodmin Parkway. "Get your bags out on the space between cars one stop before yours," the old woman next to her had advised. She had had to find out what the stop before was so that she could get her bags together near the car door. She needed to lift the mystery bag down quickly so that she could manage the heavy rolling one. It was a brief stop there in the middle of nowhere, about twenty miles from Bosinney, where she was going. Why they had built the stop outside of Bodmin itself she did not understand.

Because the train was earlier than she had told the hotel owner, who was sending a taxi for her, she was afraid she would have to wait a little while. She hoped someone else would get off so that she would not be the only person around. But surely there was at least someone selling tickets in the tiny station.

She needn't have worried. Two young women in jeans, about seventeen, were giggling next to the door when she got her bags there from the shelves just inside the car door. There were still these moments when she was a little afraid traveling alone. But not so often now. She always tried to plan ahead, in case a taxi did not show up or she was otherwise stranded. She was a little nervous when she thought about what had happened to James. *Plan B*, she rehearsed. She looked around the stop with its old bridge over the tracks. She was on the side nearest the tiny station. A sign pointed to the footpath to Llanhydrock, the great house belonging to the Roberts family, famous in the seventeenth century for furnishing money from tin to James I. Next to the sign for the path was another sheet, a posting of the foot and mouth, prohibiting the path from walkers. Yet another thing gone wrong. She had hoped to visit the house. Still, that was minor.

Her fears about having to wait were unjustified. "Afternoon, Madam. Are you the American lady for the Willapark? I am John. Rick, the hotel owner, sent me."

"Oh yes." She felt relieved that the driver was early. "I'm Ellen, Ellen Adams," she added. Minutes later she was speeding along the narrow road in a car for hire with a vigorous man of about sixty. She looked sideways at him. She could see from his muscular shoulders that he had had a more physical job.

"For many years I was a stone worker until my shoulder gave me too much pain to keep working with the heavy slate."

He had said that with a lot of regret in his voice. Slate had become the major mining industry in Cornwall after the mining of tin waned. He had that thick white hair she noticed so often on older men in Britain. Perhaps it came from Cornish stock. Baldness must be more common in American genes.

He told her about the Cornish walls that she saw all along the way, neatly dividing the farms from each other. Slates were stacked and turned in different directions to make a herringbone pattern—sometimes other designs as well. A curious patterned order, industry and imagination in combination creating beauty out of broken pieces. How many instances of order came from the need to put things back together? The grass and spring flowers grew through the cracks in the wall, and she saw the meaning of wallflower.

"Don't you miss it?" she asked, thinking about how boring just driving other people might be.

"Yes, I do," he admitted in a heavy Cornish accent. "There's nothing like that sense of making something from scratch. Something of your own." The vowels were different from those of Londoners. She remembered hearing that originally the Cornish spoke a different language, some form of Celtic speech.

"I write, myself, and I feel the same way when I look at a poem or story I have written." He had invited her to sit in front, and she felt after the exchange that they were already friends.

"My brother is in Canada," he said. "He wanted me to move there when I stopped working. He said there were no stone craftsmen there, and I could start my own business. But I was born in Cornwall, and I'll die here. This is my country." He said it with feeling, without embarrassment.

"It is beautiful country," she said. "I have been here once before, and I came back to rest and write and walk because I found it so lovely." She did not mention the other side of the experience and how she was never free of it now. How it broke into the beauty of this world.

Actually, just at the moment, Ellen could not see very much of the country. They were going back roads, avoiding Bodmin for a short cut to Bosinney. The extremely narrow road looked at first to her as if it had been scooped out of the earth with a large shovel, the sides piled high with dirt; but when she looked closely in the darkening light from the overcast sky, she saw that what she had taken for earth were steep walls overgrown with a net of shrubs, the bare branches of which stuck out in all directions. They were tall enough, however, to block the view of the countryside so that all she could see was the ribbon of the road and the leaden sky ahead.

She could tell, however, that the road was winding and hilly, and if he had not driven so surely she might have been afraid. The English books she had read all her life were full of fatal accidents on narrow winding roads. Death constantly invading life.

"We would say that these roads have no shoulders," she said. "What happens if you meet a big truck—that is, lorry—at the top of a hill?"

"You have to be very careful," he said. "You have to know the road, and you have to be ready to stop dead. Or you will be dead," he joked feebly. His name was John, she remembered, wanting to call him by it.

"This is probably why I have never tried to drive in Britain, John, in addition to the problem of driving on the left," she said. "But no matter how careful you are, things happen." She knew that now.

"A lot of young people have never learned to drive here," he said. Then there was something new in his voice. "I drive a lot of them on weekends, and they aren't like us." She noticed he put himself in her generation, though she knew she was considerably younger. "They just want to get drunk as fast as they can. They don't even stay in the pubs to talk and socialize. Sometimes they are drunk in half an hour, and then they want me to take them somewhere private where they do things I can't imagine."

He sounds bitter, she thought.

"Not to mention their language. They say things I never even saw in wicked books. And some of them don't even seem to have jobs—or perhaps they have jobs that involve them in illegal activities."

"The words don't mean the same to them," she said. "I taught at University for many years, and even though they usually didn't use language like that to me, I heard it all around me and figured out that it had become like saying 'hell' or possibly 'damn' to us. Maybe there is more frustration in the world. I don't know. They seem to feel more helpless than we did, I think. They are like lost sheep, I sometimes think. You know, wandering, not able to find their way. Perhaps the world has seemed too easy to them lately. They haven't had a war recently to remind them of death.

"But still, this instant gratification thing I don't understand. Why do you suppose they are like that?" she asked. She had her own theories but wondered how he had worked it out. "And as for jobs, I thought Britain's economy was good these days. Why is crime a problem?"

John shrugged. "They want everything in an instant form, I think. I have a strange idea that maybe they are afraid of death, in spite of no war lately. Anyway, I think they live for pleasure alone. There is easy money in theft or vice."

"I could think that too if they had known a world at war, but British and American young people of this generation have not. Unless the national memory of Vietnam is still around."

"That might be true for your young people, but not for ours." John became silent then, and the two retreated into their own thoughts. Soon they drove out of the portion of the road that seemed enclosed by the walls and hedges. As they came up to the top of a hill, the way opened out and Ellen caught her breath. Rolling hills as far as she could see, deep green meadows with houses in little clusters scattered here and there. John pulled over to a lookout place.

"I'll show you your hotel from here." He stopped for a couple of minutes, pointing over to the right. "See that clump of evergreens and the white houses? It's just on the left of that." Each farm was neatly set off by encircling or retangular walls. *Enclosure*, she thought, remembering her history. *Enclosure and the rise of the middle class.*

She peered into the distance, thinking that perhaps she saw the old estate near the trees. "How far?" she asked.

"We are about halfway," he said.

"And the sea?"

"About the same. It's on the sea, you know, your hotel, even though you can't see the water from here." He pulled the car back onto the road. "We'll be there soon."

Of course she had known about the sea. She had been dazzled by the beauty of the view of it from the dining room and the bar. Those huge sentinel boulders that so inspired Barbara Hepworth in her sculpture. Or the old films of Cornwall with always a scene in which the sea boiled below a high cliff. But as they drove down the short, lushly planted drive to the hotel a few minutes later, Ellen wondered why she had come back. It was almost dark now, no chance of a sunset. Why come back to a place that had been so traumatic?

What would she do here if she couldn't write? And now she did not even have the manuscript to return to Scotland Yard. She knew she was not up to walking all day and that many of the places to walk were prohibited because of containment of the foot and mouth disease. She just hoped she could get to the sea somehow. "Would you take me on a journey to the nearby fishing village?" she asked John.

She had an odd presentiment that the excursion would never take place. Perhaps it was left over from the last time she had been here. She shivered suddenly. The cold and dampness were piercing as she opened the door and groped for her wallet to pay the fare. *It's only March*, she told herself. Next week, when April came, it would be warmer. Maybe there would be sun. Eternal optimist. She smiled at her own folly.

"Welcome to Willapark." Rick the owner had come out to get her bags and guide her in through the sunporch. She paid John and thanked him, then turned to the dark-haired owner.

"I am delighted to be here again." It had been a long time. Three years, that mythic number, but in real life a long time. For a moment she did not recognize Rick. But his expression was welcoming, as if he knew her. As she looked at him, she saw him remembering the last time. His eyes deepened with what she took to be sympathy.

"I hope it will be a happier time," he said and smiled. "You were brave to come back here."

"I needed to have some—" She hesitated. "I think they call it closure." She might as well be clear about it.

Minutes later they were looking into her single room, as he put her bags inside, the heavy one on the rack so that she could begin unpacking. Actually there was a double bed and a nice deepset window out the east corner of the room, all done in Laura Ashley pastel print, aqua and rose, much more attractive than last night's hotel room. She glanced up to see the high barreled ceiling edged with crown molding. Such height gave the narrow room style and space. She was glad not to be in the same room she had had the last time, the one on the ground floor that she had had to go outside after dark in the evening to return to. Rick disappeared quickly, to help the chef with dinner and leave her time to unpack. *Yes, this will be a happier trip*, she promised herself.

Chapter Three

The massive mahogany wardrobe dominated the narrow room. Ellen pulled open the door on the right side and looked at her reflection in the mirror on the back of it. She was getting used to these wardrobes in the old hotels she stayed in. Often there were no closets. Renovation had extended only to the necessity of putting in bathrooms where there had been small rooms. But often the wardrobes were beautiful pieces of furniture that seemed to merit the French designation. *Armoires*, she practiced her accent.

She saw in the mirror that dressing carefully for her first dinner at the The Willow Hotel had paid a small bonus. She looked both neat and less tired. Her spirits lifted suddenly, as if she were going to a party. Clarissa and her party. She loved that section of Woolf's *Mrs. Dalloway*. Actually the aural image from the film was etched on her mind's ear: Vanessa Redgrave saying, "It's going to be a beautiful day for my party." Strong accent on "beautiful."

Laughing softly to herself, she rehearsed the line in her fake English accent. She had not felt like this in a long time. Almost as if she were young again. She sighed, wishing she were taller, like the models these days or even like Vanessa; but small she remained, and smaller as she aged. Fifty, that was her next birthday, surely the gateway to the third age, though many she knew now in their sixties were lively and active. She was thankful she was still energetic, not ill like so many of her friends. *Not dead, like James*, she reminded herself, though sometimes, at dark moments, she felt that that was a mixed blessing. Still, she was usually optimistic, probably because something beautiful always caught her eye, even in those dark moments. People had warned her she was in denial, unable to accept the reality of unhappiness, the darkness. But she believed she was simply making the best of it. What had T. S. Eliot called it? "Making the best of a bad job."

But she knew she did not want to live to be old and sick. She did not want to be a female Tithonus. Probably no one knew anymore that name from mythology to which Tennyson had given such poignancy in his poem. Poor, sad mortal lover of Aurora, beautiful goddess of the dawn. At his request, the gods had granted him eternal life; but as he aged, he withered away into a grasshopper. He had asked for immortality without eternal youth.

Most people I know had grown up reacting against Tennyson, she continued to muse even after she had been seated for dinner a few minutes later at her small table in the dining room by the window. *If they knew him at all*. Now, of course, few people read poetry. There was a certain fad for poetry slams in New York, she had read, and even in some of the remote places in the American West, but the kind of poetry that made it in performance was different—not quite as bad to her ears as cowboy poetry but still too obvious, almost campy. Like those horrible rhyming jingles she had heard from some of the poets from the International Poetry group she had met on the plane this trip.

She had chatted with one in the line for the toilet while they were flying thirty-thousand feet above the Atlantic. She had sent in a few poems of her own to the *Poetry Library* when *Poetry* and *The Kenyon Review* rejected them (*and me*, she thought). A small group of English poets who felt outside the system, the ones on the plane had been on their way back from a conference at Disney World. *Imagine a poetry conference at Disney World attended by Homer and Dante and T. S. Eliot!* She couldn't help thinking then about American influences on global culture. It was the teacher in her, she knew, who insisted on analyzing all these changes she had lived through in the twentieth century.

Ellen looked around her at the other guests, perhaps eight. She would count them later. This room with its separate tables was the epitome of a small hotel. Many of the English who came here were celebrating an anniversary or birthday, so most of the tables were small. On the walls hung a number of paintings: no prints, all original, mostly landscapes, though one included figures—it looked older than the others. But most were probably twentieth century. No abstracts. No non-representational. The selection pleased her. Just as she had caught up with the intense intellectualism of modernism with its unyielding attitudes toward the viewer, the pop movement had swept in—from her point of view debasing all the superb excellence of the aesthetic.

Gradually, of course, like everyone else, she had grown more democratic and more approving of the elevation of craft and minor arts. Still, in some ways she longed for the astringency of both the traditional and the modernist perspectives. Art could not exist along with an "anything goes" attitude. The discipline was too demanding. She liked these older forms. And yet she saw why there had to be new modes. People perceived the world differently. She remembered John's comments on the young and knew that he was too critical.

She interrupted her own thoughts. *You are here at dinner*, she reminded herself. *At least* try *to live in the moment, make some social effort, even pay more attention to food.* As she remembered from the last time, food here was very good, perhaps a little too much butter and cream for her figure but carefully prepared with lots of fresh vegetables. Instead of the lone green vegetable or salad that was common in America, there were, in addition to the usual potatoes and English peas, two or three other freshly prepared vegetables. Straight from the hotel garden, sprouts and squash tonight. But again, she had to remind herself to notice the food and the people. She was too prone to inward meditation. As she looked around her, she knew she could not resist the savoury, even if she managed to skip dessert. Tomorrow she would walk.

This was the trouble with not having James to talk to. She would both eat too much and go on too long in inner dialogue with herself. That was another reason for travel; it forced her to fit in with others. It kept her in the swim. As usual, even when she tried to enjoy all the food, dinner alone was dull, though Rick came over to pour her wine and chat, and the couple at the table next to her introduced themselves. Still, pleasure in food was something to be shared with a lover or partner, perhaps even a friend. She bit down on a fresh, perfectly cooked brussel sprout, determined to enjoy the shape of the cabbage in miniature.

After dinner when seven or eight gathered in the bar for an after-dinner port or whatever people drank these days—she had a sweet sherry—she joined the conversation. She felt more as if she belonged when she sat with the group. She remembered the first time she had been here, when there was a glowing coal fire in the fireplace. She missed it, though she was grateful for the warmth provided by the new furnace. Now that Rick had put in central heating, the couch was in front of the old fireplace.

But that time as well, after dinner had been the best part. Several of the repeat guests had helped plan two walks for an American lady who did not seem to be an exceptionally fit person, certainly not from a hiker's point of view. Then they told stories of the unreliability of the sea, how Cornish fishermen for generations had been swept away in unexpected storms and how, even in the late twentieth century, children playing peacefully with their small pails and shovels had occasionally disappeared in the incoming tide never to be seen again—to the everlasting horror and guilt of parents who had run up to the house for a hat or suntan lotion.

Tonight was no exception. Even the tone of their voices became deeper with their feeling for the stories they were telling. Perhaps an instinctive sense of Cornwall's past and the forces of nature always there. Not just the sea, but certainly its unpredictable power. Shades of Poseidon. Also that sense of a Celtic past, strange saints and mysteries that shaped Christianity as it developed in ancient Britain. What was that old Tintagel church named that she had walked to once? The Cornish had changed the accent from St. Materiana to St. "Matriana." The plaque on the door said there had been worship going on in that spot for something like thirteen hundred years, the church itself there for only nine hundred.

But she picked up from the general conversation that they were telling some story that was much more recent. The near-gale wind that had blown up at nightfall was moaning as it bent the trees, and the rattle of the windows on the east side of the old stone structure made it somewhat difficult for Ellen to hear, sitting on the edge of the six or seven regulars. She was afraid that she might not be able to sleep tonight on her side of the hotel. Even before she came down, she had heard the large window rattle from the force of the winds. But now it was worse.

"I'm sorry," she smiled at them. "I did not catch the last thing you said."

The small old man opposite her with the black lab at his feet looked across at her, his blue eyes intense as he obviously tried to draw her into the conversation He had lost his wife a year ago and was thought to be grieving excessively, she had heard one of the women at dinner mention. "I said I used to be a fisherman."

She smiled and nodded.

He raised his voice, as if speaking to someone deaf. "I began after retiring from the Royal Navy and then gave it up finally after the two boats and their skippers (who hired me originally) were actually sunk in ground seas, huge waves coming out of nowhere in the North Cornish part of the Atlantic. I almost didn't survive, and many of the seamen did not."

"Oh yes," echoed Alice, a small plump woman in a dark red, floor-length dress. "No one who lives outside this area understands what they call a ground sea. I grew up here, and I knew from a child that it meant those unexpected gigantic waves. It usually happens with the spring tides, but sometimes it surprises us at other times of year."

"Does it usually happen on a sunny day?" Ellen asked.

"Not necessarily," the old man joked. "We don't have that much sun, but it is usually a day when the ocean seems to be calm."

A woman in flowing velvet pants—Ellen vaguely remembered her name as Wendy—and a casual turtleneck sweater got up then to get another drink from the bar. Ellen noticed that she had beautiful honey-colored hair trained in a smooth style to turn under around her face. "But that is it," she said. "Often children don't see the large waves in time to get on higher ground. Now when this happened to James, it was September and nobody expected a spring tide. And the day was a calm day, so no one expected big waves."

"James," repeated Ellen. "Have I met him?" She was startled by the coincidence of the name's being the same as that of her husband.

"James is my son," Rick interjected from the bar.

That was the beginning of the story of September 6, 1998, and the true heroism of both boy and father. Everyone settled down and sat quietly as the old man continued, almost ignoring Rick now.

"Imagine it: Rick serving lunch to the locals, bow tie and embroidered waistcoat marking the occasion. The two boys are playing down on the smaller boulder, those two huge rocks at the foot of the coast walk. About twenty minutes into the lunch James's friend comes running up, dripping with sea water and sobbing. 'James has been swept off the rock by a huge wave,' says the child, weeping. 'Do something,' he says.

"At this, Rick begins stripping off his tie as he runs out of the dining room, having to go out the side door to get to the back of the house and the path down to the beach. He cuts across the back lawn, running and unbuttoning his clothes, now and then barely pausing to pull off an outer garment until he is at the coastwalk, clad only in shorts. Long ago he had lost a favorite brother to the sea, and he is afraid. Lisa, his wife, is trailing him, calling out words of warning he pays no attention to."

The older man looked down at his hands gravely.

Ellen leaned forward. "And what happened then?"

He looked at her, relishing the tension. "He dived into the sea of course. I was not there, but I was told he ran to the top of that boulder and dived in. By then forty-foot waves were rolling in. Just as he started to go, he called over his shoulder: 'Get the rescue.' It's a wonder Lisa heard. She was pretty far away, but she ran back to the house to telephone."

Ellen noticed that everyone was enthralled by the story now. The couple in the corner had stopped talking, and to a person they looked at the storyteller. His name was Mark, she remembered from the introduction earlier, and his voice had deepened as he moved into the heart of the tale.

"Did the rescue come and get them both then?" she asked.

"Oh, no, it was not that easy." Mark shook his head, the shock of white hair catching the light. "Rick said that when he found himself in the water, he realized that—good swimmer that he was—the tides were too strong. He had to struggle not to go under, and there was no sign of James. Though not especially religious, he looked up and shouted, 'God help me!'" Mark's tone changed. "The only hope he had, he said, was that the next big wave would take him into the cave that the sea had worn between the two boulders and that James would be there."

Wendy, the beautiful young woman in velvet, leaned forward: "And did that happen?"

"Oh yes, exactly that," said Mark. "Some have said it was a miraculous answer to prayer. He heard a little voice say, 'I love you, Dad,' and there was James. Rick almost wept then, I bet, but he had to rush to get James up onto a kind of shelf in the cave. Then he climbed up himself, hoping there would not be another big wave for a few minutes or seconds—I don't know the time frame. He could not have known it exactly himself."

Mark pushed up the stretched sleeves of his cream-colored cableknit sweater. "Those tides are completely unexpected. And no one can predict when they will be over. Sometimes they come from hurricanes in the south Atlantic. From America. Huge waves wash in after a peaceful surf. That is why they are so dangerous to bathers and even fishermen who ought to know to watch for them. But the point is really that no one sees them coming."

"Perhaps parents should not let the children go near the sea," said the woman with the long red dress.

What was her name? What a tactless woman, thought Ellen. *Alice, that was her name*. Ellen glanced at Rick then. She hoped he had not been listening, but he was frowning.

Mark smiled. "It takes a woman to think she can protect her children from everything. No, it is so rare that one would not want to deprive one's children of seaside experiences. It's not much different from the dangers of riding in a car—though perhaps injury or death by car is far more frequent."

Ellen raised her hand slightly as if to interrupt: "But tell, what happened in the cave? Did the rescue people come?"

"Oh yes, they came immediately, but they could not get to Rick and James. They could not even get into the cave. Their boat capsized, and one of them was washed into the cave with Rick and James. But that only meant that Rick had to help the fellow get up himself onto a protuberance in the cave."

"Then what did Rick do? Did they just stay there until the storm was over?" Alice plucked at her red dress nervously and looked over at Rick. "I had no idea I was staying with such a celebrity." She fluttered her eyelashes, Ellen noticed. Some women really responded to the heroic male.

The woman in velvet laughed then. "Didn't you see it, Alice? This story hit all the national papers."

Everyone looked happy at that, but Ellen still wanted the details. "But what happened then? How long before they got out?"

"That's the best of the story," said Mark, rubbing his hands. "It was really terrible for them. Rick said—"

At this point Rick came over to the group. "If you are really interested, I'll tell it from here. For a while I did not want to talk about it, but now I can. It's far enough away."

Murmurs of encouragement came from different directions, and several people drew their chairs closer. "Oh yes, tell us," said Ellen, knowing there was something here she needed to know. Odd how this place seemed to contain two extreme stories—good and evil personified—that happened in the same year, her husband's death and now this opposite image of something mysterious but good.

"Well, there we were, James and I, and you can believe that I had told him, too, that I loved him. But what I could not help imagining was that the waves would come in, each one higher than the last, until the cave was full of water and we had drowned. But what actually happened was different, and I tried to prepare James so that we could survive." He didn't sit down with them, but he stood on the bar side of the group, his hand on the back of a chair someone had pushed over to him.

Ellen could see from where she sat that he was tense remembering it all, as he rubbed his index finger over the smooth mahogany of the back of the chair. "He must have been terrified at twelve," she said.

"I think I was actually more frightened. Once I was with him on the rocky projection, he seemed pretty calm. Though we were both very cold and wet, of course, in great danger of hypothermia. But what I was most concerned about was teaching James to take a deep breath each time a wave came in so that he could hold his breath as long as possible until the level of the water subsided somewhat and we could breathe again."

Ellen had an image of the two clinging there wet on the shelf in the dark cave, waiting for the next wave, helpless before the force of the sea. She thought then of the story of Odysseus when he was shipwrecked off the island of the Phaeacians in rough seas and how he struggled to swim to shore, using every ounce of strength he had until he knew he was about to go under. Then just as he could swim no more Athene sent a water nymph to rescue him, tossing him up on the shore where Nausicaa was walking with her maids. Obviously, some rescue had happened, or Rick and James would not be here. "Did the rescue finally come in?" she asked.

"No," said Rick after a pause. "In fact, several times—at least twice, we thought it was over when especially strong waves swept in and knocked us off our perch. One time I dislocated my shoulder. Later I found that it was broken. And once when James was washed off the shelf, he hit his head and sustained a skull fracture."

Mark interjected here, "Tell us how long you were there and how you finally got out."

Rick nodded. "As you see, we finally got out, but we were in there for five hours; and I owe it to James holding on to me and sometimes calling out 'Dad' and 'Don't go to sleep' that I did not give in to hypothermia. But after five hours, just when I thought we could not face another wave without the level of the water in the cave rising above our heads, the tide began to turn."

Ellen shivered a little, thinking of the two clinging there in the dark, wet cave It reminded her of that story of the sea by Iris Murdoch. It also made her a believer in the old sea gods, way before Celtic Christianity in Cornwall. She saw them exercising their power to show how they control us all—and then as suddenly showing mercy. Letting go. Ellen mused aloud, "It sounds as if Poseidon arbitrarily turned and let you go. Perhaps because you had fought him so valiantly. Or, as we say, the tide started going out."

"Yes, some sort of kindness in the ordering of the universe. Not exactly a shepherd to the rescue of lost sheep, although I suppose that is what I was trying to be for James. But in nature herself, I see some tilt to the good. Every tide that sweeps in eventually goes out. Not too late for us this time. After five hours we walked out of the cave, and just outside, a rescue helicopter hovered over the scene. It winched us up and away to hospital and healing hands. The rest was easy."

"Not so easy," said Lisa, who had come in as he spoke. "You are still having therapy for that shoulder. But thank God, James has had no after-effects from the skull fracture. And of course, you received all that wonderful appreciation, as if people all over Britain were hungry for good stories after all the horrors the press reports."

Ellen could not help adding, "Even I am thrilled with it, not only for itself but for personal reasons. It gives one hope in a world that seems to work toward despair."

"I don't agree," argued Wendy. "I think there is just as much good, in spite of what literature, films, newspapers, pictures—almost everything today—tells us. That is what our religion teaches us. Not that we Brits like to talk much about religion."

"I'm not sure of that—I mean, what religion teaches." Ellen tried not to be disagreeable, but this was important to her. "There is so much suffering in religion, I don't think we can tell that. No, we can't prove by mere reason whether the good and the bad are equally dispersed or whether one is dominant." Ellen frowned. "But perhaps you are right in one sense. Certainly, religion helps us look for hope. But in ancient times those nature gods seemed more arbitrary and more frightening."

Wendy laughed. "Oh, no one thinks in terms of those superstitions anymore. Or perhaps it is fairer to say that I don't want to think that. It scares me."

Rick interceded: "Who knows what mysterious forces of nature exist? We still haven't figured that out. Somehow Cornwall has nature gods and Christianity mingled. All that Merlin tradition. I know he came from Wales, but he hovers over us with Arthur and Guinevere. I only know that our rescue, in spite of my efforts, seems miraculous to me."

After that the conversation became general, and Ellen went up to bed, tired from travel. As she switched off the light beside her bed, she smelled the scent of English lavender that wafted from her gown. She kept a sachet in her luggage. There was something magical for her about that scent that had been with her since her mother introduced her to Yardley years ago. She was home. England was another home.

Even if bad things happened here, so did good.

Chapter Four

Ellen felt as if she had been shaken awake. Her heart pounded as she sat up. No, no one was in the room. She knew immediately that she was here at the The Willow Hotel. Was this only her first night? It seemed so familiar, as if she had never gone home and come back again. She reminded herself, breathing deeply—and yet again—to calm herself, that James had been dead now for three years. But what had awakened her? Then a shrill scream rang out from the corridor outside.

What a strange, unbelievable start to my holiday after such a pleasant evening, she thought irrelevantly. She suddenly found herself reliving the moment when she had walked down the two steep steps from the train at Bodmin Parkway, still breathless after handing down her heavy bags. The first sound she heard as she looked around the platform was a shrill cry—the screams of seagulls mounting the sky. She had felt then that it was an omen. But this present scream was the beginning, the real beginning that had been prefigured by the screams of those seagulls wheeling about the sky—only more agonized. Whoever was screaming was suffering some sudden and unbearable torture.

She got up quickly and belted on the chenille robe at the foot of the bed. She wondered then that she had been sleeping peacefully for what felt like years. All due to that story of Rick's heroism. For a moment there she had tried to talk herself into being happy for the first time in a long time. It seemed to her that she might wipe out what had happened here before. Or perhaps Rick's story had brought back for her a balance between good and evil in the world. The world was a mixture of good and evil. Where the balance lay was the question. Did nature tilt towards death or life? The story of Rick's heroism and the love between father and son made it seem possible to triumph over evil. But now the world was tilting back to normal. Normal for her was pain, and surely that was the cause of the sound. Her James and his story. She shook her head. She needed to stop thinking. She opened the door and peered out. Down the hall, she saw several people. Someone might be ill, though the scream boded worse.

Ellen walked hurriedly towards the others, several people who seemed to be hesitating outside the door about the middle of the hall. Rick appeared out of nowhere and intercepted her. "Please go get dressed," he said. "I'll need you downstairs. I'll need a cool head there. We'll talk then." He was almost curt, obviously worried. She returned to her room and surfaced about ten minutes later, according to her small Seiko watch. She walked carefully down the wide stairs, noticing with one part of her mind even then the various plants on the sills at the landing that were banked in front of Tiffany stained glass windows. It was a lovely old manor house.

The scream had been no more than twenty minutes earlier, she judged as she approached, but there were already people in the bar. She heard the low hum of voices as she stepped down on the hall red carpet and walked toward the cosy room. They would surely be able to tell her some details about what had happened—even the main event. At least the bare facts. Or perhaps Rick would be there now. She paused at the door, smoothing her gray sweater at the hips. She had dressed hurriedly. The two men and one woman inside looked towards her coolly, surprised at her presence, she thought. One of them made a comment in a low voice that she could not hear. It was the woman in the long red dress who had stood near the fire the night before.

The eyebrows of the dark-haired man rose like half moons, and the woman, about fifty—her name was Alice, and she had deep crow's feet around her eyes as if she had laughed or perhaps cried a great deal over the years—began to shake her head slowly as if to say, "No, you don't belong, you American tourist. This is trouble for us to handle."

But then Rick came up behind her and touched her upper arm lightly. "Let's talk in my office." The words were mildly comic, as his office was a big desk in the hall between the bar and the dining room. She turned and followed him, happy to escape the feeling that she was an outsider. If he wanted to consult her, perhaps she was not such an alien after all.

"I am sorry, Professor Adams—may I call you Ellen?"

She nodded, and he went on quickly: "We have had a terrible accident. I know from the last time that you are aware how important it is not to panic or to let the guests become hysterical. If you could help by taking the others into the dining room for tea while I talk with the police, I should appreciate it immensely."

"Of course," she said at once, adding almost in the same breath, "what happened? I heard a scream, possibly two."

Rick did not answer immediately. He looked down at her, seeming to select his words. As usual, she was smaller than anyone, though he was not especially tall for a man. "A woman is dead; her name is Marie Deschamps. She was in the bar last night, but I am not sure you met formally. She was wearing purple, I think. She was a librarian. Perhaps that is all I should say until the police come."

Ominous past tense in the description of the woman. Ellen somehow could not summon up an image of the woman. She knew she had glimpsed someone who was very quiet somewhat on the edge of the group. She had also seen her walk towards the bar during the story of the rescue. Suddenly she wanted to cry. Another death. It seemed to follow her. But she tried to reply like the adult Rick thought her. She was a middle-aged woman now, and people looked to her for experience and stability. This was part of who she was, the good part of being almost a senior. She sighed. "I'll take the others in the dining room whenever you say. Just exactly what do you want me to tell them?"

The dark-haired man frowned. He was clearly still worried. After all, in spite of his confident manner he was only about fifty, maybe late forties, and the reputation of his hotel was now in danger. He had been here, she knew, about twenty years, having owned a hotel in Gloucestershire as a young man. This hotel was extremely important to him.

"Just take their orders for tea and ginger biscuits. If they ask—and they probably will—tell them Miss Deschamps is dead, but don't speculate with them. Tell them the police will talk to them later. The local constabulary is here, and an inspector from Scotland Yard is on the way."

She knew from experience that the involvement of Scotland Yard meant that this was murder, not an accident, but for the moment she did not say anything, just moved toward the bar and collected the now larger group for the dining room. She would rather have heard what was going on with the the police, but she was grateful to be busy, especially in a way designated by Rick, who had the full respect of all the guests, most of them repeaters to the The

Willow Hotel. Obviously, the heroic stature he had achieved in the event of the rescue had added a certain glamour to his already strong image. She would do her best for him. He had been so kind to her when she really needed it.

But it was always difficult when people were afraid. When everyone knew or would know that a murderer was abroad. She could imagine how it might be if some of the anxiety was translated into interaction among the guests. Tempers might flare as they had when James's body was discovered seven years earlier. Two of the men at the hotel that fateful twenty-four hours after the police had come had had an actual fight in the bar, with their two dogs getting into the fray. She shuddered as she remembered it. She would certainly do her best to keep things as calm as possible. Luckily Brits were good at keeping their feelings under wraps. Not like the Irish she had known so well in her home town.

But what had happened exactly? Ellen was curious. Perhaps she was becoming an old busybody like those fictional mystery characters Miss Marple or Jessica Fletcher. What could she possibly do? Nothing, of course. The police would do the important things. She felt her own palms grow sticky with perspiration even in this cold hall when she thought of that scream, possibly screams, that had awakened her. Without thinking much about it, she walked toward the stairs and diverted a small group coming down into the dining room. Rick came in behind her and announced to the people still standing there that they should settle at their usual tables.

She scrambled in her purse for her small filofax notebook that she had bought at the pen shop on Turl Lane near the Bodleian the last time she was in England. Already she had English telephone addresses in it and sketches for poems that she wrote when she traveled. Another use for it! Tonight she would keep track of what people wanted in the way of tea and water and even biscuits and sweets. If only she could also find the small pen she used with it. She knew she needed it. At her age she might well scramble tea and coffee orders, a bit like giving the diabetic sugar or sweet ginger sauce. Then she would be suspected of murder herself. Not funny, when she was in the midst of the real thing, but she couldn't resist dramatizing. Best to begin here and cease and desist from flights of fancy.

"Bill and Jane Markham," they said at Table One. After breakfast they would face the windows looking out to sea. They would both have tea, they said, Earl Grey, if it were available. They were from Sussex and had come to Willapark first on their honeymoon, probably about fifteen years ago now. They had actually discovered the body, they told her, after they heard the first scream. There had been two, as she thought. "But we don't want to talk about it until after we talk to the police," Jane had said, as if she were used to speaking for both of them.

"Absolutely," she said, unconsciously aping the California certainty of her son-in-law. She did not want them to report to the police that she had been trying to extract information from them. She moved quickly to the next table, knowing that she could not spend a great deal of time with each group or she would not have finished her task when Rick and the police came in to talk to them.

Ann and Dickie at the next table lived in Portsmouth now. He had been in the Navy at one point. They were in their fifties and probably were involved in a second marriage for both of them, she had thought from something Ann said last night. Or perhaps they were recent partners, not yet married.

"Tea and biscuits?" she asked. "Or would you rather have coffee?"

"Dickie will have anything you have to eat," teased Ann, subtly putting him down, Ellen thought.

"And you?" she managed to say coolly. Ann was wearing a floor-lengtb skirt in a bright print that looked Carribean.

"Oh, I like to eat, too, but not like him," she said. "He ate all afternoon in the car, chips and leftover Cornish pasty, and four candy bars." She laughed, a little too loudly from the expressions of those at the tables nearby. The woman on the right was already looking down her nose, Ellen could see from the corner of her eye.

"I do like to eat," Dickie agreed, oblivious to the condescension from the other part of the room. "Not like when I was a child in Cornwall. I grew up here, and sometimes I would eat the slices from a whole loaf of bread for breakfast. You know, for my morning toast."

"This hotel is the place for you then," said Ellen. "The food here is delicious, and there is always a lot."

"That is how I know he did not do this dirty deed," Ann said, laughing again. "No criminal could have that easy a conscience."

"I'll tell the maid to bring an extra large serving of biscuits." Ellen ignored the reference to the crime deliberately and moved on to Table 3. Yes, those two at Table 2 with their raillery were too happy with each other to be married. That particular kind of sparring tended to diminish.

Here at Table 3 the couple were celebrating their thirty-fifth anniversary. No rough teasing here but a kind of quiet warmth of which Ellen felt a little envious. She had hoped that her own marriage would arrive at this plateau of content. Too late now. The woman, Barbara, looked worried, however. "We'll just have the tea. At our age we don't need to eat in the middle of the night." She was a tall blonde woman with wavy shoulder length hair, obviously still trying to hold on to the way she looked when they had met so many years ago. "We are Barbara and Dennis from Devon. He's a decorator, and I stay home with the children. Only one left now, an afterthought," she said ruefully. Her husband said nothing but looked over Ellen's shoulder, more solemn than his wife. In fact, he looked depressed, as if he were not listening to the conversation. His wife looked up at Ellen with wide eyes. "Could you tell us just exactly what happened?"

"A woman in the hotel died," Ellen confirmed in a matter-of-fact-tone, "but Rick doesn't want us to say anything more about it until we talk to the police."

The conversation around the room continued much in the same vein, people wanting to know more but generally bending to Rick's rules and asking for tea and cookies for the most part. It seemed on the surface highly unlikely that any of these ordinary people might be the murderer, but she knew that police work demanded a slow and tedious collection of facts. Perhaps she could help with those. Ellen hurried to the kitchen when she had collected the orders and returned quickly just as Rick entered the room again.

"Chief Inspector Brown." He gestured towards the door, and a slender redhead entered, curls that escaped her hat around her face making her look younger than she could have been at that rank. "She comes to us from Scotland Yard."

Following her was a tall gray-haired man, slightly bent as if he had borne a lot of the burdens of the world. "And this is is retired Chief Inspector McInery, who lives in in Oxford but also part-time in Tintagel now. Ms. Brown has asked him to sit in."

"And this tall young man is Sergeant Ted Jones of the local constabulary. He will be staying here now for the next two days to oversee the investigation as closely as possible." The newcomers blinked a little at the early light coming in through the dining room windows. Beside them, Rick looked unusually dark, still with the remnants of his tan from a recent holiday in the Canary Islands.

"Ladies and Gentlemen," said the tall redhead, looking solemn and, if possible, younger than when she first entered, "I regret to tell you that we are beginning a murder investigation." Although virtually everyone knew this already, Ellen heard something like a sudden intake of breath at the announcement. "This morning at approximately two-twenty a.m., Marie, or Helene (we don't actually know which), Deschamps was hit with a blunt instrument that led within minutes to her death. Usually we wait for the autopsy to tell you that, but there is no way the blow that smashed her skull could not have been the immediate cause of death."

Perhaps it came after death, thought Ellen but then chastened herself for being argumentative.

"There is also no way such a blow could have been self-administered, which leaves out suicide. Before this day is over, I shall need to speak to each of you."

Jane raised her hand, like a child in school. Just as she began her question, Ellen noticed the gray-haired man who had been introduced as the retired Douglas McInery. He was looking down at his shoes with a scowl on his face. He must have felt her looking at him, the way one sometimes responds to staring eyes on the street. His bright blue eyes met hers with a look so searching she was for a moment mesmerized. Then he began to make his way quietly around the edge of the room towards her.

Chapter Five

Ellen stood there, waiting for the slender man to arrive at her side. At first she thought he had a shock of white hair, but when she looked at him again she saw that it was only white around his face. It became darker towards the back of his head, as if in some way he were a Janus figure of an elderly man as he moved towards her but possibly much younger at the back. But she could see from the way he walked—easily and without the knee difficulties she had noticed that seemed to affect the aging in this damp part of the world—that he was not old. She knew from the way he was looking at her, as if he knew her, that he was deliberately, if somewhat unobtrusively, she thought, making his way towards her.

Where had she seen him before? He looked familiar—perhaps not exactly familiar, but she knew she had seen him somewhere. The obvious answer was that he had been involved in the brief investigation of James's death. But she knew that he had not been the major inspector involved. That had been a man they called Spenser—no first name. A very blunt Englishman who, for all his lip service to various polite forms—always addressing her as *Madam*, being very careful not to press the questions into the area of the personal, even after he found out that she and James had been in the midst of a divorce—that he suspected her. It was perhaps because of his manner that she had not told him everything. Anyway, in the end the case had been closed as an accidental death, although the questions remained.

She had heard since that Spenser had died of a heart attack. In some sense that had given her the courage to come back with what she had found among James's things. She would not have to face him again, although she had little idea whom she would ask for at Scotland Yard. Perhaps this man would walking towards her would give her information that would help. Oh yes, the image flashed across her mind, but she couldn't hold it—his face in that dim room in Cornwall where she had gone to make a statement about the body in the creek. It was vague to her whether he belonged to the Cornwall police or to those who had come down from Scotland Yard.

Perhaps this Douglas McInery had inherited Spenser's unsolved cases. She would ask. The questioning began, and Ellen tried to pay attention. There might be important information. But Chief Inspector McInery was finally at her side, lightly, just touching, her elbow as he said quietly, "Mrs. Adams? May I have a word in the bar?"

"Shouldn't I hear the rest of the questions?" She smiled up at him. He was quite tall. "Have we met?"

"Once briefly," he answered the latter question first—then "I'll catch you up later on anything you need to know."

Like most men, very sure of himself, she thought, bristling, but she followed him into the bar and lounge off the dining room. *James had not been so brusque,* she couldn't help thinking.

He gestured to the green velvet wingback chair just inside the door of the lounge where she had felt so unaccountably happy the evening before. Some stories had happy endings. It was almost dawn now, but it was pitch dark outside the large window that looked out upon the back garden and beyond its wall down the gently sloping hill to the coast path and the mysterious sea beyond. It was an ancient landscape weathered and softened by how many years she could not imagine, even though the house itself, the hotel, had been built as a manor house by a wealthy man around 1900. Rick, the present owner, had told her a story the last time of how the son of the owner, who had eventually lost his fortune and sold the house sometime in the twenties, had written to him when he read of this present sale fifteen years ago. That was a story, too, of a child who had lived in a small room and wanted to return to it in his aging years. Unfortunately, the room had become a bath in one of the remodelings since.

It occurred to Ellen that one of the reasons she loved to come to Britain was that stories of the past were told again and again, treasured and passed on. Poignant stories of loss and change. But somehow change that did not obliterate. If it were light, she knew that she could have stood at the window and seen the huge boulders and the blue Atlantic itself. When she was a small girl, she had walked the shores of the Atlantic from the other side, but her Atlantic was warmer and kinder than this; and in those early mornings when her mother let her walk alone outside the cottage set in the gentle dunes, the sea had yielded up beautiful, almost tropical, shells that had been brought up by the moving tides of the Gulf Stream to the middle Atlantic state where she and her mother had spent lazy sundrenched summers. She had heard that the Gulf Stream moderated the climate of Britain and was in danger, ironically, from the global warming that was melting the North Pole. If that happened, scientists speculated, Britain would actually be much colder.

But here, in the Cornish darkness that would soon be gray light, the ocean seemed more dangerous than her Atlantic, more sudden and more arbitrary— she thought of the story of Rick and James that she had heard the evening before. The sea here was guarded by irrational sea gods like those in the *Odyssey* she had read about all her life. Suddenly she knew that, however much she loved Britain, she was a foreigner; and this was a foreign sea, much closer to mythology than to the domesticated Christianity that took her to an Episcopal or Anglican Church on major holidays. She shrugged off the unwelcome personal feeling. And of course now the brutality of murder and the embedded suffering of that primal scream had wiped out the reassurance of the love and heroism between father and son.

She opened her purse and searched for a tissue. She blew her nose, as if to clear her head of fanciful thinking. She would use that detail when she wrote her next short story. She wanted to convince herself that the sea and the room here were simply places where she had spoken to policemen or members of the constabulary and even these more elegant officials from Scotland Yard. She looked up at the inspector almost covertly. She did not want him to see her staring. This room was a place where people questioned and analyzed the latest murder. This one tonight and the ostensible murder of James that had not been a murder at all, but had somehow involved the seamy side of life, even criminal behavior, on both his and her parts. In different ways, of course. But she would think about that later.

"I met you briefly in the investigation of your husband's death," Chief Inspector McInery was saying. "Of course, I was not deeply involved in that, as you know. Spenser was the man. But since I have been retired here in Cornwall, I have been asked to confer on some of the more interesting cases."

"Yes, I thought I remembered you." So he had been with Scotland Yard. She looked into his blue eyes with frank interest, but he glanced away, all business. "I am here visiting again. Since the case was not resolved, I have had some difficulty coming to terms with it all," Ellen spoke firmly. She too could be businesslike. "Actually, I had come to bring the police something I came across later in my husband's things, but unfortunately the bag I brought it in was mixed up coming from the airport luggage. Anyway, I expect you want to ask some questions about tonight…." Ellen paused to allow McInery to lead the conversation.

He did not pick up the conversational ball immediately. He took out a pipe from his pocket and then replaced it. Then he got up from the chair and walked toward the bar, looking for an ashtray. He turned. "Do you mind?" he questioned, taking out his pipe again.

"Frankly," she said, "I have always minded smoke since my parents used to make me carsick with their cigarettes."

"Yes, I'm sorry." He put down the ashtray and returned the pipe to his jacket. "I have almost given it up," he laughed wryly, "but when I am anxious I'm afraid I revert."

"And why should you be nervous? I should think the shoe would be on the other foot." She noticed then that although his blue-gray tweed jacket, probably hand-tailored, was slightly frayed around the edges of the sleeves, he wore what was clearly an almost new and freshly ironed burgundy shirt that contrasted with his dark gray trousers. Although he must have dressed hurriedly to get here at this time of the night or morning, he had taken care. A care that spoke a certain self-respect in his generation. And hers, she thought, with a flicker of surprise at the revelation.

"Yes, I know. But even after all these years and murder investigations, I sometimes feel restless before I begin. It is as if chaos has come again—and somehow it is up to me to bring order." He sighed then and fingered his tie. It bore the insignia of some college. Ellen did not recognize it. He must have realized than that he was was straying into the personal. She almost saw him thinking that this woman was intrusive.

"Shall we start the questions?" He sat down firmly then, all business again.

"I am ready, though I know very little. But first, would you be able to tell me why you called me aside?" She must stop taking control. Perhaps she was getting used to being alone. Sometimes when she entered a restaurant with a friend or male relative these days, she would ask for the table before she thought. After all those years of waiting for a man to take the initiative. It had been almost second nature.

"Yes, I shall be happy to, but first let me get these other routine matters out of the way."

Ellen nodded and remained silent. She did not want to irritate him or make him think that she was simply a garrulous and bossy American. The combination of teaching all those years and now being alone made her naturally independent, but that did not mean that she should be rude. She would follow the forms.

"Where is your room in the hotel in relation to the room of Miss Deschamps?" McInery took out his pad and a black Waterman pen.

"I am on the first floor, as you call it. The first level above the ground at the north end of the Willapark. There is a small stand of oaks outside my window, and the last time I was here I heard a lark sing in the early morning. I was in a different room then, but I think the birdsong came from a different direction. My room is on the very end, and Miss Deschamps was about three doors down towards the middle of the hall."

Douglas looked at Ellen closely. "You make a good witness—we like precise detail. Then I take it from what you say that you have no hearing problem—but you wouldn't at your age." He looked at her then as if he really saw her, taking in her bright hair and lingering just slightly at her lips. Perhaps, she thought, he was noticing the deep lines of sorrow on either side of her mouth.

"Obviously, if you can hear the lark in the early morning, you should be likely to hear any intrusive noises in the hall—as well as any loud noises from the room just three doors away?"

"I am not sure, Inspector—I was sound asleep, and I heard the lark three years ago—remember, time passes. I am also suffering from jetlag still. I only arrived two nights ago. But I don't mean to argue—I think I hear as well as I ever did, except perhaps in crowds." *Oops.* She was talking too much again. Was it in the nature of the teacher always to give answers that were more than people wanted to know?

Douglas McInery was silent for a moment, as if considering her answer. "What you observed is important, particularly because the rooms between you and Helene Deschamps were not occupied. Too many people this spring are staying away from Cornwall because of the foot and mouth disease. No one is allowed the coast walk, you know. But tell me in your own words what you heard."

Ellen paused, trying to frame her statement carefully, though she knew from past experience that he would question her further, wherever she started.

"I can only say that I awoke startled, as if I had been awakened by a noise. Later I decided that it was the first scream, but I did not actually hear it, so my supposition may be wrong. For a few moments I lay there quietly, listening and wondering. And then I heard what is often described as a bloodcurdling scream. I am not sure what that means, but it sounded to me as if whoever made it was in agony."

Now Ellen was rubbing her forehead unconsciously, feeling as if a headache might be in the making. Her emotion at the scream had come back to her, and the world seemed dark again. She sat up then and looked toward the window of the room. It was not a large room. Sometimes it seemed too small for the guests, as it had the night before. But perhaps that was part of the cosiness. She still missed the fire. The gray light was beginning now. She saw it through the lounge window, a western window that was still quite dark, but perhaps it was the mist over the Atlantic that made it so.

"Did or do you have any idea what time it was when you woke?"

"Not at first, but after I lay there no more than three or four minutes I looked at my wrist watch on the night table. It was three o'clock. For me that is a time I often wake these days, since I am alone. So perhaps I woke without hearing any sound. And yet my heart was pounding—In Hopkins' beautiful line, 'I woke to feel the fell of dark, not day.' Or is it 'wake'?" She looked at the quiet man across from her then, more fully returning to the context of the questioning. She was surprised to see a look of warm sympathy in his eyes.

McInery smiled at her, his blue eyes turning cloudy. "I know—but I don't know which poem that is," he said gently, as if he really did read Hopkins. Odd for a policeman. And then he leaned forward in his chair as if the next question were important. "But my dear Mrs. Adams, you have said you were sleeping soundly, so it is most likely that something external woke you in this early morning. And, of course, the second scream bears that out. What time did you get to Miss Deschamps's room? I understand that you came out in your robe, and that Rick told you to return and dress because he would need you downstairs."

"Yes, it was only about five or six minutes after three, I think, that I arrived near Miss Deschamps's door. I did not quite get there, if it matters. A couple from the other end of the hall were standing at the open door, and Rick more or less intercepted me before I arrived at the room."

"Who were the couple?"

"I was a little flustered, and they were in their night clothes. But I think it was Ann and Dickie. They live in Portsmouth—I don't remember their last name, but I have it here in my little notebook." She took the mini-filofax out of her purse.

Doug McInery frowned and tugged at his right ear.

Ellen laughed, "Don't look so gloomy, Inspector. I am not keeping close records of everything. Rick asked me to help the non-existent staff by getting orders for tea or coffee to keep everyone together until the police came. The only way I could keep up with it all was to match people and table numbers and take notes on the orders. With milk, with cream, biscuits or not." She deliberately used the English term, not cookies. She sat up straighter. "Actually I only made one boo-boo—or do you say it that way?"

Doug McInery laughed sheepishly. "No, but I think I understand you. Of course, and you are a writer, too. I imagine you often record aspects of your experience?"

"Of course—I do. But I think I have enough material of such things from last time." It occurred to her that he was an exceptionally attractive man, late fifties, perhaps sixty, whatever the contradictions of youth and age in his appearance. She especially liked the impression of energy restrained, as he sat quietly, asking her questions and concentrating on his thoughts, but a kind of leonine grace in the muscles of his upper arms as he leaned towards her. It was early, surely, for retirement, or was Scotland Yard like the US Army, where it was of little benefit to continue after twenty-five years if one were not going to make general?

She had missed a question thinking about frivolous things. Somehow it helped to distract her from the horror that threatened to bring back unabated the anguish of the last visit here. "I beg your pardon?"

His eyes crinkled as he smiled. "You must be tired. Your sleep patterns all disturbed by the trip. And this situation must be particularly painful after last time."

Amazing how he seemed almost to read her thoughts. But of course that was his stock in trade. He would have to be a very observant man to have risen so high in his profession.

"No, I have enough from you for the time being, but the reason I drew you aside was that we have reason to believe that Miss Deschamp is involved in the manuscript, fine arts, ring of thieves that—forgive me—your husband seemed to have some connection with."

She couldn't believe it. Was it starting all over again? "Are they still active?" She wet her lips and smoothed the back of her hair, shifting slightly in her seat.

"More than ever. These last few years have been prosperous times, and collectors want to obtain things that often are unavailable outside libraries and museums."

She leaned forward, suddenly intense. "What do you mean unavailable? Surely they could arrange private sales and go to Sotheby auctions like anyone else?" If possible, she did want to understand. She had been agonizing ever since James's death about how he could possibly have been drawn into such criminal action in the very area of his deepest loyalties, books and learning.

The inspector reached into the inner pocket of his jacket and took out a photograph. "Would you by any chance recognize this person? She seems to be an international agent of the concern that has within it curators, professors, collectors that seem on the surface eminently respectable, but who work at least part time with this group."

She took the photograph, fumbling for her reading glasses in her purse.

Instantly she recognized the face but not where she had seen it. The face looked out at her, seemingly a newspaper photograph much like the engagement pictures of her youth. Now both the man and the woman getting married were pictured, but then only the woman, the prize of beauty for the deserving knight. She looked again—dark hair, perhaps brown eyes, certainly dark, an unusually forthright and intelligent face and expression. It was not someone she knew well but someone she had seen recently.

"I know I have seen her." Ellen took her glasses off and then put them back again. She struggled to place the face. Traveling so much seemed to exacerbate the natural aging principle that would cause her to mix up the people she met casually. Was the hair different? Women so often changed their cut or style. "No, I can't place her, but perhaps it will come to me later when I am not so tired." She took her glasses off and rubbled her eyes. The allergy that made them itch often suddenly seemed worse.

Chief Inspector McInery got up. "I think I've bothered you enough. Just don't leave for London yet. We'll talk later."

"I plan to be here for a week," she said, "then to Oxford for a little research on funeral sermons for women published in the first thirty years of the seventeenth century."

"Then we shall meet again. I shall be delighted." He spoke in an old-fashioned formal way. "I shall be here about that length of time if all goes well, but I have retired mostly in Oxford. Though I have a small cottage here, also. Remember to take care. There is a murderer abroad, and I can't be sure that he does not in some probably remote way have you in his sights."

"Can you be sure that he is not a she? Not me, of course," she laughed faintly as she saw his expression change.

"It is not likely, from the blow that Miss Deschamps died from. Though you are right, when people are angry enough, the adrenalin can make them very strong. A woman could have smashed something very heavy against her right temple."

Ellen rose and held out her hand. Was it the proper thing to shake hands with a Chief Inspector? He had certainly treated her very graciously. He was clearly a sensitive man.

He shook her hand firmly, holding it perhaps a fraction of a second longer than necessary. "Thank you for your cooperation." Was she imagining that there was a special tone in his voice?

Why had she always felt this way about voices? She judged people by their voices. She smiled to herself. She had been in danger constantly throughout her long life of falling in love with film stars because of it. Radio earlier, of course. And here in Britain, shades of Dylan Thomas, Richard Burton, even Gielgud as an old man—those lovely English or Welsh accents, all Brit to her and wonderful. Perhaps she was into her second childhood. What friend had made a case recently for life as a succession of adolescences? She must be in some odd phase such as that to be thinking such thoughts when another murder had taken place.

"Oh, my God!" Ellen suddenly said out loud. She remembered where she had seen the face in the photograph. It was the woman on the plane with a shorter haircut and slightly lighter color. A shiver passed along her spine as if someone had walked over her grave. There did not have to be any connection, she told herself. But she knew there was.

Chapter Six

Here she was again, walking along the fast-running creek of Rocky Valley after three years. She had called it Happy Valley when she had been there before, when James's body had surfaced. By some curious confusion, she had arrived at this misnomer, and it had taken her almost a year before she found out the that the real name was Rocky Valley. Perhaps because of her odd initial reaction to the body when she had last seen it: *Free at last.* With a surge of relief. Only days later had the terrible grief come through, and she had lost that sense of freedom in pain. Today, three years later, she let her mind go back to that morning, after not letting herself think about it for so long. She looked around her, pausing a moment just to take it all in.

Straight ahead now was the huge waterfall, breaking through the towering rock that guarded the hollowed-out space of the valley behind the wild Atlantic surf. It must have taken thousands of years of erosion before the water had first seeped through the huge boulder and then another thousand before finally it made enough inroads in the stone to form a trickle. From the first trickle gradually a narrow stream and then finally this bubbling fall that came straight down to smooth out this creek bed along which she walked. Who knows then how long the whole process took before the full creek was running along happily until it joined some Cornish river and then looped back to the sea?

She had never seen the end of it. She knew the stream was diverted somehow when it met the farm through which she had entered.

This early in the morning the mist still rose from the water, almost as if it were rising up to hang on the low branches of small trees and shrubs that grew along the edge. Not far to the left of the path she had followed since leaving the hotel she saw now the slate stones that someone had designated as steps up to the coast path at the top on the left. Yes, she remembered now, those were the steps that had a small marker beside them. They were a memorial to someone's daughter. She had felt those years ago that somehow this bronze plaque was an intrusion in a place where it seemed that she as walker was just discovering the beginnings of civilization. But it was not the only indication that others had been here.

There was the marker across the little bridge—even the bridge itself—but certainly the marker beside the primitive drawings of the labyrinth scratched on the wall from prehistoric times beside what might be a cave. She had not followed that path, after the cave, that led up the cliff on the right to join the coast walk as it went towards Boscastle. She had seen one other hiker, but he had moved on quickly. No, obviously others had been here over many years, hundreds, thousands, but she still had felt, irrationally perhaps, that she was among the first. She had also felt safe, she remembered, until James had shown up.

It had not happened exactly the way she told the inspector three years ago. She was afraid to tell him the whole story. Then he might not have believed she didn't have anything to do with the death. But it was time now for her to think about it. Perhaps her refusal to confront the scene had kept her from getting over it before. Her anger when James spoke had overwhelmed her. She had come to England itself to escape the feelings she was having about him in Pennsylvania. She could not stand to stay where they had been together for so long, the beautiful crooked old nineteenth-century house. They had loved each other there.

But when he had told her about his double life, that seemed a mockery. Indeed she had come to England on leave, hoping to resolve the feelings of betrayal she had felt when he asked her for a divorce. Even when he finally told her how long he had deceived her—two years at least—with the younger woman, he could not hide his excitement. He was too accustomed to sharing that with her. Even as he told it, he was caught up in that new passion with the beautiful secretary in geology. Though she had the one little girl, she had looked even younger than she was. Later the greatest humiliation she felt came as she thought about how he had expected her to empathize with how much more alive he felt. He actually said that he felt as if he had been given a gift.

She was suddenly back there in Pennsylvania, standing in her yellow kitchen with the morning sun streaming in the window. With retirement still ten years off, she was already dreaming about where they might travel. She looked at her hand holding the spatula. For the first time she noticed how large the veins on the back of her hand had become. *Ravages of time, I hate them!* Of course, she was already conscious of the depth of the lines around her mouth. She had tried some of those expensive creams, but nothing helped much. Maybe James was tired of looking at her across the breakfast table. Someone had told her once that that was the answer to all these second marriages. Men wanted to see a young face looking at them there and be reassured about their own youth.

For many years he had gone without her in his hunt for medieval books of hours throughout European libraries, getting small grants that were just enough for one person's expenses, or that was what he said when she suggested going with him. But she had believed that someday when they retired he would take her with him and show her some of the things he told her about that made his blue eyes light up with excitement the way they had when the two of them were still in school and danced all night to the big bands that were popular in the fifties. They had planned to be travelers and students of culture their whole lives.

Here she was in England now, actually Cornwall for the first time, England for the fourth, the only place she had been with him because she had been able to get grants for this library. But she had been without him this time, getting used to the idea that she would be alone forever. She had made a big investment of her now dwindling savings after he had moved out. And suddenly now today when she thought she was alone, this time happily so, his voice invaded her space. So angry. She knew she was angrier now than when he had told her. She could hardly say how angry she felt to see him. Perhaps because she knew when she looked at him that she had not become used to being alone.

She ached at the sight of him, grieving as freshly as she had in the beginning. Her throat tightened, and the pulse in her forehead beat like a drum. Perhaps she was going to faint or have a stroke. All those promises of forever. Had she never known him at all? They had talked so often about the foreverness of their relationship. Sacramental and all that. Bitter, bitter, she tasted it in her mouth, the gall of betrayal. She could hardly hear him, her own thoughts were so loud.

"Oh, Ellen!" He had looked at her, pleading. She could still see his face in her mind after all this time. "I am so sorry. I was just a fool." She had noticed that he wore one of those buttoned down blue shirts that brought out his eyes. He also had on the usual khaki pants most of the professors affected, though she would have thought he would have worn flannel in Cornwall this time of year. She could not have said why she was noticing such superficial things when there were more serious things to think about. But somehow she could not speak. She felt very distant from his apology. What could it mean? There was no way back from where they were now.

Ellen started up the stone steps, but they were so far apart, each one at least twelve inches from the last so that her weak thigh muscles began to cramp. She stopped at about the third step and looked down at James.

"I don't blame you for not trusting me," he interpreted her silence. "How could you after all this? I can only think I have suffered from some kind of madness. Could we go back to your hotel and talk?"

"Have you been there?" She hated to think of him in her hotel, her refuge. "But of course, they must have told you where I was."

He shook his head. "No, I was driving a rental car and saw you turn in at the farm that is the entrance to this creek. I just happened to see you at the foot of the hill before I turned in to the drive to Willapark. That is, when I saw you there, I didn't turn in but followed you in the car. I left it with the woman who was feeding the pig. She said it was okay. I have been just behind you until you paused a few moments and let me catch up." He looked up at her. "Where are you headed now?"

"Up to the coast walk and around to the back of the hotel," she managed to get out.

"Come down, and I'll drive you back."

"No, it's a circular walk I'm taking. They helped me map it out last night around the fire." It seemed important to her to complete it, her first real hike in the area.

"If that is what you want," he said. "I'll walk with you, and we can talk on the way."

She nodded, indifferent, and began to walk up another step, feeling the pull in her thighs. She stopped again. "I can't talk and climb at the same time."

He had climbed up two steps quickly, closing the space between them. He touched her back lightly, and the touch of his hand burned. "Don't," she warned sharply. "I might fall."

"It is steep here," he agreed, "but maybe we should just turn around carefully and sit on the steps a while."

"I'll do that when I get nearer the top," she said. They were both silent while they pulled up cautiously until they were about two-thirds of the way. The slope was almost straight down, with jagged slate jutting out of the grass at uneven intervals. Or perhaps he was half way, two steps behind her. Then they turned carefully and sat down without saying anything, neither of them used to climbing, not even to hiking. All those years sitting in libraries. They weren't athletes, although James had been a serious gardener part of his life and she knew his leg muscles were stronger and more flexible than hers.

She heard his voice, low and quiet now that they both faced the opposite cliff and looked down at the rushing water. It helped not to have to look at each other.

"I have broken with Marlene," he said. "She was not important."

"Important enough to deceive me with. To leave me for, to make me feel worthless," she added, unable to resist the overkill.

"I thought you would have gotten beyond so much anger. But of course it's unforgiveable." He tried to backtrack, knowing the argument could escalate. "I could not have known what I was doing. I thought I was being honest. That you would want me to be. But of course the whole thing was cruel and mad. Think of it—it was totally out of character for me."

"I'm not sure what your character is," she murmured. "I must have been wrong." She got up then. What was the use?

She started to move farther up. "Wait," he said. "I haven't told you the rest. Maybe you will understand."

Was there more? She could not believe there was anything else. She had been living in a dream if there were more that he had been keeping from her.

For a moment he remained seated there and put his head in his hands. "This is almost worse. The other—the girl—is after all a common malady. Midlife crisis, I think the shrinks call it."

Yes, giving it one of those cliché labels tamed it a bit, made it more acceptable to him, though she felt the hot fire still burn in her chest. What next?

"There is no other way to say it. For almost five years I have made extra money by selling manuscripts on the black market. That has supported my travel and some luxuries. I have no excuse for that either. It is entirely contrary to my values."

She knew he meant that he had needed the money—expenses for the woman. *Perhaps there had been earlier ones*, she thought for the first time. A chain of deceptions. "But where did you get the manuscripts?" She thought of those beautiful medieval manuscripts he had shown her reproductions of. Once she had spent a week in the basement of the British Library sitting before the librarian, who watched her to be sure she turned the pages correctly. Now they made you look at microfilm unless you were printing a new edition. She thought of those borders painted centuries ago, seven or so, the strawberry blossoms painted by some monk, the vivid red old fashioned roses, many in honor of the ideal of the purity of the Virgin.

James sighed and shook his head slightly. "The first one was almost an accident. I met a man who needed to sell one secretly from his private collection. It is a long story."

"And later?" She looked at him, not believing her thoughts.

"Later, after I knew the contacts, I became more involved. I was a very desirable contact for them. Finally I took a couple from libraries."

How could he? How could he have violated all his loyalties? She looked at him with cold eyes. Then the rage began to build. A lifetime with this stranger, or had he changed? And then she remembered when she first met him and how he had cheated on a small quiz. Never afterward. Always words that asserted an opposite point of view. But somehow, underneath, this soft spot of decay. A sheep that could be led astray. God, he needed to be rescued now.

"Let's go now." She hoped he would get up. On second thought, she did not really care.

"But, Ellen—I'm in trouble. I spent an advance, and I have to repay it. I thought if I could borrow from our retirement funds—"

So that was why he had come.

"That is not why I came." He seemed to read her mind. "I needed to see you, to let you know I loved you." He stopped, seeing the look on her face perhaps.

She turned around fully then, trying not to let her foot slip on the stone. "I don't think I know you. Probably I haven't known you ever, or not for a long time. But of course the retirement is yours as well as mine. Take your part; I'll sign."

He moved towards her then, smiling, using his charm, it occurred to her. She shrank back, not wanting to be touched, conscious of the precarious slope. Just as he made an effort to pull up the steep slope, he slipped, his right foot that had most of his weight sliding down the wet grass and then his left leg buckling. He reached out for her, but she stood frozen, perhaps knowing instinctively that his weight would pull her down too. Ellen stood there almost in a dream and watched the clumsy way James fell now backwards, cracking his head about halfway down, gathering speed as he fell until he bounced once at the bottom and tumbled into the creek, his clothes catching between two rocks. At first his face was up, held by the collar of the blue shirt, his long body submerged. From where she was, she could not see his expression.

What should she do? Run for help? She just wanted to run, to get away from him. As long as his face was out of the water, he could breathe. Perhaps she should go down now and try to pull him out. If he were conscious, he could help her. If not, he might pull her in. Ellen looked down the steep bank. She was afraid to start down it, lest she fall herself. "James," she called, not very loudly. Now the only sound was that of the waterfall. She looked at him. He was not worth risking her life for. But he needed to be rescued. She remembered thinking that. Perhaps that was why she sat down again to gather her thoughts. She would watch him. Perhaps someone would come along, she told herself, some rare good shepherd. Not her, though. Not after all that. Once she thought she saw him move, but it must have been the current. She watched until she saw his face turn down into the water.

Oh, yes, that was how it had gone. She may have forgotten a detail or two, but she thought it was all etched on her mind. She had been able to postpone thinking about it until now, though she often dreamed about it. The dreams softened it somehow, as if the whole thing were a dream. She had not been to blame, had she? Not really. It wasn't fair to blame her. And then she heard a voice behind her.

She stood there, then turned slowly on the path. The slender man with the gray hair was coming towards her, his once shiny black shoes now spotted with mud. "Ellen, I wanted to talk to you here in this setting. About your husband's murder. There are things that puzzle me about it." The chief inspector looked sympathetic, but she was frightened.

She took a breath. "I am a little out of breath," she said, playing for time.

Chapter Seven

"You should tell me straight out," she said. "Or rather, you should ask me what you want to know about it all."

The inspector looked puzzled. "Ellen, if I may call you that—and Douglas, not Doug, please. Call me also by my first name. You are of course not a suspect in this murder, though in some sense everyone on the scene is until the murderer is apprehended. But in this situation I can treat you almost like a visiting consultant. Whatever—I don't know what you mean—you haven't heard about it surely, walking here in the morning."

It was her turn to be confused. She had been so certain. "Heard about what?" She realized that she was standing beside the creek, near the point at which James's body had gone in to the water three years ago. The mist had cleared with late morning sun and the cold that made her shiver. Perhaps she had stood there long enough to get chilled.

Douglas ignored her question for the moment. "Why are you here anyway? It's posted, you know, just like the coast path."

"But it is not the coast path," she argued irrelevantly, knowing that he had specific information. "There are no animals here. My shoes will not be contaminated by this mud." She knew her lips must be blue. "I came back to settle some things in my own mind." She tried to stare him down. She raised her hand to her hair and irritably patted the bangs (or fringe, as the Brit hairdresser called it) that had blown to the side.

"Nevertheless it is posted," he said reasonably. "Let's go back the way we came. We'll have coffee at one of the places in Tintagel. It's not far." When she did not answer immediately, he put his hand under her elbow. "Have a little pity on the representative of the law. I can't be seen to be refusing to obey the government. The Cornwall farmers are already threatening to march rather than obey the order to kill their livestock."

She sighed a little as she gave in to his reasonable coolness. Perhaps she should not be here anyway. She began to get in stride beside him, to match his pace. There was just room on the path for two as they made their way back through the farm to the road that led to Tintagel. That was where she would have to walk this next week. Probably the only place, unless she took some excursions to nearby towns. Maybe to John Betjeman's grave. "You forgot about the sow on the farm," Douglas said as they emerged from the wooded path and entered the farm itself, walking past a small boy standing on a stool beside the farmer's wife and helping to feed the enormous pig in the enclosure.

Ellen barely kept herself from calling to the child to be careful. She had read in one of the British newspapers about a three-year-old who had fallen into a pigpen and been eaten.

"Going through the farm is surely reason enough to post the Rocky Valley. Poor farmers. These anyway will suffer doubly because they also run the little coffee shop along the way." The inspector looked solemn. "We have not yet begun to imagine all the consequences of foot and mouth."

"That is the way it is with evil and death." She had meant to offer this as an irony, but it came out deadly serious. They walked along in silence for awhile, as if conversation had been stopped.

She wanted to explain the seeming insensitivity of her last comment. "I don't know whether it's important, but I am something of a specialist on death—not exactly death in the abstract, but death in seventeenth-century England. Only the last few years have I begun to see what it can mean. In real life, that is."

"It is of course my specialty in a more concrete way." Douglas looked down at her kindly. "I think I have always seen it in terms of consequences, but I can see that as a scholarly pursuit there are other angles. Still, there are times when macabre humor is the only response."

"Yes. And I have come to see that Donne's frequent punning on it is often at points where he is most serious. But aside from that—more academically, at least, I have studied a kind of tradition that grew up after the Black Death, an art of dying that focuses on a somewhat peaceful, inner preparation for one's own death (and the death of others) as it scrolls out over a lifetime."

"That must be interesting—I always wanted to spend more time in libraries, digging into odd aspects of history." Douglas smiled down at her.

"But this is not an odd aspect—or that is what my researches show. For people in the seventeenth century and two hundred years before, at least, death seems to be somehow at the center, drawing other values under it. The art of dying is not merely a tradition, a kind of musty old ritual—it becomes embedded in visual images that mark people's deepest feelings. You know, almost icons in poetry and other forms of literature. Oh heavens, I am lecturing again—it is one of the dangers of asking a question of an old teacher."

"Not so old—at least not in relation to someone like me." Douglas frowned. "Please go on—I am really interested."

"Really such ideas become the foundation of a development of an art. Socrates and many others pointed out that we die daily. Under time.

"But now the whole notion of time has changed in modern science. Not that I really understand it—but aside from that, I wish I had had more experience of the kind of dying you are talking about." Douglas increased his pace slightly. "My job shows me too often the suddenness of death by violence. It is a more vicious thing than what seems the often kindly release of the figure of death at the bedside. After all, in that situation someone has lived a long rich life and is perhaps suffering the pains of some wasting disease from which he might quite like to be free." He paused while she made a murmur of assent.

"Yes," said Ellen, "even in the seventeenth century they knew that such circumstances as death at sea or even the violence of death by childbirth required a different ritual."

"Let us stop at this pub just around the curve on the right, just after the Arthur Centre. As I recall, it has an open fire. We can have a drink and talk there. The young man who runs it just moved down from London. He is worried sick about the tourist trade." Douglas gestured ahead, where the sidewalk gave way to road only.

"How do you keep up with the village as well as you do? You only arrived after the murder." Enough about death and dying.

"No, I came down yesterday to see a friend who was ill, and they called me in the night from the Yard. They like to have someone who understands the village and might help the inspector they send down. But in a small village like this you soon hear almost everything, especially when you are visiting."

Overhead the sun shone in a blue sky. The morning mists were gone, and it was almost noon. As they walked up the path to the pub—The Boar's Head, a seagull flew off the chimney with one of its crying calls.

Douglas looked up at it as they stopped in front of the door. "Did you hear your lark this morning?" He remembered what she had said about the earlier trip.

She was oddly pleased that he had listened. "Yes, but only as I was just coming up from a meager hour's sleep after our session most of the night. It was a glorious song, though, extremely complex in melody. It almost reassured me that there was a principle of good in the world, in spite of all the recent events. I wanted to spring up and make notes on it, try to capture the notation, but I was just too far down in sleep to move."

"Perhaps you'll get it tomorrow." He opened the door for her and then the inner door into the main part of the pub.

"Oh, Inspector McInery, I wasn't sure we'd see you this time." The owner came out from behind the bar. To Ellen he looked about twenty-nine, blond, stocky and square, and grinning broadly. Clearly his accent was London with its lilts, not Cornish. She noticed that the only other customers were a woman with a pint at the bar and a spindly man in a scruffy woolen shirt playing the machine in the corner. It looked like one of the casino machines at Vegas, the dollar one to which she had lost thirty dollars in her only visit there.

True to Douglas's promise, there was a wood fire in the fireplace, flames new and bright as if fresh wood had just been piled on. There were four tables close by, with a booth in the corner. "I wouldn't leave without coming here," said the inspector, shaking hands with Mike, the owner. "I want you to meet my American friend, Mrs. Adams."

The innkeeper looked at him meaningfully. "Any friend of yours.... How about a bottle of chardonnay for the two of you?"

Douglas looked at Ellen inquiringly. She reached out a white hand to the young man, and he pumped it briefly then turned towards the bar. "I am so cold and sleep-deprived," said Ellen, "I think I'll have coffee—filtre."

"Make that two." Douglas gestured to the booth in the corner, and the two of them sat down facing each other. She could see the fire from her seat.

It was time to tell him now. But first, what had he followed her to say? "I have two things I want to talk to you about after our conversation early this morning. But you obviously have had some startling news, so you go first." She smiled at him tentatively.

"Okay, as you say in America. That, by the way, was the first American word I learned. It came into English usage during the last war." She noticed that he did not seem to count Korea or Vietnam, certainly not the Gulf War or other interventions since. He sobered. "I almost hate to tell you now in this pleasant setting. But I must. There was a murder in Oxford yesterday afternoon—a young woman who teaches sixth form in Wales. She was house-sitting for a friend in the general neighborhood you stayed in last time you were there."

Ellen shuddered. Not another one.

"The friend was a librarian, or rather an assistant one, at the Bodleian. She seems in the clear, as she was en route to her cottage in Normandy when it happened." Douglas looked down, running his fingers over the smooth oak of the old table. "We have no other suspects at the moment. Or that was true when I had the phone call this morning from Scotland Yard. But they want me in on that case in two days."

Ellen looked puzzled. "Are you sure you are retired? And what would that have to do with me? Or with the murder here?"

"Perhaps nothing. Almost certainly nothing," he answered the second and third questions, ignoring the first, as it was largely rhetorical. He sounded unsure, however. "But there is perhaps a vague tie-in. The Bodleian missed a manuscript from their open shelves in Duke Humphrey's. It seems to have gone yesterday afternoon. It was not terribly valuable, as those things go, or that is what they claim. But something tells me there is a connection."

"Ah, the network strikes again, but why—and what is the connection with Miss Deschamps?"

Mike brought two coffees with large filtre pots. "You didn't say, but I brought cream. Would you like Demarara?"

Douglas shook his head, but Ellen nodded. Then Mike moved away discreetly, sensitive to the apparent seriousness of their conversation.

"That is all I can tell you at this moment." Ellen guessed that if there were more it was part of police confidentiality. "Now it is your turn," he said quietly. For a moment she thought he might touch her hand, which lay on the table with the fingers spread out, her wedding ring gleaming in the sun. But almost imperceptibly he drew back.

"First of all, I need to tell you about the lost piece of luggage and the link with the photograph. On the plane from Kennedy International to Heathrow, I sat in a group of three seats with the woman in the photograph you showed me earlier. We shared the empty seat between. She told me her name was Jean. We did not exchange last names. She also told me her husband was an international banker and that she was going to him in London to spend two weeks there in a flat that the bank was providing while he accomplished his business with them." She stopped in case he might have questions.

He looked delighted. "I was right about you. You should have been a detective. One of the things I miss now that I've retired is my sergeant with whom to talk over the case. Not that I think of you as a subordinate, of course." He laughed in a friendly way.

"You won't say that when I finish," she said sadly. "I had no suspicions of Jean at all. In fact, I stopped talking to her simply because I wanted the time alone. But since then I have had cause to suspect that she might be the one who took my small leather case that had—and here's the big news—a stolen manuscript I found in James's things."

Douglas sat back and put his coffee cup down carefully.

"We need to get this sorted," he said. "Let me see. At home, you mean, in Pennsylvania, you found a manuscript in James's things. What was it? Describe it for me—I know very little about such things."

Ellen drank the last of the coffee in her cup, and Douglas poured her another. As she stirred, she thought back, trying to get it all in order. "The manuscript was small, or perhaps I should say 'thin.' It was a *Book of Hours* commissioned by a French Duke of Burgundy for his wife who was apparently ill—a thirteenth century manuscript. It was the love match between the two that eventually gave rise to the memorial hospice for the poor that he built in Beaune after her death. One of the loveliest stories I have gleaned from my travels. Have you been there?"

Douglas shook his head. "But the book?"

"Yes, I don't want to get off the track. As I said, a rather slim volume, even the decoration not as elaborate as one might think. You know, those border paintings that make the hand-painted manuscripts so valuable. I could not help thinking that this one was perhaps done in something of a rush so that she might have it in her illness. Perhaps they knew that her death would be soon. Anyway it seemed to me from my limited knowledge—I work most with early printed books—that the value of the thing lay most in who commissioned it and the historical story surrounding it. Perhaps that was why James still had it."

"Oh, Mrs. Adams!" The strident voice was close by, and Ellen looked up to see the woman who had worn the long red dress in the bar the evening of the heroic story. "Here you are with one of the principal detectives," she said meaningfully. "I might have known that such a lovely American lady would zero in on the source of information. Especially such a distinguished source as Detective Chief Inspector McInery. Shades of Morse, how jolly!"

How irritating. Her English friends were usually very thoughtful about not making some big deal about her being an American. She looked up at Alice—

was that her name? "Inspector McInery was just asking me some official questions," Ellen slipped around the truth a little.

"Won't you sit down, Mrs. Helpers?" asked Douglas with a raised eyebrow.

"No, I shouldn't want to disturb official business. The sooner we get all this over with, the sooner we can get back to normal. I am due at a friend in St. Ives on Sunday."

"You're quite right," said Douglas in his most policeman-like voice. "I shall be speaking to all the servants at the hotel later this afternoon."

"But none of them were there last night. At least, as far as we know," said Alice. "I shall go on now. Don't monopolize the inspector, Mrs. Adams." She laughed maliciously as she turned towards the door.

Douglas and Ellen exchanged a look and smiled broadly. No need for comment. *We understand each other almost too well*, Ellen thought. But then she had thought that about James. When would she ever stop comparing other men to him? She stretched her neck a little and rubbed the tight muscle on the top of her shoulder. The lack of sleep made her sore all over.

Douglas tapped his empty coffee cup with his spoon. "Where were we?" His fingers were long, but strong. Somehow he had the hands of a musician, Ellen observed. She would have thought a policeman's would have been more blunt and stocky, but then he was not the usual policeman—sensitive as he was to poetry, to history, almost like some of the academic men she had known. But with less ego. Somehow less feminine, if the term meant anything these days.

"We have perhaps covered it all," Ellen said. "I think I need a nap now. And you have the servants to interview."

"Not really," he smiled. "The Cornish constable will do that, but I do need to confer with the inspector from Scotland Yard and fill her in on the Oxford murder. She has invited me to dinner at the Castle Hotel down the street. But before that, I shall go back to my friend's house. He has flu, and I shall do some simple food preparation."

"Could I help? I could shop for you?"

"No, I shall need to make a list first. No, go and take those forty winks. It would be a shame to get overtired at the beginning of your visit." He spoke kindly.

Perhaps he thought of her as some ditzy younger sister. It came to her that she knew nothing of his background. Perhaps he had sisters, but she would not presume on such an early acquaintance. She needed to remind herself, she knew, that the English were more reticent than Americans. This was a small island after all, and keeping up with friends for a lifetime must be reserved for people one came to know slowly and with a certain amount of caution.

"I'll say goodbye then, and thank you for the coffee. It was a lifesaver after my morning walk in the dampness." She realized then that she had not told him about James. It was too close to a confession. Perhaps later. But was she turning into James herself, presenting herself as entirely innocent when she was not? An image of Masaccio's Adam and Eve flashed into her mind, the one in Florence, *The Expulsion from Eden,* with the grief and agony etched on the face of Eve particularly as the two of them were barred by the angel at the gate.

Shrugging on her down jacket and tightening the scarf about her neck, Ellen moved out the heavy door of the pub. Eve had told the truth about her sin, taking on herself the responsibility for all that followed. It was a hard life after that, according to the old myth. But no harder perhaps than what had happened to James.

She reminded herself that he too had finally told the truth. *Yes, after over two years of deceptions, maybe more*, she argued with herself. Certainly he had seemed to feel that the deception itself was unbearable—or why had he finally told her? "I am so sorry. I was just a fool." And then later just before he fell—the words came back to her: "I needed to see you, to let you know I loved you." It was an agonizing necessity to confess, to tell the truth.

As soon as possible, she must, Ellen decided as she walked as close to the edge of the narrow street as she could. She was seized again by her neurotic fear that some speeding English car would come along on the wrong side of the road—she could not help it; it was the wrong side of the road to her—and smash her as in those childhood roadrunner cartoons. Only a few more places left before the turnoff to the driveway of the Willapark Manor. Her feet were hurting already. Why could she not find shoes for walking that had more inner cushion? She did not want to resort to running shoes, what the English called trainers.

But she knew now that she must tell the inspector when they had a quiet moment like the one this morning. Soon, if they were going to be friends. She wanted him to know who she was, even the elements of cowardice and deceit.

Chapter Eight

When Ellen first entered the front door of the The Willow Hotel the next morning, she would have sworn that the murder of the night before had never happened. Everything seemed quiet in the way she remembered. The small bright porch at the front was bathed in sunlight, and even though the wind was still high and the air cool outside, within the small enclosure that was like a porch surrounded by windows, it was as warm as spring. *A spot of paradise*, she thought fancifully, *in the midst of life*. She remembered how shocked she had been to see a palm tree planted along the drive, but when she mentioned her surprise to Rick, he had told her that Cornwall was renowned for its mildness of climate.

So far she had not noticed that herself, but now she began to see that there was some truth in the reputation. The windows on the little porch trapped the sunlight and held the warmth, and the light wicker furniture looked inviting. Ellen was tempted to pause and put her thoughts in order, but her eagerness for a nap moved her on.

She opened the heavier inner door into the dim hall, inhaling the scent of some lemon furniture oil that the maid from town had spread on the banisters of the stairs. A dull feeling of dread began to invade her chest. A basket of cleaning materials stood beside the table near the entrance, but the maid was somewhere else. Ellen could not help wondering if anything else could possibly have happened. Did someone know, for instance, that she was here? But why would anyone have it in for her—especially now that they had her hand luggage with the manuscript? Could they believe that James had told her things or given her materials that implicated someone? Perhaps there were indeed other ostensibly respectable people involved who were desperate to protect themselves. That was surely what James had been trying to tell her along the slope when they were climbing, when she thought he was only trying to excuse himself.

The door to Rick's lounge was open, and she heard a low murmur of conversation inside—probably Rick and Lisa in private communication. Ellen coughed lightly to let them know that someone else was in the hall, and then she started up the stairs to her room.

"May I have a word?" Rick called to her just as she reached the first landing. She had not heard him come out of the lounge, and at first the sound of his voice startled her. She must be getting nervous—no wonder with all that had happened. But she turned and walked downstairs, being almost superstitiously careful not to fall. She was not used to steep stairs—there were so many in Britain, while at home there were elevators, or lifts, as the British called them, everywhere.

"I am sorry to disturb you. I know you must be tired after last night, but the inspector from Scotland Yard would like a second identification of Miss Deschamps. I, of course, did the initial one, and they have not been able to find family; but because her face is badly swollen from the blow to her head, they would like to have a second identification in their records."

"I can only say that I was introduced to someone of that name in the bar." She made a feeble attempt to avoid seeing the body, but she knew she would have to assent.

"Really, that is almost all *I* could say. She has never been here before. She booked over the telephone. When I asked her how she heard of the hotel, she had no personal recommendation, just a vague story about seeing it listed in a travel book on small hotels. Since I have listed it in several such publications, I offered her the booking." Rick smoothed his moustache thoughtfully. "I really think the police may suspect that she was traveling under an assumed name. Marie Deschamps is a bit fancy. And unusual."

"Anyway, I will do it," Ellen agreed without enthusiasm. "Could we go now so that I can return soon for a nap?"

"I think they want it done as soon as possible so that they can get on with the autopsy. I was just waiting until you returned from your walk." Rick turned toward the lounge. "I'll just get my jacket, if you want to wait here."

Ellen nodded, still in her own walking suit and green down ski jacket. While she waited, she walked over to a painting on the wall of Neftan's waterfall. It was a small original by a local artist, and she wondered if it were for sale. But perhaps she did not want a souvenir of the place. Oddly enough, she found herself wanting it. Of course she wanted it. Here was the last place she had seen James, who in spite of everything was the only man she had ever loved, the father of her only child. She would ask herself later what the psychology of that feeling was—betrayed as she had been in so many ways.

* * *

Minutes later, she found herself standing in the Cornwall morgue, Robert Griffiths, pathologist, standing slightly behind her. Rick had been asked to remain outside, perhaps in case he might influence her in her judgment. Just a few feet away, a female assistant was pulling out one of the drawers that lined the wall. Shades of her grandmother's mausoleum, though larger. Her father's mother had built a small marble building to house the dead of her family. Its construction had been triggered by the suicide of her eldest son after he returned home from World War I, gassed and shell-shocked. She felt that he had suffered enough from the constant rain and mud of the trenches, and she wanted him to rest in the shelter of the small building. When Ellen was growing up, she had resented the Sunday family visits to the cemetery—after all, she had never known her uncle; but now that her grandparents and her father and mother lay there, too, she actually had made an excursion all the way from Pennsylvania during Easter season. It seemed appropriate at last to visit, now that she was head of the family.

But this cold room in Cornwall with its dingy marble floor was hardly a welcoming place of shelter. Suddenly it seemed to her almost mad to be here, so far from any home that she had known. Though, like many Americans, she had several. Academics were a nomadic people, following schools and positions from place to place. Though now, after all these years, Pennsylvania seemed the most important home, where they had lived happily together for a time.

Her wandering thoughts stopped abruptly as she shivered, and the pathologist moved toward the slab on which lay the victim of last night's murder at the Willapark. She must focus on the present. He gestured to her to come closer.

"Take your time," he said in a neutral voice, having done this so often. She knew he recognized her churning feelings.

The assistant—Karen, he had introduced her, without last name—was unzipping the body bag, exposing the upper body. Ellen tried to make her expression neutral as she looked. Was this the Miss Deschamps she had met the night before in the lounge? Already her limited experience with dead bodies had prepared her for the curious way that, once the life has gone, the person looks very different. She remembered the deep lines of anxiety around James's mouth in contrast to the youthful looks he had shown in life.

The terrible smell, probably from the brown crust of blood about the right side of the woman's head, wafted towards her, and Ellen felt her stomach turn. She tried not to breathe deeply. That side of the head was so damaged, dented in, that she could not have sworn it was Helene. The rest of the face was hard to recognize, also, the mouth twisted and swollen. Ellen remembered the anguished scream she had heard. But there was something about the left side of the face that was familiar, aside from the odd expression of the mouth. Surely the scream was there in the twisted lips, still open as if a sound might emerge even yet. Ellen glanced at what was revealed of the body. Not that there was much that could be seen. The body bag still covered the lower part to the waist, and a sheet inside made a modest covering for her nakedness.

Except for where it had slipped down and the surprisingly seductive left breast protruded, almost rakish, a large aureole of nipple uptilted in the direction of Griffiths, who waited without saying anything. It was as if that breast were a part that refused to die, that waited insistently for resurrection.

"Naked thou came into the world," quoted Ellen, wanting somehow the dignity of the King James prose in this barren setting. Then she was quickly more aware of her surroundings and their official reason. "Yes, this is the woman I was introduced to as Marie Deschamps last evening in the hotel lounge. It's just that everyone looks so different when the life goes out." She felt her voice tremble, as if it were the voice of a stranger, and the image of James floated up in her mind, those curious lines in his face like a map of the years. Even James, whom everyone had thought looked years younger than his age. Her thoughts seemed to repeat themselves.

"Are you all right?" The pathologist moved closer to her side.

"Yes, quite," she said, consciously using the English idiom, but swaying just slightly as the smell of decay came up into her nostrils, in spite of the temperature maintained in the morgue.

"No need to prolong this, if you are sure. We can move into the outer office for a cup of tea, and I'll have you sign the form." Dr. Griffiths smiled up at her. He was half a head shorter, and considering that she was small herself, that made him look like an elf of a man. *But a kindly one*, she thought

She did not mention that she had been here once before, but she felt that he remembered. Surely there were not that many deaths in this small town that required investigation.

"It is difficult when you have only met someone once to identify her," she said, "but I don't think that taking any longer would help much. One must compensate for the death blow and the swelling of the face, especially the distortion of the mouth. And then there is the color of death, that gray green that is so different from even unhealthy pallor." She brushed her hair off her forehead and sighed. "Yes, I can imagine the woman as I saw her last night. She was wearing a becoming rose wool jumper with a navy skirt, and her makeup was rosy, too, I remember. No lipstick—most people don't wear that now—but a shiny gloss on her lips. Perhaps it is her mouth that is so different."

"Yes, she seems to have felt the blow to her head as agonizing." Griffiths looked uncomfortable.

Ellen was sitting now, the identification form before her. She took her old Waterman out of her purse. It was the pen she always used for significant signatures. She was a little superstitious about it, always afraid she might misplace it when she carried it in her purse, but at the same time wanting it with her in case she had to sign something important. It seemed a mark of respect for the dead in this instance. She signed quickly, suddenly feeling foolish. What could she know of it, the Marie or Helene of the slab inside? She had lived, perhaps been a member of James's ring; now she was gone, so little trace of her past that strangers were identifying her. Perhaps her passport would lead to someone who could tell them more.

Rick entered now to take her back to the hotel. "I had to move the car," he said. "I was in a thirty-minute parking zone." He looked at her sympathetically. He knew she had not wanted to come.

Later in the car, she told him, "It was far worse than I thought it would be. Does every death trigger memories once you have experienced one? Once someone told me that grief was impossible to heal, that all the losses of your life would emerge at every single loss. I didn't believe it at the time, but now it begins to feel that way to me, beginning with the death of my father. And now this woman I don't even know."

"It is perhaps your own death you fear each time," he said slowly. "And surely, there is something more frightening about a violent death. Some of the old ghost stories suggest aspects of that. Even Hamlet. Don't you think so?" He looked solemn, feeling it too, she knew.

"Oh, do you mean the idea that spirits suffer if they die without absolution? That ghosts are perhaps those who can't enter heaven or perhaps even purgatory if they die by violence without having made their peace with the Almighty?" Some of her research on early modern thinking about death was coming back to her.

"I don't know the theology," he said, "but I think it is something like that. But it must have arisen initially out of the way people feel about the dead. Whenever anyone dies suddenly, we can't accept it, I think. In my own experience…." He hesitated.

"Yes, what happened?"

"If you will forgive a personal example, my adored elder sister was killed in a car accident. For a long time, I literally could not remember that she was dead. I would look for her as I came into the house. I would lie in bed at night—I had to be in bed at eight—I was only seven years old—anyway, I would lie in bed and wait for her to come in and kiss me goodnight. It was a ritual with us. And then when she did not come, I would cry myself to sleep with anger and grief."

"Thank you for telling me," Ellen said, knowing it had cost him to reveal that much to a virtual stranger.

"I don't feel that you are a stranger," he said as if reading her thoughts. "Lisa and I were talking last night about you, your courage in coming back here."

"I was almost afraid to come, afraid that you would think I was bad for business. It does seem to have turned out that way." Her tone was ironic and sad at the same time.

"These things are not in any one's hands, I think. I am a fatalist that way. And besides, think of all the good publicity I had from the James event. I don't think a murder is going to close us down. Besides, my business is almost all return clients—people with dogs who come to walk every holiday and during the summer especially. Sometimes I pretend I am an old-fashioned lord of the manor who simply entertains a few more guests now that my fortune has disappeared." Rick laughed to let her know he was not being pretentious.

They turned into the driveway, and a few minutes later she was crawling under the duvet for a nap. At last. But as she was falling down into the longed-for sleep, Ellen wondered: *Who are the suspects?* Not Rick, not herself, of course, not Lisa. But of the guests? Or perhaps someone who had come into the hotel. But no one had. Rick locked the outer door after the guests were in. It was still possible for a guest to have let someone in. An accomplice within? She decided to postpone thinking about all this until the evening, when she got up for dinner.

A twinge of disappointment still kept her from sleeping. Douglas would not be there this evening. He was having dinner with the inspector from Scotland Yard at the Castle Hotel at the end of town. She had not been there yet, but it was a more pretentious establishment—a "Victorian pile," one of her Oxford friends had called it.

Ellen stretched luxuriously, warming her feet on the bright green hot water bottle with which she always traveled. She tried to stop her thoughts. They kept unrolling, and she was tired to the bone. She needed to sleep, she told herself. But almost too much had happened. She tried counting: one, two—three. Her eyelids fluttered.

When she woke two hours later, it was dark outside and the smells of onions, broccoli, and lamb roast were seeping under her door. For a moment she did not know quite where she was. She almost expected her mother to call her for dinner. How ridiculous. She shook her head and sat up on the side of the bed. Somehow she was still groggy. Perhaps light would help. She switched on the lamp beside her. The pink shade made for a rose glow in the room, dim but warm. But the air itself was not warm. Usually the central heating came on morning and evening, but it only really was warm about five in the afternoon. It took a while with these high ceilings to permeate all the rooms.

Ellen stood up. What should she wear tonight? It would not be a festive evening like the one last night. She could not imagine that many would gather in the lounge after dinner. People would be suspicious of each other, perhaps depressed. Like her, they had spent most of the day thinking about the murder. She could imagine that several would be eager to leave for home or other places, but the police would have to agree.

She walked over to the radiator in the corner. Sure enough it was warm, almost hot, to the touch, but the heat did not seem to go very far into the room. Perhaps she would dress here in front of it.

Then she heard the knock. It was Barbara of the anniversary pair, she saw when she cracked the door.

"Come down and join us when you are dressed. We thought we would have champagne before dinner."

"What are you celebrating?" she asked, puzzled.

"It is our anniversary, you know. We can't let it all be spoiled, even if we spent all day thinking about that poor woman."

Ellen smiled. "Yes, how thoughtful of you to ask me. Perhaps it will cheer us all up. I'll be down in ten minutes." She could always dress quickly when there was a good reason. After all, no one had known the woman. Perhaps there was no necessity for a very long period of solemnity. Perhaps they might even forget it for a few hours of innocent pleasure. During World War II, she knew, from programs on Radio 4, the British had known how to keep the spirits of the armed forces up with entertainment. A theatre culture like this one knew about the ritual of drama, how acting out a story could expel the shadows, bring about some sort of resolution. Wasn't that what catharsis was all about? But these were modern times, and no one knew any longer, as far as she could see, what tragedy was all about. Perhaps it was some form of romance they were planning here in the hotel, celebrating an anniversary after the world of decent order had been broken by a brutal killing.

Her thoughts went back again to the body at the morgue. Who could have wielded the blunt object with such force as to smash in one whole side of a skull? The human head was not an eggshell.

Chapter Nine

"And here's to thirty-five years of happy married life! Taking the bad with the good—all those burned toasts, all those kindly cuddles. To my darling Barbara—and, more seriously, for all those good talks through the night and day—and on and on [much good-humored laughter], it's been a wonderful journey with the right woman." Dennis Lofton, the graying man in the maroon sweater, raised his glass high.

Ellen, moved unexpectedly at the sincerity of the less-than-eloquent toast, raised hers, as did the other six in the lounge. Yes, it was good to celebrate an apparently happy union. Even if hers had not worked out quite as they both had hoped. She saw an old snapshot in her mind of the rehearsal dinner Aunt Beatrice had given at the country club. She and James had cut the heart-shaped cakes for the guests, and the toasts that night had hardly been poetic. James at that time overly tall and thin, she small and almost slight as a child, both of them with the charm and awkwardness of youth, and two enormous linked cakes with pink icing: on one the word *Wedding,* on the other *Joy.*

That they had never lived up to the beautiful ornamented cakes was surely more bad luck than anything else. Her best friend Tessa would say that they could have done better, but her heavy sense of responsibility left little room for accident. Certainly they had been immature, though they had not known that. In fact, they were somewhat solemn and pompous. Ellen saw from this distance her own mistakes, but at this moment she was filled with admiration for those who had managed a lifelong relationship—whatever the accommodations and compassion she felt for her young self, now so far away as almost to seem another person. *Not quite*, she thought—they had not been quite up to it all, but even so she would not have missed it.

Still, if theft and murder were the outcome, there was more wrong than her personal betrayal, she admitted. Though she was sure James knew nothing of murder. Was it the nature of the world? It was too easy to say that. Where had it all gone wrong? Or was it in something people had once called character—James's character and her own, perhaps the combination? She had lived long enough, if she were honest with herself, to know that nothing was ever just the fault of one person.

"Let us have a toast from the American lady," said the older man Mark, who had told the story of Rick's heroic act.

"Of course." She raised her glass, and everyone followed. "To those who have stayed the course, may they share more years of joy and companionship." Best to be conventional—humor too dangerous a maze in a foreign land. Then she remembered Shakespeare's tragedy from which she had taken the central image of her toast—not a very happy allusion: something like "I am lashed to the mast, and I must stay the course." Perhaps the others would not remember, though her experience in Britain was that most people she met seemed to remember all the quotations she knew—possibly the chestnuts of English literature.

And if they did, life was indeed somewhat like a storm that required real persistence. Shouts of "Hear, hear!" and then raised glasses raised higher throughout the room. Then Rick was at her elbow. "Well done," he said, "but I'm afraid I must interrupt—there is a telephone call for you."

* * *

"Mrs. Adams, this is Left Luggage at Heathrow. We have your bag. I regret to have to say that it is empty. Whoever took it probably removed the contents. We found it on the counter this morning, abandoned but still with your tags on it. There is a folded piece of paper inside with your name on it."

"Thank you very much for calling." Ellen felt weak. If she had had any doubt that the mix-up was planned, probably even part of this new spate of violent happenings, she saw she must have been in some sort of denial. "I am not sure when I can pick it up, but within the next week to ten days. Can you hold it for me? I do want it." If nothing else, she needed to examine the folded sheet. Perhaps it was a note. She wanted to speak to Douglas, ask his advice.

"Of course," came the woman's voice on the other end of the line. "You are in Cornwall now. There will be a small storage charge—depending. Do you know when you will be back in London? Did you say you had a bag you took by mistake?"

"No, I'll let you know later." Ellen slipped over the mention of the other bag. "What is your number, please?"

Oddly, she heard a click. They must have been cut off. The woman seemed inquisitive. Perhaps it was difficult to store such things and to be held responsible.

Ellen hung up and returned to the lounge, but everyone had broken into little group of two or three, ready to move in to dinner now. "Friends," said Dennis, the happy husband, "let us continue our celebration at dinner, and I shall invite you all to join us in the lounge afterwards for a brandy or other drink. Wendy here tells me that her favorite on such occasions is B&B, a mixture of brandy and Benedictine. The ladies particularly may like the sweet." Some laughter at such old-fashioned patriarchy. None of these kindly people, she felt reassured, could be involved in the murder.

Just then a presence at her side she already recognized, even out of the corner of her eye, even before she looked up to see Chief Inspector Douglas McInery. He looked down at her. "Chief Inspector Katherine Brown came along with me. She wanted the three of us to have a word. As you recall, I took her away before she could meet you last night."

"Good," said Ellen, "I am eager to meet the feminine contingent from Scotland Yard. There has been a new development—nothing major, but I just had a phone call I should like to tell you both about."

"Perhaps you should come with us for dinner at a pub, the Sheepshead Inn—we gave up the idea of the Castle Hotel after seeing what a big empty place it is. We thought it would depress us," Douglas explained with a smile. "Otherwise you'll miss your meal, since there is only one seating for this one."

"All right," Ellen agreed, though she knew the pub would not be as good. The chef at this hotel was part of why she had come back. She sighed as she hurried to catch up with Dennis and Barbara in order to excuse herself from the rest of the anniversary festivities.

* * *

"Yes, they seemed a little disappointed that the odd American lady would not be around for induction into English or Cornish celebrations," she was telling the two inspectors as they ate fish and chips and ubiquitous English peas at the Sheepshead Inn, "but I am actually eager to get on with the investigation." Ellen hesitated. "Not that you aren't doing that without me." She reddened a little, knowing they would think she did not think them competent. "It's just that you had not heard about my phone call before dinner."

Inspector Brown looked serious. "Who called?" Her blue eyes grew steely and her voice alert. Ellen sensed that, in spite of her youth, she was both intelligent and tough.

"Someone from Heathrow's Left Luggage. By the way, does that mean luggage that someone checks there to travel light—perhaps to pick up on the way back from Afghanistan or somewhere, or luggage that gets lost or misplaced?"

"The latter," Douglas said quietly. "And...?"

"It was about my lost hand luggage." She looked at Miss Brown. *Jane*, she must remember. *Chief Inspector*, that was best. "Chief Inspector Brown, I imagine Mr. McInery must have told you—or perhaps he has not had time?"

"The chief inspector mentioned something, but I should like to hear it from you."

Ellen knew she was being gently disciplined for not having used Douglas's title. *How could I work in my own title?* she wondered but then mentally slapped her own wrist for her pettiness. In England they were still more careful about such things. She tried to compress the information and be clear at the same time, but what she said was more or less a repetition of what she had told Douglas about arriving at her hotel in London with the wrong bag.

Then she added, "The main thing was that I remembered the woman in the photograph he showed me, but only after I had gone away for a few hours. I knew at the time she looked familiar. I had sat next to her on the plane. She had a French name—though she told me she was originally from Brazil and now lived in Bermuda, the wife of an international banker. I can't help feeling she was the one who switched bags with me."

"Do you have the other bag, or did you leave it in London?"

"Yes, I have it, but I did not tell the woman at Left Luggage. I thought perhaps you would like to examine it."

"We would," said the young woman as she looked over Ellen's shoulder thoughtfully. "Actually, I doubt that the Yard can find out anything from it. It was such a setup, but nevertheless, something may provide a clue. Old Alec, who goes through such things with a fine-toothed comb, can sometimes come up with amazing things—a matchbook that leads us to a certain restaurant, even once a prescription bottle."

Jane put down her fork then; they had made quick work of the fish and chips. Ellen noticed that Jane had left half of her chips. That must be how she stayed so slender. "I'll give you the bag when we go back to the hotel."

Douglas was quiet, sipping his Guinness, but Jane sat up to continue. "Actually, now I would like to go over some painful material. As you know, I was not around when your husband died or was killed. I'd like to ask you a few questions."

"Of course." *Here it comes.* Ellen wished she had told Douglas earlier. Perhaps she would wait for that, though she knew that the longer she put it off, the worse. And was it not after all obstructing justice—something she could be imprisoned for? She felt herself looking guilty. Or at least sullen.

Jane's eyes were sympathetic, however, when Ellen forced herself to look up. "First, just tell me in your own words what happened that morning in Rocky Valley. As if you have never told it before."

Ellen glanced at Douglas. He was looking down at the oak table, but he felt her eyes on him apparently and looked up to nod reassuringly. She fixed her eyes then on Jane's left shoulder and began, reaching down into her memory, but with a certain cool part of her mind standing back and listening: "It's been three years now, but I think I remember it all, every detail. Let's see—first I started out from the hotel to make a circular walk. Around the fire the night before, the experienced walkers had planned for me an easy hike. They saw that I was somewhat out of shape from spending months in the Bodleian working on my project—you knew, I think, that I was here on a grant that spring, living in Oxford and getting used to being alone."

"As I understand it, you were going through a divorce?" Jane looked at her somewhat sternly, Ellen observed.

"Yes, although not yet officially. We planned to do it, but we had decided simply to separate formally for six months." Odd, it was still difficult to admit that to a stranger. "We separated because of another woman. At that time I knew nothing of the theft of valuable books."

"When did you learn about the books?"

Here it was then. "After I came to Oxford." Ellen paused. "But back to Cornwall," she fudged a little. "I made my way from the Willapark down the hill towards Boscastle, turned left at the farm when I saw the sign they had told me the night before to look out for. I must admit I thought I had passed it when I suddenly saw it and knew I was on the right path."

"Yes," said Jane Brown non-committally. Her social manner had disappeared. She was all business now. "I don't know the path to the creek and the waterfall. As you know, I was not in on that investigation. About how far were you from the creek?"

"Not far at all. I saw it again this morning when I walked back there. I only walked through the land at the front of what I think is the farmhouse. The way lies past the pig pen, where the woman (the farmer's wife perhaps?) and the little boy were feeding the pig. I suppose it wasn't strictly a pig, but a sow. I saw one this morning that was enormous—I don't remember how large the one was three years ago. Anyway, I remember saying good morning to them and fearing that they would resent a stranger walking through their land. But they did not seem to. Later I found out that they run a coffee shop along the way for tourists—so, I suppose, they were quite happy to see me. Though, actually, I never stopped for coffee."

"And then about how long did you walk in Rocky Valley along the creek?"

Ellen wrinkled her forehead. "I am not sure. I walked along the creek fairly briskly until I reached a small bridge. I crossed the creek and looked at the ruins of a house. Apparently someone lived there at one time. Possibly the late nineteenth century. Nearby was a cave that had drawings scratched along the rock outside—labyrinthine designs, prehistoric, I thought. I was thrilled. I felt as if I were an archaeologist who had discovered a great find but then saw a small bronze plaque that labeled them as ancient drawings by a cave-dweller—so much for being the first on the site to recognize such things.

"All that may have taken twenty minutes or so. I remember that I had started out at about nine fifteen or nine twenty. It was probably no later that nine forty when I crossed the bridge again to the other side and started up the slope to the coast walk on the completion of the circle as I went back to the hotel."

"You had not seen the body yet, then?" The inspector frowned.

"No, I did not see it until I was about halfway or two-thirds of the way up the hillside. I stopped and very carefully turned around to sit on one of the steps that were a memorial to someone's daughter. Just as I sat down, I saw it surface in the creek. There was something about the head that looked familiar. And then as the face was turned up by the current, I knew it was James. At first I thought it must be a trick of my imagination. There was absolutely no reason for him to be there, as far as I knew. Later I thought he might have come looking for me."

"Yes, this all checks out with the earlier information of the investigation, but did you or anyone ever know where he had come from?"

"Yes," Douglas broke in for the first time. "The farmer's wife had allowed him to park a rental car on their property shortly before that. After Mrs. Adams had walked by."

"That is curious," said Jane without elaborating, but Ellen knew it put James with her in Rocky Valley, alive at the same time. "You did not see him before you saw him in the creek?"

"The creek memory is etched upon my mind," said Ellen, trying not to lie directly. To her surprise, Jane did not pursue the matter, although Douglas seemed to look at her oddly.

"I won't ask anymore. I think we have the rest of it. Except for one more question on time. How long before you climbed the steps up to the coast walk?"

"I am not sure. I was of course very upset, and I laboriously climbed back down first. Then when I really saw that it was James and he was dead, I went slowly back up. All that may have taken another twenty minutes—maybe longer. I had to sit down again halfway up. My thigh muscles simply were not strong enough for those steps, which are at least twelve inches apart, perhaps more."

"Why didn't you go back through the farm? Surely that would have been easier."

Ellen laughed a little and pushed back her hair. It was warm in the pub. "Yes, I know—I thought about that earlier. But it was as if I simply absent-mindedly followed the plan the guests in the hotel had laid out for my walk. I called the Cornwall police as soon as I arrived at the hotel and spoke to Rick, the proprietor."

"Yes, of course, you did the right thing. I think that is all I need to know. I have enough on my hands with the new Willapark murder. I just don't want to miss any connection there might be. Chief Inspector McInery has something, however, that he wants to talk to you about. I am going now—I need an early night after last night." She stood up and put on her long overcoat. "I'll leave you two now; thanks for the fish and chips." She smiled at Douglas and held out a perfunctory hand to Ellen.

As she left, Douglas paused a moment, following her with speculative eyes. "She could have asked you more questions—but she is thorough. Still, I feel we missed something last time. Anyway, we won't this time, if you will agree to do something for me."

"Anything." Ellen trusted him. *How could I?* she warned herself firmly.

Thus began her second career, employed as what she thought of as a double agent. They wanted her to see if she could get inside the manuscript and rare book ring that was devastating libraries across the world.

But first she knew she must come clean to Douglas about the murder of James, that strange accident that she had been part of.

Chapter Ten

Whenever Ellen entered Oxford from the train station, the other times she had arrived would flow together into the experience. She had not expected to leave Cornwall quite so soon, but here she was. Her friend Cordelia had not minded her coming a few days early. When she had telephoned, Cordelia said that she herself was going to Thailand the next morning, and the house would have been empty anyway for the next few days before Ellen's previously agreed arrival. Now that she was here in Oxford, it seemed as if she were always arriving. Almost as if someone had happened to bend time around to where it had begun (was she beginning to understand Einstein at last?), and she was spending her life riding through town to somewhere in Oxford on Kingston Road, where she usually stayed. That one luxurious time she had come with her historian friend to do some research, and they had had rooms at the Randolph, with all the other American tourists, in the newly decorated room—Laura Ashley patterns everywhere, wallpaper, curtains, duvet—it had all been too touristy, even with the bonus of being just across from the glorious Palladian architecture of the Ashmoleum Museum. She much preferred the north Oxford neighborhood where she could imagine she lived here.

She had come only once with James, perhaps six years ago, when they had been on sabbatical and had rented a small flat near Summertown for a month. Then they had been doing some research, but he had also had some things to do outside the library. God knows what forms of deceptions he was practicing. *Was he already involved with the manuscripts then?* she wondered.

Probably. She had never been suspicious. Not even when he told her about taking a quick train to Banbury and having dinner in an elegant restaurant, but no, he would not like to go again when the two of them could go. Yes, probably that had been some sort of meeting. Funny how sharply she remembered these things.

She must have wondered at the time but talked herself into suppressing her fears. And how about the time he told her he was going to Burford overnight just for a lark? And no, for her to continue her research; he felt like getting away. He must have thought her stupid. *And I was*, she admitted, aching. Again now she felt the anger pouring over her, some hot molten liquid. At the same time, some of it came up into her throat. She had denied earlier how angry she was. So much deception—it was hard to believe of someone you lived with. The thefts ran together with the sexual deception in her thoughts: she could not bear to think of all those times he had slept with that woman, putting his body into hers and then coming home, defiling their home. And lying about it literally for years. But that was in Pennsylvania, not Oxford—only the thefts were here. Though who knew, when he stayed for weeks, sometimes a month, without her?

But that time when they were together she still thought it must have been at least primarily the arrangements for theft he was working on. Still, it was not impossible to think that perhaps there had been someone here. Once she had glimpsed him in the café with a pretty dark young woman. Sex for him after all was nothing—an appetite he must satisfy. When it came down to it, he was capable of spending only a brief hour somewhere with someone in a completely casual way. Even making love with her had become that way, except for rare times. She tried to remember one, and for a moment she could not. Perhaps she was blocking out the good now. She did not want to grieve for him any more.

Getting away from Pennsylvania had helped when the big break between them had come. When she had come here alone at last, she had really enjoyed Oxford most—staying in the small house she rented from a friend, there on Kingston Road, almost at the end of it. Near St. Margaret's Church, where she could look out her front window from the bedroom and watch the magpie dive off the top of the steeple, golden in the rare late afternoon sun.

But here she was now, once again going in that direction from the train station over the Hythe Bridge Street, then up George Street past the entrance to the coach station where the famous Oxford Tube waited, an express that would take one not only to Heathrow and Gatwick, those temples of American tourists, but also to the city of London itself, where once and awhile she would glimpse Donne or Shakespeare down some twisting alley. A return ticket for £7.50 that would allow her to run up and see *Seeing Salvation* at the National Gallery. Or even the theatre she preferred, such as that last *King Lear* at the new Globe on the Thames, that joint British-American achievement. After either delight, able to be back by seven or eight to have dinner at home and watch the newest Pascoe and Daliel murder. Somehow the mere mechanics of doing all those things kept her from thinking.

Not really, of course, he was always on the edge of her mind, but at least she would not fall straight down into the pit where her darkest dreams would take over and sometimes she would weep and cry out with harsh sounds that waked her. They seemed not even to come from herself, but from somewhere in the universe where old women in black sat around dingy walls and keened.

And the coach for London left every twenty minutes, so that all she had to do was walk down from the Duke Humfrey's in the Bodleian or the house on Kingston Road and get on, paying the coach driver at the time. Of course she knew that most Oxford visitors would not wax so eloquent on the means of public transportation. Most of them came on their own huge tourist buses, but she, traveling alone these two times and staying for the longer period of several months, had delighted in learning how Oxford people themselves traveled. The others considered Oxford a beautiful medieval town, she knew, filled with colleges, most of which they never saw because they were all built around courtyards and, during term time, had strictly limited times for visitors to enter. Even then, visitors were mostly limited to chapel, library, and refectory for viewing. Of course, they were always introduced to the Memorial and the hotel and the Ashmoleum Museum.

She was just passing the museum now, as the taxi took her down towards St. Giles Church there at the fork between the Woodstock and Banbury Roads.

On their tours, the tourists would drive into the University to see the Clarendon Building and Blackwell's, that venerable bookstore across the way beside the New Bodleian. If they got out at that point and strolled further into the area, they would perhaps have a glimpse of the Sheldonian Theatre and the old Bodleian with Sir Thomas Bodley's statue out front, and the Radcliffe Camera would catch their eye even more before they moved out into town.

But she was just as glad to be going the opposite way from Cornmarket with its Covered Market, where they would surely go for shopping, after a stroll down Broad Street or maybe even High Street, if they were good enough walkers to approach the most beautiful sight in Oxford, she thought, the curving street as it ended in Magdalen College and its graceful tower at St. Clement's and the bridge.

But mostly, she knew the buses would enter and leave Oxford on that street so that most of their riders would not take the walk. Perhaps in the late spring they might be encouraged to, however, when the Oxford Botanical Gardens across the street from the tower were in such glorious bloom. Oxford, though a small market town, was nevertheless so filled with interesting and historic places to visit that she felt she would never grow tired of it. Perhaps that was why so many people retired there from all over Britain—and perhaps the world.

Surely it would give most newcomers chills when they realized that they were eating their pizza in a restaurant on the site where Cranmer had been held before his execution in the sixteenth century—that venerable author of the *Book of Common Prayer. Or perhaps not*, Ellen sighed. Most Americans no longer knew much about English history unless they themselves were teachers at some level of the literature.

Now the Arab taxi driver was taking her up the Woodstock Road toward St. Margaret's. She looked at the exotic Islamic symbol on the mirror, wondering momentarily about religious differences. It was curious how now the growth in religions was coming mostly in Islam and evangelical branches of Christendom. She always told the drivers to go down Woodstock, especially since all the speed bumps had appeared on Walton Street. This time she would not have as much chance as usual to explore Oxford and its wonders. Of course, she would do some writing and visit the Bodleian.

That was her cover for her new job of trying to infiltrate the manuscript ring—a job she was not sure she liked anyway, but after all, she was in the midst of it simply because of the manuscript and James. And how was she connected to these last murders? She tried to convince herself she wasn't, but Douglas had thought they would be contacting her. The fear rose in her throat as she remembered the murdered woman's scream at the Willapark.

What now? she could not help asking herself. How could she possibly act as some kind of double agent when she did not know anyone involved in the business of stealing valuable manuscripts now that James was dead—except Jean, whom she had met on the flight. She had actually liked the woman, even given her a bit of marital advice about doing things with her husband before it was too late. She would have to give up that persona she had affected about being the widow in a happy marriage. All those suggestions of grief and a lifetime loving relationship. She was not being honest—perhaps had not been honest with herself

But back to Jean Marie, as Ellen thought of her now to herself because of the salutation she had read on the letter in the substituted case. In her mind, Ellen had also connected the double name with the woman's pin in the shape of a letter M and guessed that Jean probably used the name Marie when she needed a cover. Jean Marie had let drop the hotel she was going to stay in, the Strand Palace, in the section for business class travelers. But of course she would not be there now. She would have gone on to the flat the bank was giving to her and her husband. Assuming all that was true, of course. Still, perhaps the place to start was the hotel. She might have left a forwarding address.

The taxi pulled up to number 179. Its blue door looked familiar, as did the steep gray stone steps that had had been glassy after that rare Oxford snow the last time. But March was surely too late for that now. And the foot and mouth disease was worse because of the cold. Perhaps it was only the beginning of someone or some terrorist group spreading disease in the world that would precede the end time prophesied in every generation. People were hoping the warmth of spring would put a stop to it, but she thought that was a kind of whistling in the dark. She had done enough of it herself to recognize the symptoms. The government warned that only the killing of massive numbers of sheep, anywhere the virus might lurk, could prevail.

She handed the driver five pounds and a fifty pence coin. She wanted to tip generously because he had helped her put her large bag in the back. "Give me your card. I shall be here several weeks, and I'd like to have you come most mornings to take me to the Bodleian. Would you take an advance booking to pick me up every morning except Wednesday at 9:30?" She could always cancel.

"Thank you, madam. Yes, the card." He handed it to her but did not get out this time to help with the heavy bag. "You had better call the night before to book. We have stopped booking too far ahead. Sometimes we are busy in the morning. Businessmen going to work, you know." His heavy accent exaggerated the *r* in work.

As Ellen dragged the black roller bag up the steep steps, she decided that her excuse for contacting Jean Marie would be to take the bag to her—although really it was now in the hands of Scotland Yard. While negotiating the double lock she heard the phone ringing inside. She stashed the luggage by the door. "Hello," she said huskily, controlling her heavy breathing from the exertion of getting in.

"Douglas McInery here," said a deep voice. "I hoped you would be in by now. I called to see if you would have dinner with me down at Loch Fyne on

Walton Street." He paused a few seconds. "I thought we might go over some things."

Her spirits rose unaccountably. She knew he meant to help her map things out. "I should be delighted." She looked at her watch.

"I'll come by at seven-thirty. That way you will have time to get unpacked and settled in your house."

And take a short nap, she thought. "Fine. I am glad you called. Until seven-thirty, then." Ellen was glad not to spending her first evening in Oxford alone. She would call her friends tomorrow.

* * *

"We are always sitting across a table from each other," she joked mildly as she looked at Douglas McInery. He looked tired this evening, the lines around his mouth and eyes more etched than she remembered from two days ago at the pub in Tintagel. She looked down quickly. She did not want him to think that she was studying his face. "And now, I suppose, you want to tell me what my new job of 007 will consist of—how I shall have to seduce the top executive of the arts in Britain—would it be a Chairman of the Board or a Minister of the Government I should have to play Mata Hari to?"

Douglas looked faintly shocked, and she regretted her humor. Why was it that humor seemed the most impossible thing to transfer across the Atlantic? Suddenly she felt like a brash and ugly American. "I am sorry," she apologized. "I know, of course, that you would not think such a thing about an aging widow. You are too much of a gentleman."

"On the contrary," he said, bristling a little, as if she had attacked his manhood in some way, "I often think of seduction." He seemed to look for a moment at her lips. "But I am hoping that you trust me not to put you in so dangerous a position. This is a very limited position—a very limited task I should like you to do for us."

"Of course. I am vaguely disappointed," she could not resist saying. "I had hoped that I was moving into an exciting and glamorous new second career. In a year I shall be finished with my part-time transition to retirement." She looked around the room of Loch Fyne—the freshest seafood in town. It was crowded at this time of the evening, though it was a week night. Their table in non-smoking, a table which seemed ridiculously small, was nevertheless a bit apart from the tables nearby, as if Douglas had asked for one in which their conversation might not be overheard.

Douglas looked serious. "No, it is not much we want you to do—and you may not get to do it if you do not get in touch with Jean or if they do not get in touch with you in some way. We are actually banking on their getting in touch with you."

"I know you have said that. I am not so sure."

"We think, for instance…." He looked down at the table, tracing a circle thoughtfully on the wooden surface. "That they already have contacted you—that it was some one of them calling, not Left Luggage at Heathrow."

Something clicked in her head then. Yes, there had been something odd about that call. She searched her memory of the conversation. For one thing, the woman had been too inquisitive about when she was coming to London. For another, she had inquired about the other bag. Perhaps there was some thought of an exchange, at least using that other bag to set up the meeting. "Perhaps that is so. I felt something odd about the phone call. And remember, she hung up suddenly, or the connection was lost. I can't remember what I said just before that. That is one of the problems about being Miss Marple's age."

Douglas laughed. "Of course, you aren't, but perhaps it is the early onset of Alzheimer's. I have had it for years myself," he added to let her know that he was joking. He had already let her know how much he valued the quality of her mind.

"However, I do remember that Jean told me the name of the hotel she would be staying at in London until her husband had the flat ready for them—the Strand Palace. So what should I do next? Simply wait or what?"

"I suggest that you inquire over the telephone at the Strand Palace whether Jean left a forwarding address and go on from there. You might also call Left Luggage at Heathrow. Perhaps if you do those two things and leave your Oxford number, they will get in touch with you." Douglas picked up the menu then. "In the meantime, let us just enjoy ourselves. This place has lovely food. And by the way, feel free to treat yourself. This is on Scotland Yard."

Ellen looked down herself at the large rectangle of the menu. She had never broken her habit—from years of cooking—of reading every item, weighing the possibilities. The rack of lamb caught her eye, but it seemed too close to all those dying sheep. Then the sea bass, but that reminded her of James. Best perhaps to put herself into the hands of Douglas McInery. *Capable hands*, she thought, with a flutter of desire. Ridiculous! Really, she was getting too old for such things. No wonder all the middle-aged men she knew married sweet young things. Only if you grew old together could you get past the soft flesh around the waist, the breasts somewhat pendulous. Who was she kidding?

Certainly not herself. Her breasts were large and heavy. She sighed: "Why don't you order for me? Something with seafood, and I love spinach."

"A bottle of the white Bordeaux," Douglas said to the waiter. "We shall order in a few minutes." He leaned toward her. "I need a bit more guidance. I only know you like coffee and fish and chips. First now—what starter? How about the moules with wine and herbs—just a half portion?"

"Please have that yourself and give me one—I'll have the leek soup." Ellen found herself drawn into his thoughtful planning.

The evening had proceeded pleasantly from there. She liked him more and more. Not an academic, he did not monologue. She had a theory that people had jobs that they chose out of some aspect of their personality, and then the jobs themselves tended to reinforce and exaggerate that characteristic. For example, James had loved to lecture. Although he had not gone on and on in conversation like some of his colleagues, never giving anyone else a chance, he had nevertheless developed a way of talking that was something like a mini-lecture, and he would grow very angry if she or anyone would interrupt in the middle. Sometimes, she confessed to herself now, she had done that when she knew what he was going to say, hoping to save herself boredom. But there was no danger of that with Douglas. There were occasional pauses, but generally there was a leisurely but genuine conversation.

"Have you never married?" she asked him over the small espressos they had allowed themselves.

"Yes, when I was quite young. I was married for ten years, and then sadly my wife was killed in an auto accident. With our seven-year-old son."

He paused then, looking at his hands. "I was driving."

"How terrible!" She willed him to look up at her, but he seemed suddenly remote. "Forgive me for asking. It is terrible to feel even remotely responsible for death."

"When it is the two people who mean most to you, you go over it again and again, asking yourself questions. What if? Could you have changed the outcome?"

"Yes, I do know, believe me. And now I need to tell you something. I have been over it again and again, and I don't really believe I was responsible." She stopped, trying to think what exactly to say.

"I think I already know, Ellen," he said. "You saw James die?"

"How did you know? Yes, he had come there to see me, and the long and the short of it was that he slipped and fell, hitting his head on some rocks and almost bouncing as he slipped into the creek. But how did you know?"

"We suspected it last time. That is why Spencer was so aggressive in questioning you. We were almost certain from the time of death; and also, you remember, there was the time at which your husband asked Mrs. Gentry, the farmer's wife, if he could park his car in her farmyard. You had to have been in Rocky Valley at the time he died. But of course someone else could have been there also."

"Then why would you have let me go back to America?" She could not bear to think of how long she had worried over this. "I felt horribly guilty, but I didn't think you would believe that I was innocent if I told you."

"We probably would have suspected you less if you had told the truth. Why didn't you?"

"I think because I felt that I could have saved him if I had really wanted to. Or at least I could have tried harder, even at risk of my own life. But gradually I came to see that I was simply helpless in the situation. I was guilty of two things, perhaps: at the moment of his death feeling a sense of relief and then later not telling every shred of what happened. Insofar as the police were forced to spend more time investigating, I suppose I actually owe money to the government. I have worried over that. Perhaps that is why I have made such an effort to return the manuscript."

Douglas was silent. For a few moments Ellen was afraid that he now despised her. He looked across at her then. "You were wrong, of course, not to tell what you knew. Technically, you were withholding evidence."

"I know—and I have lost sleep over it. I felt like a murderer in Cornwall, though I had nothing to do with the death of that poor woman."

"I know that, of course, and I don't think your holding back that information at your husband's death had anything to do with this one or the one in Oxford. And we have already said among ourselves at Scotland Yard that you are repaying the Yard by helping in this investigation." He smiled at last, his blue eyes losing their cloud. "I suspect you have paid your debt to society in your own struggles with conscience."

He spoke lightly now. "Now that everything is out in the open between us, I'll give you this folder. It has some photographs of people involved in fine arts theft or suspected of it. I think, however, that they are mostly art, not book, thefts, but the two are somewhat related. The buyers of such hot goods tend to overlap."

Ellen sighed. "Thank you for believing me. I'll look at these later, unless you have something you want to tell me about them."

"No, I am going to get you home now. I am sure your trip today makes you feel in need of a rest."

"Yes," Ellen agreed, "but I think I'll walk to the house from here if you won't mind—just to blow away the webs from my brain." That would solve any awkwardness at the door. She was not used to going out with men. She was happy to be friends still, with everything clear between them.

"Of course. The way is well lit. Please call tomorrow night to let me know what you find out. I am going in to the Oxford police in the morning to see about the investigation into the murder here." They were walking to the coat closet near the door. He held her coat for her.

"Fiona—yes, I should be interested to hear more about her. And again, thank you for dinner and the pleasant company. And for understanding."

He shrugged on his own black overcoat and opened the door for her. "Take care," he said and laid his hand lightly on her shoulder.

Chapter Eleven

She stretched her legs luxuriously. It gave her something like joy—at the very least an unusually sustained burst of intense pleasure—not to have to spring out of bed. All these years of teaching, grading the last five essays before breakfast, having to be out of the house early, doing a hundred domestic tasks before she could go, rushing home to take her daughter to the dentist—always juggling six oranges at once—life was different when you were on leave. However the day ended, the beginning was good.

Perhaps the emptiness she sometimes felt now when her family life seemed to be over—James gone and her daughter no longer needing her, even the teaching winding down—would be compensated gradually by such self-indulgent pleasures. Something dark hovered on the edge of her mind. She knew it was the murder at Bosinney and more pressing, here in Oxford, at least, the murder of that girl—Fiona somebody. But she would not think about them now. Later when she could face them. These small pleasures would give her a cushion, but she needed to balance them with a serious purpose. She was going to London today. An edge of excitement just at the thought of going to London. " Pussy cat, pussy cat, where have you been? I've been to London to visit the Queen." Being in London even now belonged to old rhymes and fairy stories. She had spent her life with English books, and, she admitted, she was still something of a child in her discovery of the place.

Her own life (mostly elsewhere) had not been what she expected in either direction—towards the good or towards the bad. Not dull, as perhaps the

Cinderella story would have been after the slipper was found to fit. Extremes both directions, but the daily ordinary things, like the warmth of the duvet and the great English bread waiting to be turned into toast with black current jam, seemed better really than all her successes—modest ones but surprising, such as snagging a few academic prizes and getting the PhD, in an age where few women succeeded in doing either. Both of which seemed cancelled by James's betrayal and then death—she shivered—but not the joy and achievement of teaching and mothering. Surely nothing could wipe those out. Now, however, the ordinary and smaller things were best, mattered most, she sometimes thought, when she couldn't bear to think about the big things.

What was life all about anyway? Love and death and going on in the face of loss. Those, of course, big things. But the words did not touch it—certainly not love, which had taken her unawares and dragged her along strange paths. She wondered at how she saw it in those helpless images. Then death and loss. Early in her life she had started to think about them. After all, those were what poetry and novels were about. Once a friend told her she had written two full novels about the worst losses in her life, trying to exorcise them—work through them, as they say in pop psychology books. And the outcome had been that the griefs still lay there untouched, like heavy stones. *Inconsolable*, that lovely word that expressed her friend's state of being. But no, words could never touch some wounds. Ordinary people had a common sentence: "You never get over it," they say about such things as loss, betrayal, suicide. Some wounds remained. Scabbed over at times. Still, one went on. But perhaps the words in poems were different. They were for her, when she read them and even when she wrote them.

She must stop that voice again. This was not a morning for depressed thoughts. She must realize, anyway, that truth, however hard, was valuable. Knowing things through experience should not cause depression. Maybe acceptance, if it turned out to be possible. Depression was too inactive. One must build on truth, another structure, however fragile.

Another side of her mind saw this moralist attitude as naïve. *Shut it off. Go back to the small and the ordinary.* She would get her breakfast, drink her coffee in bed, listen to those beautiful English accents speaking the news from BBC1. Then she would go to London, meet Jean Marie and see what happened. Something stirred then, a spirit of adventure perhaps. If the Queen should happen by in her golden chariot, that would be a bonus.

By the time Ellen was walking down Kingston Road towards the Walton shops, she was determined. She even had a small plan about her procedure.

I am going to be working for Scotland Yard, she thought in wonderment. She realized also that she was happy because she had finally told Douglas the true story of James's death. She relied on him, maybe because, when she had grown up, figures of authority were strong, thoughtful men. She knew also that he was right. Strictly speaking, she should have come earlier to tell the police the truth, but somehow she had been too unexpectedly full of grief for James. If she were really honest with herself, she was full of grief more for the failure of their life together—her fault as well as his, she finally had come to realize. *Though his was the greater betrayal*, she insisted to herself.

And if she had come to England before now, then perhaps she would have had to talk to an entirely different sort of person. Someone harsh. She might even have been charged with something. In some ways, she knew, Douglas had not wanted to hear how cowardly she had been; his own integrity was too deep. But in the end he had seemed to understand and did not seem to believe she would have been held technically responsible.

She walked down past the shops in Walton, pausing only once to look in the small gallery with its original watercolors of Oxford scenes. Perhaps the one of Port Meadow in the morning with all the black birds winging across the pale sky would be her souvenir. She needed something to remember her adventure by. She was still sorry she had not bought the one at Willapark of St. Neftan's Waterfall. But then the image of James's body turning in the rushing water of the creek came back to her, and as his face turned towards her with the staring eyes, he seemed to smile in a particular sardonic way. Perhaps it was just as well. She wanted to stop dreaming about it all. The nights when she woke at three to shadows in the corner seemed to be fewer in number, although jet lag made it more difficult to sleep through. Once she had dreamed he was there in bed with her, penetrating her in a harsh and brutal way. She saw his face then, as it had been when they took the body out of the creek, gray as putty, with lines graven beside his mouth: "I have graven you in the palms of my hands." Was that in the Psalms?

Somewhere else there was something about heaven and earth forgetting you, but not her—she would not forget. But she wanted to forget James. It was time. *Think of other things, new things*, she told herself. *Follow the plan for today*. Just what would she say at the Strand? And if she found out Jean Marie's number, what would she say when they met at the British Museum? When she had called Left Luggage at Heathrow, they seemed to have no record of the call to her. So Douglas had been right in what he told her at Loch Fyne last night—there it was, by the way. She looked into the interior as she walked by. Yes, he had been right about the call. One of the ring had probably made it, hoping for more information.

When she finally arrived at Gloucester Green and the station, she was glad that she could step immediately onto the London Express. She was tired, but she felt virtuous. She had restrained herself from taking a taxi—spoiled American that she was. But here at least she walked and walked; after all, there was plenty of time. She was still in the waiting game. She looked behind her once as she climbed on the coach. Perhaps someone was following. But for the moment at least, she saw no one shadowing her even if some flesh on the back of her neck had signaled strange eyes staring.

Sitting near the front among the scattered travelers, Ellen folded her long black coat so that it would not wrinkle and settled in to read her mystery novel about Oxford, this one by a woman, now that Morse was gone. She almost thought of him as a real person—another one she had mourned recently. But she comforted herself by starting over again with the series. It was a little like going back over one's memories. Death was not so final after all unless it went along with a real change in your life like the one she was working on now.

She dozed off then when the green hills of the countryside surrounding the M40 seemed to run together. *Not very exciting*, she remembered thinking, and when she jerked awake, they were stopping in North London at Baker Street. Shades of Sherlock Holmes. She smiled to herself. Now that she was a double agent of a sort, she belonged to that great tradition in England of solving crimes and cleaning up the world, eradicating evil wherever it lurked. She knew she was being naïve, but she couldn't help it. Besides, there was truth in the notion. She knew Douglas felt the importance of his work in that way. If she felt a twinge of fear, well, there had already been two murders, and the image of Miss Deschamps floated up into her mind. It was not the image of her that night in the lounge but the one of her twisted mouth, like the silent scream of the painter Munch that threatened still to come out of it. That image she had seen in the morgue, or whatever they called it in Cornwall, the place that had always seemed to her like a large filing cabinet but with cold dead bodies on the slabs when the drawers slid out, bodies sometimes zipped up in bags that made them even more sinister than if they had been lying there naked with a clean sheet around them. What was she doing talking to herself about it all as if she had been in hundreds of such rooms? Actually, she had only been in one twice—the same one there in Cornwall. James and Helene Deschamps, probably part of the same ring of manuscript and rare book thieves.

Ellen grabbed a taxi quickly at Hyde Park corner. She had hailed it almost as soon as she stepped down from the bus, remembering the nice English custom of thanking the coach driver. "Strand Palace, please," she told the cab driver, almost giggling as she resisted an impulse to say, "And speed it up, Buddy," like some New York private eye in a Hollywood movie. Sometimes she really felt as if she were play-acting, a little girl again who loved doing theatricals and dressing up, though her life had not been like that. It had all seemed to go deadly serious for the past fifteen years. Yet she knew that this current situation was more serious than she was really equipped to deal with. Still, it was exciting. One of her cousins who was amazingly in the context of her materialistic family had told her that for every death there was a resurrection among the living. She wasn't sure what that meant, but she felt as if she were living a new life now, somehow related to James's death.

After checking into the Savoy, Ellen nervously emptied her purse onto the bed, suddenly remembering that Jean had given her a business card at the airport, which must surely provide her last name. Why had this so completely slipped her mind when she told Douglas that they had never exchanged last names? It must have been because she could not find her own card to give Jean at the time. Anyway, now she knew Jean's card must be somewhere in her purse and would have the exact name she should seek out when she went to the hotel.

There it was: "Mrs. Marie Deschamps"! Suddenly the pin Jean had worn flashed in front of Ellen's eyes, the medieval "M" that didn't seem to fit either her first or last names, and the card confirmed that "Mrs. Marie Deschamps" was indeed the same person. But "Deschamps"? That poor woman murdered in Bosinney had given Rick the name "Miss Marie Deschamps." What was the connection? If both women were involved in the manuscript thefts, did they simply borrow each other's names for a cover? Or was there more? Were they related? Ellen wished that Douglas were here so that she could ask him what he thought, but he would not be arriving until later. She would just have to trust her own judgment for now. She gathered up the contents of her purse, checked the room carefully before she left, and walked down to the Strand Palace.

When she entered the Palace, Ellen walked directly up to the familiar desk—she had stayed there at least three times when she wanted to be near the theatres and not to have to pay the prices at the Savoy. She was glad this time, however, to be staying in a world that seemed cocooned from modern business. This time Scotland Yard was treating.

"I am trying to locate a Mrs. Marie Deschamps," Ellen told the young woman behind the desk. "She must have left the hotel now, but did she leave a London forwarding address?"

The woman looked among some papers. "What date did she arrive here?"

"March 3, I believe." She knew the date of her own arrival, thank goodness.

"Are you her sister Desiree? Desiree Helene?"

Ellen nodded, crossing her fingers.

"Then, yes, this is her number, " she said, handing her a card. "Let me check and see if she also left a note."

So the dead woman's name was not Marie at all, but Desiree Helene Deschamps. And she and Jean Marie were sisters—or were they sisters-in-law, since Jean Marie's card read *Mrs.* Deschamps? *Either way*, Ellen concluded, *they were clearly related, at least as sister thieves!*

The young woman returned quickly. "No, the card was the only thing."

"Thank you." Ellen looked at the card, walked to the pay phone in the lobby, or lounge, as they called it here, and placed the call. Fifteen minutes later she was walking to the British Museum. Jean Marie had agreed to meet her there to receive her bag back. The call had been pleasant but remote, as she maintained the fiction that there had been a simple mix-up in the bags. It was still remotely possible that confusion at the airport was the answer, but Ellen did not think so now as she walked along the shortcut she knew through Drury Lane.

About fifteen minutes later she was climbing the broad steps to the British Museum. How many summers had she and James done research there early in their marriage? She always thrilled at the romantic notion that Karl Marx and Virginia Woolf had also sat under the beautiful blue and gold dome in the reading room. Now of course it had all gone to the brilliant new British Library juxtaposed to St. Pancras Station, the bright colors and modern rectilinear forms of the new library in stark contrast to the Victorian fantasy of the station. It was wonderful, however, that now everyone, not just scholars, had access through the new surrounding remodeled area to the old reading room in the British Museum.

This time when she entered the museum, however, she turned left instead of going straight towards the dome and walked through the bookshop towards the Egyptian collection with its shriveled mummies and other treasures that her daughter had loved as a girl when they visited. The café was down at that end near the Elgin marbles that Greece was still trying to get back—she could never remember exactly how to get there but knew that she would finally see it. *That is the secret of happy travel*, she thought, *not worrying too much if I know I am headed in the right direction.* Many times one discovered other things along the way, and somehow, what one discovered was more fun than the great objects one worked so hard to find.

She was startled at first when she entered the café to see the dark woman sitting near the cash register. She recognized her easily, in spite of having seen her so briefly on the flight when she was thinking of so many other things. She herself had dressed in the bright blue suit she had worn on her trip so that Jean Marie would know her, but Jean Marie had on different clothes, a smart red and gray muted plaid suit. Perhaps her husband had rewarded her for coming.

"Hello," Ellen greeted her quickly. "I am so glad you could make it." As Jean Marie looked down at her hands, obviously empty of the bag she was supposed to have brought, Ellen quickly improvised an excuse: "I left the bag at the Strand with the chief bellhop, as it was too heavy to carry here. I thought that perhaps when we part you could pick it up there on your way back to your flat in a taxi. If that is a problem, I could go with you in the cab and hop out there and hand it to you while you wait with the taxi."

"Yes, I was noticing that you did not have it with you, and my husband wants his shirts. He has been complaining that I was terribly careless." She smiled.

"I must have picked up your bag; you left it when we were talking. Did you not just take mine by mistake? They were much alike."

Jean Marie frowned. "No, I didn't," she denied, shaking her head. "I just walked off without my small bag. I must have been thinking so hard about getting a London taxi. Haven't you found your own bag?"

"No," said Ellen, hiding her surprise at the lie. She had clearly seen Jean Marie settling two bags on her trolley before moving the other two, which she had assumed were both her own. "And unfortunately, there was an important item in it," she threw out, hoping for a response.

Minutes later, after a brief cup of coffee and a polite exchange about Jean Marie's welcoming husband and Ellen's unfortunate visit to Cornwall, where she was prohibited now from walking the coast path, the two walked out of the British Museum to catch a taxi for the Strand. Jean Marie had seemed upset when she heard of the murder that had occurred in the hotel. *And well she should be,* Ellen thought, then wondered if indeed Jean Marie had not known about the death of Helene before this moment.

A taxi seemed almost waiting for them as they arrived at the curb. Ellen hardly felt the needle in her arm there in the back seat of the taxi. She was conscious mainly of the scent of Guerlain as she drifted off—was it Shalimar or something else…?

PART II

Chapter Twelve

When Ellen awoke the second time, she found herself gagged and tied to a small chair near the window. She thought at first that the room was over St. Ebbe's Street in the pub where the poetry group had met. The Backstreet Poets, they called themselves when she had joined them. But as her head began to clear, she remembered that she was not in Oxford but in London, where she had gone to meet Jean Marie. The window was open from the top. These English with their desire for fresh air! She was freezing. Then she corrected herself, in her exhaustion: *My captor is not entirely English anyway, so such cultural stereotyping is wrong, as it always is in some sense.* Why she should stop to speculate in this situation she did not know. *That inner voice never turns off,* she thought now with some irritation. She shook her head to clear it and tried to figure out some way to help herself. Her hands were tied with a heavy cord behind her, and both her feet were bound, but not so tightly. She could shift in her chair, thank goodness, but she could not really move away from the cold draft. She knew that if she sat there very long she would grow cold and numb. Hypothermia would make her sleepy.

But before even she felt the prickles start in her feet, the door opened, and Ackman came in with an older man she had not met. But that it was Desmond Boyer, she knew at once, having seen his photograph in the file Douglas had given her. *Curator of the Museum in Lyon,* she remembered, *frequently in London for the Sotheby sales.* Apparently buying, according to rumors in the art world, both paintings and books for a rich American couple from North

Carolina who collected late Italian baroque—the husband loved the paintings, but the wife wanted seventeenth-century Bibles and books of Common Prayer. Until twenty years ago the latter were easily available, but the wife had been interested in religion only recently.

From their low-voiced conversation, Ellen gathered that Ackman had been dismissed from the room. Ackman had told her earlier that he was a courier for the outfit but sometimes moonlighted by doing rough jobs, such as getting her here. *Kidnapping me. I must learn to call a spade a spade, not a gardening instrument.* That gentility she had cultivated all her life was no help at the moment.

"It is regrettable that we must have you in such a situation," said the older man as he removed her gag, his small eyes hard but his voice carefully soft. His English was perfect, if somewhat stiff, as if he had learned it in a foreign school. *Which he probably had*, she thought.

"What were the choices?" she asked, her voice cracking slightly.

"Ackman is sometimes over-zealous," he added, frowning as he bent down and untied the cord around her ankles. "It would have been enough to detain you here under lock and key." He went around behind her and began to cut the bonds on her hands.

"Thank heavens," she said meekly, as she rubbed her hands to restore the circulation. "May I move away from this window?" Standing up, she carefully only stretched where she stood, awaiting his permission.

"Of course," he assured her, gesturing towards the green plush easy chair in the corner and moving the straight chair out of the draft and closer to it as she crossed and sat down. She looked at him closely then. Of average height in his neat gray suit. No one would immediately take him for the double player that he was—halfway between criminal and gentleman. Perhaps there were no gentlemen left in the world. Of course that was not true—after all, *gentleman* was not a class delineation but a matter of courtesy, which itself was a matter of kindness, gentleness.

He sat down gracefully, unbuttoning his suit jacket as he did so. Adjusting his trousers at the knee so that he did not lose the crease in his flannels, he finally addressed her: "Mrs. Adams, surely you know that all we want is your cooperation. Not even that. Your late husband is out of it. We have the manuscript now, and we are willing to compensate you generously if you will just go home to Pennsylvania and stop playing this dangerous game. I and the people I work with do not want Operation Leonardo to become associated with crime or violence—certainly not. It is bad for business."

When you have people such as Ackman working for you, that is hardly avoidable. She kept herself from saying that aloud. "Of course it would be, since you have such highly respectable people in your network." Her voice was dry.

"I am going to let you go now. You will forget you ever saw me. If you meet me somewhere later you will not know me. Probably you don't know my name yet, but you will go about your business as a tourist and professor doing research in Oxford at the Bodleian or in London at the British Library or in the various art galleries and theatres you visit with that taste that allows you to enjoy things you cannot afford. But you must forget your husband and his unhappy end. Believe me, we had nothing to do with that."

* * *

Later, with Douglas, she had been angry. Ackman, without speaking to her again, had returned as soon as it was dark and blindfolded her, walked her down a steep stairway and driven her to the train for London. He had actually given her a train ticket to Oxford and walked her on to her second-class car, knowing that she would not say anything then. "Don't get off, bitch," he had warned under his breath. "You are too old to fuck, or I would go with you to Oxford." He laughed at seeing her fury.

But she did get off at Reading and took a return train to London and then a taxi to the Savoy. All the anger she felt and had not been able to express came out when Douglas arrived at the hotel to meet her. They had agreed earlier that he would come to her room as soon as she called so that she could fill him in on all that had happened. She walked straight up to him as he stepped into the room, and he put his arms around her. "I am so glad you are safe. I blame myself for getting you into this." He looked down at her.

"There was no choice," she said, breaking free of his arms and beginning to pace. The frustration and anger caused her adrenalin to rise. Then they sat down before the lovely Tiffany porcelain on the mantle, each in one of the overstuffed chairs beside the imitation Edwardian tea table. She had been disappointed that the Savoy did not have the real thing, but she was very comforted by the safety of this old lady of an Anglo hotel that welcomed Americans with money.

As an academic, she had usually stayed in shabby places in Bloomsbury, but her strange job as an undercover agent for Scotland Yard had given her the privilege of staying at the Savoy. She had not questioned the meeting place.

It was easy to get to, though the halls felt too empty to be entirely safe. Next time, she found herself telling herself, she would see if they would allow Claridge's or that small elegant hotel where they had snubbed her when she and James went once to lunch. The lunch was better at Claridge's now anyway, one of the elegant bargains in town.

But as soon as she sat down, to her humiliation she began to cry. "I am so mortified," she snuffed and mumbled into her handkerchief. "I was very brave when I was kidnapped. But now—you would think I would be more grown up at my age."

"Of course you are. This is just the after-effect of nerves," said Douglas, handing her his large pressed handkerchief. "Women's handkerchiefs are only good for one sneeze," he smiled.

"Oh, don't be condescending," she laughed. Humor always works. Or it did for her in tense situations. She handed him back the enormous white square. "Sorry. I am all right now. The best thing about all this is that now I have it straight in my mind what the choices in life are. Perhaps you always knew—maybe that is why you are a policeman. There are those who live for themselves first: greed writ large, perhaps enormously overlaid with money and taste, even sometimes good intentions, but always honoring the desire of the self."

He looked at her seriously. "My initial need is to hear your story, but actually what I like most about you is the way you are always looking for meaning out of new experiences, even the painful."

"Especially the painful." She looked thoughtful. "But first let me tell you the other choices in life that all this has highlighted. Indulge the teacher in me."

"If not the moralist," he laughed softly.

"Don't make fun. I am deadly serious."

"Thank God you are not *dead*. I should feel responsible. But go on—I know how serious you are." He looked serious now, too, his blue eyes darkening.

When had she begun to notice the ways his blue eyes changed with his mood? Ellen tried to cheer him. "Afterwards I will let you examine me for every practical detail that might help with the investigation. What I like about you, by the way, is the analytical bent of your mind—that you do not let me float off into meaning when we need to sift evidence first." She leaned a little away from him then, gathering her thoughts. "Given the number of people who live for self, it is a wonder that there are other kinds, but there are. I have always noticed how many ways there are of responding to a basically self-driven world, but at last the categories seem to be coming clear to me. Categories of response, that is.

"You belong to an important one." She looked over at him then, meeting his eyes directly. "You focus on what is wrong and attack it as a member of a group organized and designed to do so—one of the better parts of society. You work from within to do what you can. And yet, you probably ignore corruption within your own group."

He did not trouble to argue about the presence of corruption. "Perhaps I would have more serious problems in the regular police force. But I went directly into the special forces at Scotland Yard. Still, you are right. I assume the force has integrity."

"Yes, that is the way most of us live. We don't want to join protests against society. We rationalize (or perhaps it is true reason) that despite whatever corruptions, the group to which we belong—especially those groups based on idealism of some sort—is doing good. As we grow older and come more often in contact with how little good can be done at one time, we correct that a little. We accept that our group, our base for improvement and change, is doing as much as it can."

Douglas got up and walked to the mantel, leaning there and looking towards her as she spoke. "Ellen, are you all right? You aren't hurt in some way you haven't told me? "

"Only in my mind. No, really. I was frightened at first, but then I realized they did not want any more violence. Just let me finish what I thought out when I was waiting in that room, hoping you would come." Ellen sighed, thinking of the university system and its attempts to protect professors from politics. In a lifetime, she suspected no one could be protected from the evil in the world. It came from different directions. After a death, it seemed somehow that the other evils were small, but she knew they made a network or a web, with death often at the center.

In a university, evil focused on different things: tenure and its value, tenure and its abuses—also a kind of indifference to the personal needs of its faculty as they grew older and began to lose their idealism, which had been the problem with James. "The police deal with immediate justice—in some ways an enviable end, whereas the university with its long range vision for changing minds has more difficulty. Of a sort, anyway. But in both, I suspect, most of us maintain a kind of naïve faith in the institution.

"That has a great advantage. It allows the order of society and leisure for western achievement, but there is a profound defect. We wear blinders to the enemies within. The art world is the same, and evil there is somehow tamed by the beauty of the operation. Not really, of course."

"Yes, I see that. Even as a policeman, I find myself thinking that stealing a work of art or a manuscript is not so bad. It is done by people who have good taste."

"Exactly. You see where I am going. Greed in other areas is much uglier and more immediately frightening. Selling arms to terrorists or sending infected wheat to the third world seems much closer to the sin of greed, much more likely to involve hoods and criminals. The merely personal desire to own a great work of art or a book—a desire that becomes obsessive—seems of a different order."

"But fighting the greed that somehow corrupts even the best of enterprises—that becomes the problem. Isn't that what you mean?" Douglas looked at the clock on the mantel. "It is almost lunchtime. Shall I order sandwiches and tea?" He walked to the phone and called room service, then came back and sat down across from her. "Sorry to interrupt—I do want to hear it all. I sense you are building towards something."

"Yes, and that—fighting the greed—demands a different kind of person with different modes of approach from that of you and me carefully addressing each problem day by day in an orderly way. Sometimes at least, when greed threatens all the good the institution can do, the situation requires people to take on the system—sometimes to fight violently, sometimes to use questionable means, sometimes to risk death, sometimes to die. But what it is going to require me to do is to go underground, to lie, to convince the world of the library—perhaps the art world tangentially—that I am one of them. That kind of approach is against my principles, and I can't know how it will change me. But I have to do it, to make up for James."

Douglas leaned over and took one of her hands, holding it between both of his. "You are still frightened. I can see that. But don't jump to conclusions. Sometimes our quiet analytic way can work. And it helps us avoid the trap of becoming too much like our greedy opponents. Not in the greed but in the violence. Sometimes in the callousness towards the harm or death of an individual in the face of the death of many."

"But we must fight actively. In this sheep thing, for instance, it is right that people are protesting the deaths of sheep that show no sign of the disease. Even in a good cause, there cannot be too many sacrifices."

"What do you mean? What happens if there are too many? How would we know?"

"The balance shifts then—people begin to talk about how the overall justifies everything. It is that old argument—whenever we begin to think that a good end is justified, whatever the loss of humanitarianism or even human life, then propaganda has taken over truth." Ellen rose and crossed to lean on the mantel, too restless to remain sitting. "Such talk is a sign of institutional corruption. That is really what I am afraid of personally. If I begin to think that the lies and the double dealing are justified, then I shall become somewhere deeply corrupted, like the rest of them. But I don't see any way out. This has convinced me that such corruption has affected the art world—and the university world with its experts and bibliophiles is being drawn in. Not everyone of course, though many are influenced, but those in arts and books who have felt really cheated out of money and the way of life it buys."

Ellen stopped then. "I'm so tired of puzzling over it all. It is too close in this new job you have given me, but I need to go on with whatever it takes, even if I get my hands dirty…." She ran her tongue over her dry lips. "Or even if I become some sort of sacrifice. This experience was enough to make that possibility real to me."

"Yes, I see that. But I don't want you to think that way. Tell me first what happened from the beginning. Then we shall talk about what to do. It may be time for you to go home where it is safe." He frowned.

"In a sense, what I am saying is that I *can't* go home leaving this unresolved. It has too many tentacles that reach into the institutions I value—libraries and universities, of course, but also museums and art galleries, the whole world of valuable and beautiful achievements that are just about the best memorials that human beings leave behind." She felt a stubbornness creep into her voice.

"I know how you feel, Ellen." He used her name to let her know that he valued her seriousness. "I am not trying to persuade you against your better judgment. It is just that we all have our part to play, and I think you have played yours. That is, you have been extremely useful in pointing out some important players, but now that they know who you are…."

"I know what you are trying to say—it is too dangerous now for me to go on."

"Not necessarily. You simply won't be very useful. They won't believe that you have gone over to their side." He spoke slowly and firmly.

"I know that is a danger and a complexity, but I think that with your further help we could set something up that they would believe. I do have a scheme—you can tell me whether it is practical. First, though, I shall do as you ask and tell the narrative of my day as carefully as I can. It begins with coming to London to meet Jean Marie in the café of the British Museum…."

Douglas pulled his chair so that it faced hers and took her hand. "Go slowly—don't be nervous. Just try to remember it all." There was a new note in his voice, she noticed, and she thought irrelevantly of the way he had held her earlier. But no time for the personal now. She was a witness, and it was important to remember and to be accurate.

After they had talked and said goodbye, Ellen found herself in need of a long soak in the tub and a good night's sleep. When she woke late the next morning, the previous day hung over her like a nightmare, but she was still determined to carry through with her scheme, which Douglas had somewhat grudgingly agreed to support. To clear her mind, she decided to attend a play before making her way back to Oxford again. Afterwards, coming up all those steps from the National Theatre to Waterloo Bridge made her pause breathlessly. It was five fifteen and already dark. She had thought that by March the light would last longer, and she still had to walk to the Strand to get a taxi to Victoria Coach Station, from which the Oxford Express left at six-thirty. Oh well, the coaches left every thirty minutes this time of day. She would take her time and think about the play, or rather the reading of lines about Homer's Achilles that she had attended at the Cottlesloe. It was rush hour and people were pouring over the bridge. She stopped at the edge of the crowd and looked towards St. Paul's. What a splendid view of the Thames with the buildings lighted dramatically! She would have taken a picture, but she had left her camera in Oxford.

Chapter Thirteen

Ellen was already back in Bosinney, or, to be more accurate, in Tintagel, having her hair cut and blown dry. She had left Oxford the next morning after the London episode.

"Don't forget crime in Tintagel," said Sharon at Snip 'n' Cut, a small house on the road into the shops. The beauty salon was in a large outside room that brought in light with a multi-paned window. She laughed as she held the blow dryer away from Ellen's head so that she could hear. Most of her earlier words had floated over Ellen's head, literally blown away, but Ellen had herself brought up the subject of crime and was trying now to have a more serious conversation. Wherever she traveled, she had found that hairdressers knew more about what was going on in town than anybody.

"Well, of course, I know the town is not used to murder. Probably the two murders at the Willapark were the first in a hundred years. There hasn't been another since I was here, has there?" Ellen smiled up at Sharon.

"Of course not. I meant the latest crime, nothing so bad as murder, but something everyone is upset about. I only heard this morning though. A bloke in a long poncho stole the postman's bike when it was sitting outside the tourism center. Somebody said it was two men, but the postman was inside only for about five minutes delivering mail."

Ellen could not help smiling. What a typical crime for Tintagel. People there often did not lock their doors. But what a violation of the trust by which everyone left bicycles unattended or baby carriages in front of shops. "Have the police been called? What has happened since?"

Sharon blew Ellen's bangs, or fringe, as she called them, for about ten seconds, then she turned off the dryer. "You must know from the Willapark incident that it is hard to find a constable in Tintagel. We share our constabulary with Devon. You've seen those brilliant green, white, and blue cars—some even with checks on them. But getting someone to come when there is trouble is different."

"Maybe they hang out at the Falls or somewhere." Ellen shook her head, puzzled.

"More likely in the back room at the pub." Sharon put down the hairdryer. "And to be honest, there aren't many of them. We don't seem to have the robbery and other minor crimes they do in the city."

"When I watch those Midsomer Murders, it makes me think that the villages are as bad as the big cities. But it really can't be. It's probably just the literary attempt to set crimes in even more surprising places. Anyway, when they finally came, what happened?"

"The police have been by twice in one of those cars, patrolling the streets looking for a chap in a long poncho with the postman's bike."

"Maybe someone loaded up the bike in a small truck and hauled it away." Ellen was getting into her new role as detective. Then her normal self surfaced. "Poor postman, he must be dragging around by now with all that mail."

"At least he is one of the good guys in town who believes in serving the community. I hate to think if old Robin were the postman. He would probably just throw away the mail in a fit of rage and make the town fathers pay to get it back. And he would have received a payback from some of the men at the Sheep and Goat."

Sharon teased Ellen's hair slightly at the crown. "There, that puff helps a little."

Ellen smiled at herself in the mirror. Yes, that was a nice touch, not the old bubble, but a slight fullness at the crown made her face a better shape, and she was meeting Doug at the pub later. "Yes, I like that. But hey, I don't know Robin, do I?"

"You know him—of course you do. He's the man who charged you to go down and see St. Nectan's Falls. I've never been myself. Most of us in town were so mad when he started charging we all vowed not to go out there. That's been almost ten years ago."

"How can you not go to see those Falls? They are the most beautiful thing in the area. I almost agree with those New Agers that it is also a really sacred place, almost as if it is haunted by old Cornish nature gods. They have made little altars—miniature reproductions on a ledge there." Ellen patted her hair gently. She and Sharon both had auburn hair that gave a faint glow to their skin. "Hey, I think this is the best styling I have had in England."

Sharon blushed with pleasure. She gestured modestly. "Oh, I bet you've been to some fancy places in London that do wonderful things. You're lucky to have such heavy hair. Some of my ladies I have to struggle to cover balding spots.

"But back to greedy Griffith. No, I won't go there till he stops charging. Other people call him that, you know—Greedy Griffith. We live on tourists—I know you are thinking that about the town, but suppose we all started charging for all the entrances to the Coast Path near where we live?"

"You might need to after this foot and mouth lets up."

"I know—so many people have canceled their spring walks in Cornwall."

Ellen frowned. "But I know it is no joking matter. Rick says he has had cancellations for summer already."

Sharon sat down in the extra chair beside Ellen. "I didn't know that, but it's May now, and the whole town is worried sick. If we don't have tourists in the summer, the rest of the year will be awful from an economic point of view. My old ladies keep coming in for hair—regular customers, but some businesses are utterly dependent on tourists. Still, I don't believe in charging for the beauties of nature—it's okay to sell ale, but not the Falls. God made them, after all."

"You are right, of course. I couldn't resist saying to Robin, after I climbed to the top of those steep steps that led past his house and then down the steps to the path along the Falls, 'Aren't you going to pay me for that climb?' I could see he was not amused by that. He said he had heard that before. But really, to be fair, the National Trust charges at all their entrances."

"I have thought about that, but it is really a different situation. The Trust is trying to keep up a huge architectural heritage all over Britain. Even our Arthur's Castle in Tintagel is such an enormous ruin that it needs constant care for tourists to be safe wandering around. Falling rocks are always a problem."

Ellen nodded. "Of course you are right about the distinction between the Falls and the National Trust, but Robin does have to maintain his steps and keep up the path."

"Most of what he maintains, however, is part of how he is blocking off the whole thing to force people to pay his charges."

"I give up," laughed Ellen. "You are absolutely right. You have convinced me if I needed convincing. Who is Robin anyway? Has he lived here all his life?"

"No, like many people in the village, he came to Cornwall from London, I think, about seven years ago. Someone said he had run a small art gallery in Hampstead that went belly up. Nectan's Falls used to be open to everyone who walked along the creek from the side of the road opposite to Willapark."

"I was mixed up the last time I came. I thought Nectan's Falls were in Rocky Valley. After all, there is a waterfall there where the sea has eroded a sentinel boulder. But later I found out different."

"Yes, I can see that that is confusing, but they say the stream in Rocky Valley comes from Nectan's Falls originally and runs under the road and farm to bubble up just at the coffee shop the farmer runs. I don't understand the relationship of the smaller falls at the sea end of the valley." Sharon had gotten up now and was straightening out combs and putting the curling iron back in its holder.

"I've argued with you enough, my friend. We both have other things to do," said Ellen, taking the gentle hint. "Tell me the damages." She took out her red wallet and fished for a ten-pound note, then added another five.

"That is way too much," said Sharon, "but next time I'll trim your fringe free."

* * *

Minutes later Ellen was walking towards the shops that ran along the main street of Tintagel. Perhaps she would not be late to meet Douglas in the Sheep and Goat. It was unusually warm today for that time of year, about 65 with sun and a few high clouds. The foot and mouth had been worse during the winter and the cold spring, but now so many sheep and even other creatures had been slaughtered that there was little news about animals being added to the list.

Someone pushed by her suddenly, and she almost tripped. Strange, people were usually so careful not to touch anyone on the narrow sidewalk, but this man was in a hurry and almost broke into a run. One of the bright-colored police cars braked quickly behind her almost simultaneously, and a young policeman jumped out to run after the man who had jostled her. Could it be the thief who stole the postman's bike? Ellen stopped in the path, not wanting to become involved as the constable caught up with the smaller man, taking him roughly by the arm and walking toward the car that had crept up almost beside the two men. Then the brightly colored car drove off, the man stowed in the back. She would have an adventure to tell Douglas about, if nothing very relevant about the arts scheme they were working on together.

She shifted her purse to her other shoulder and noticed a folded sheet of paper sticking out of the top. What could this be? Had the man left it there when he bumped into her? She unfolded it carefully. It was strange, words cut out of a newspaper, a headline first and then a brief text:

VERONESE STOLEN BY ART THIEF

A Veronese has been taken from the National Gallery: a Venus and Adonis image that was hung with three others in a small room there. Louis Gerard, Curator, said that the theft was discovered by a guard who arrived at 8:30 a.m. this morning.

Ellen was not sure whether the report was accurate, as it was not the printed continuous text from the *Independent* but was made up of separate words cut out of a newspaper and pasted on the sheet individually. Only the headline was a continuous phrase cut out from a newspaper. Thank goodness she was seeing Douglas in a few minutes. Perhaps he would know something about the theft and have some ideas about why the sheet should have been stuck in the top of her purse. Clearly the man who shoved her had been aware that the police were following him. But why he would have put this in her purse she could not imagine.

There was almost no traffic downtown as she approached the Sheepshead Inn. The Information Center had seemed deserted, and only a few scattered tables were occupied in the Tea Shoppe as she passed. Her feet were sore from the cobblestones already. She must buy some sturdier walking shoes tomorrow. One of those tall handsome Englishmen with a shock of white hair hurried up beside her to open the door to the pub, and she walked into the dimness. A fire was burning in the corner, and she hoped that Douglas was there before her, but the place was even more deserted than the Tea Shoppe.

The young owner appeared at her elbow and guided her to the booth in the corner near the fire. "You won't be too warm, Mrs. Adams?"

"I am almost never too warm in Britain." She smiled at him. "In America we always keep the heat on. And besides, I love the look of the fire."

"Would you like to have a glass of wine or an ale—maybe a hard cider?" He seemed to remember her tastes.

"I'll have a glass of merlot, but after the chief inspector comes." Just then Douglas came striding in, his plaid jacket a jaunty touch in the plain room. "Ellen." He leaned down and kissed her cheek lightly. "It's good to see you. I have just returned from London." As he spoke, he slid into the booth opposite her. "How about merlot for both of us?" He smiled at his friend the owner.

Ellen realized how glad she was to see Douglas. She almost felt safe, but then she remembered the man on the sidewalk. "It is good you have come. I wasn't sure your train would be on time."

"I didn't come on the train, you know. I had taken my car to London so that I could get back in a hurry."

The cleft in his chin is really quite attractive, Ellen mused, almost surprised she had noticed. "I suppose I should tell you my small adventure, but tell me first about London."

"As you know, I went mainly to consult with the London police about whether there were connections between the Oxford murder and the Willapark murder. And even Professor Adams' death." He looked at her apologetically. "I had to enlarge a bit on that, you know, but everyone is satisfied with all you told me. They are also grateful to know that you are working further with us on trying to make contact with the ring of rare book thieves."

Ellen twisted her hair unconsciously until she remembered that she was ruining her new "do." "I don't know whether I should be back in Cornwall or in Oxford. I leave it to you to decide, but here I am, and already crime is running rampant in the quiet town of Tintagel. Have you heard about the man who stole the postman's bike?"

Douglas smiled broadly. "Of course! It was the first thing the gas station attendant on the edge of town told me as I came in. They haven't caught him yet, I assume?"

"Oh yes, I think I was happily at the scene. I may even have made him more obvious to the constabulary pursuing him."

Douglas's smile turned into a look of worry. "Are you all right? I see I can't leave you alone even in this remote place."

"As you see, coiffed and happy." Ellen reached over and touched Doug's hand lightly. "But starving. Could I have some chips to restore me from my fright?"

"Of course, but tell the story first."

"It is not much of a tale. I had just come from the beauty salon and was walking down the sidewalk on the main road to meet you. Suddenly I heard steps hurrying by me, and a rather small man actually brushed against me. At the same time one of those bright Devon police cars zoomed up, braked suddenly, and the young constable jumped out, raced after the man, captured him, and took him away."

"Perhaps I should drop by the police station."

"Stay awhile. There is a bit more," Ellen teased.

"Hurry so that you can have your restorative chips." Douglas relaxed a little at the lightness of her tone.

"There is one strange detail that appealed to my new detective state of mind." Ellen reached into her purse and pulled out a folded sheet of paper with the words pasted on.

Douglas with customary care opened it and read. "Yes," he confirmed, "I heard about the robbery in London but thought it too important a painting to be linked to our rare book ring. After all, rare books bring small profit in comparison to master paintings."

"Perhaps it is not linked," Ellen said, "but why would he stick the paper in my purse? Coincidence?"

"Simply to get rid of it before he was picked up by the constabulary. After all, how would he know who you were?" Douglas drummed his fingers nervously. "I never should have let you get involved."

"I am an independent woman." Ellen drew her hand back, a little stiff at the implication she was in his control.

"Of course," he apologized, "but I am the professional in this field and must use my judgment when potential danger is involved."

The owner appeared then, asking them if they would like another drink or something else. She ordered her chips and Douglas a second glass of wine.

"I am going, after I drive you safely home, to the police station in Devon and see what I can find out."

"Let me go with you. I'll sit quietly in the waiting area, but you can tell me what you learn on the way back to the Willapark."

"All right," he agreed, "but if it drags on, I'll send you home in a taxi. John is always around somewhere."

The chips arrived, hot and delicious, and the two shared them, knowing that dinner was probably some time away. "Tell me now," said Ellen, pausing to wipe her salty fingers on a large napkin, "what you learned in London, both about the theft of the painting and the European network that seems involved."

"Not much about the painting. It is still too recent, and they weren't sure about any link to our project. But there was a little new information about our friend Ackman—that he was involved, for instance, as a courier taking a rare manuscript of the Duke of Burgundy to the buyer, probably the one your husband took the last time before his death. It was not in the Bodleian, by the way, but in the British Library. The buyer has since that time died in a remote town in Burgundy, and Ackman's fingerprint was found on the manuscript, along with that of the owner. How the international police traced it I don't know, but they had notified Scotland Yard.

"We had, of course, the glass you smuggled out of that dingy room in London, where they held you for almost twelve hours, and that had a matching print. These days forensics are a wonder with fingerprints."

Douglas got up then and wrapped a burgundy muffler around his plaid shoulders. Then he walked over to pay the bill and came back to drape her cape around her shoulders. "Ready?" He looked down at the small woman as she straightened and started out of the pub.

"Good evening, friends, come again soon!" The owner was hearty, encouraging, they knew, the few people in town this chilly spring. But he also seemed genuinely to like them. There was something about Cornwall that was warm and welcoming, whatever else might have happened here.

Ellen began to think about their walk the day before along the path to St. Nectan's Falls. Douglas had arrived a little after lunch, and they had driven together down the road to Boscastle, parking off the road across from the farm where the path to the Falls began. This time she would not go all the way to the Hermitage where Griffith sold tickets at the entrance. The two of them just needed a quiet secluded place to walk and talk about the case, and of course both of them found the walk along the the sparkling clear stream a satisfying experience. Nature's purity helped sometimes when the world seemed so filled with impurity.

She had come earlier with Mark Johily and actually seen the inspiring Falls, almost thirty or forty feet high. When she first arrived at Willapark this trip, Ellen had bumped into Mark, the old man who had told the story of Rick's rescue of his son James. It occurred to her that Mark was someone to ask about the evening of the murder, and she had spontaneously told him of her desire to visit Nectan's Falls. When he politely offered to take her there, she had jumped at the chance, but his continued silence during their walk defeated her purpose. The two of them had stood silently on that rough slate that Griffith had put across the stream just where it began to flow from the dark pool made by the powerful cascade of water. She had not been able to stop wishing that either she were there alone or with Douglas, not with a man that she mistrusted for some reason. Maybe it was just that he had spoken so little on their walk. Gone was the lively storyteller she remembered from their first meeting. She even shivered slightly in the cold air as it occurred to her that Mark could shove her in the deep pool, and no one would ever know. But of course he wouldn't— why would he? He had no motive.

Then she recalled that Mark had only been at the Willapark for the evening and had left after the conversation in the lounge to return to his own home across the meadow, so he could not have told her anything about the evening of the murder that she didn't already know. That memory eased her tension, and she smiled at him as they had left the scene and come upon the small gifts New Age people had offered in this sacred spot—perhaps offerings to St. Nectan or just to mark the power of nature in the Falls. One that particularly caught Ellen's eye was a small constructed scene made out of chips of slate that suggested the character of Cornwall with its slate gravestones and elaborately designed walls.

No need to think about the awkwardness she had felt with Mark now, when Douglas was comfortingly present at her side, even touching her arm occasionally as they walked in rough spots, where the early spring mud made the rocky path slippery. The water was so clear in the shallow icy stream as it moved over the stones in the winding creek bed that, in most places where she walked, she could see the pale earth on the bottom. So far she had not glimpsed any of the trout she expected, not on either walk. Perhaps it was not the season for leaping along upstream to lay their eggs that she had read about and been fascinated by.

"Have you seen the white tails?" asked Douglas, drawing her towards him as he pointed across the stream near the richly dark rockface on the other side. "See how their tails bounce up and down? They seem to be leading us along, if that is not too fanciful for an old policeman."

The falls would always be a vivid memory for her, she knew.

"Where are you woolgathering?" Douglas asked as they started up from the booth in the pub.

Chapter Fourteen

As they left the pub, a salty breeze blew up from the sea and overwhelmed the mingled smells of food and beer wafting out of the pub and the restaurant across the street. Ellen breathed deeply, recovering her sense of the freshness of the sea.

Douglas put his hand under her elbow to guide her to his car, parked in a lot a few shops down the street. She was often admiring of how drivers found parking in a town with such narrow streets lined with buildings that had all been there before the invention of the motor car. Even in Oxford, Kingston Road had almost no room for cars, though houses were a mixture of solid two-storey single dwellings and even luxurious Victorian three-storeys in comparison to the bungalows of the Cornwall village. Still, they too had been built in the time of horse-drawn vehicles. And there were no garages.

Just as they turned into the lot, Ellen glimpsed Rick driving by in his elegant old Jaguar convertible. One was sure to see all who were out and about, as there was only one main street in Tintagel. He must have been shopping for the chef for the evening meal at the hotel. She found herself changing her mind about going to the Devon police station. She wanted to talk more to some of the guests at the Willapark, a few of whom had been there the night of the murder.

"Perhaps I should go back to the hotel," she said, after they were settled in Douglas's gray car. "I want you to be free to find out all you can from the Devon police, and I really need to ask some questions of some of the guests.

Last night at dinner I noticed there were still three or four couples there from the night of the murder. They might have remembered a few details since they were interviewed."

Doug nodded. "Perhaps that is wise. I doubt that I shall be long in Devon, but who knows when I show them the note from your purse? If they need to talk to you, they can come back to the hotel with me afterwards." He turned the car quickly to the left and headed down to the Willapark. The two were silent for a few moments in the darkening of the mid-afternoon sky. One lonely seagull flew over the black road in front of them, crying as if it were searching for a lost mate.

"I love the gulls here," Ellen said quietly. "It is as if they knew we were searching out some of the darkness in the world. When I was a child, I believed they followed me on my morning walk on the beach where we spent the summer. I imagined they were protecting me from the stinging jelly fish in the shallow water, but then I thought their cries were warnings. Now they sound more like laments."

Douglas looked at her quickly, then back at the road. "You sound sad. Are you sorry you agreed to this?"

"Oh, no. I just always feel a little low in the late afternoon. It's my body clock, I think. I am up—that is, really cheerful—in the early morning, and as the day wanes I do as well. I'll bet you are more steady in your feelings."

"I think so, but I need at least seven hours sleep, and the life of a policeman did not always allow for that."

"Of course not. It is a luxury to have a job that allows you to follow your energies. Mostly teaching did that, though when I was younger, I sometimes taught a late afternoon class for teachers. Sometimes I felt like falling asleep during student reports. I never did, of course. And after that evening I made a real effort not to teach at that time again.

"But then, teaching never had the satisfying closure of solving a case and finding the villain. It had other good things, but not that. I am a little excited about that aspect now. In college-level teaching we were always hoping we were laying land mines—you know, planting some seeds of knowledge that years later students would find when they grew more mature. Or even when something really puzzling about life happened in their experience. Do you see what I mean?"

"Oh yes," Douglas nodded. "I once thought of teaching when I was younger, but I wanted something that would come to clear conclusion. The only problem is that sometimes it doesn't. Crimes are not always solved."

He slowed gradually and turned in to the long drive, planted with exotic trees, even one or two palms. At the end was the main building of the The Willow Hotel, the old manor house, next door to an annex that had once been the stable. *That was the trouble with the town houses in both Tintagel and Oxford. There had been no room for stables*, she thought. By now Ellen felt almost as if she were arriving at a second home. Even the unpleasant events did not change her affection for the place. As they drew up to the entrance, Douglas reached across her and opened her door. "I'll just throw you out here and head for the Devon constabulary." He laughed softly. "I hate to lose your charming company."

"Likewise—or rather I hate to lose yours," she corrected, a little surprised that his hand brushing her dress made her pulse race. She got out quickly, and he leaned towards her. "I'll be back around 8:30, or I'll call."

"Safe journey," she said, consciously imitating the British phrase she had picked up.

* * *

As the guests went in to dinner, Ellen tried to pick out the couples who had been there a week earlier when the murder occurred. There were at least three, she saw as she looked around the dining room, one near her. The man was a native of Cornwall, she remembered. Dickie and Ann, she remembered, but not their last name. They were living now in Portsmouth; he had said something about working in the shipyard—in what position she did not know. She stopped at their table before moving to her own.

"It is nice to see you still here—familiar faces are welcome."

"We have missed you," said Ann. "I thought you must have gone back to America."

"No, I still have a few months, but I did make a flying trip to Oxford to visit a friend, who was leaving for the summer." Ellen smiled at them. "By the way, I love that painting just behind your table. Have you been to Nectan's Falls yet?"

"I used to go as a child," said Dickie, "but I heard that some foreigner had bought the property and was charging for entrance."

"Yes, that is true," Ellen said. "Not exactly a foreigner, I think, except in not being a native of Cornwall. His business had failed in London. Sharon, the hairdresser in town, said that townspeople are boycotting it."

"Oh, I don't know that I feel that strongly, but I don't live here anymore. I just felt I had been there many times."

"I would like to have the painting, but I am not sure it is for sale," Ellen looked towards it again just as Rick came up to the table to take their orders. "I'll move on then. Perhaps we might chat after dinner in the lounge."

Ellen crossed to her own table, prepared to order. While she waited, she took her small notebook out of her purse and opened it on the white tablecloth. She needed to frame some questions that might have bearing on the crime. Perhaps later she would ask Douglas what the relevant questions were that the police focused upon for interrogation. When Rick arrived at her table to find out whether she would have fish or lamb, she had already begun to write.

"Welcome back, Mrs. Adams," he said pleasantly. "I wasn't sure you would make it when you called on Monday."

"Nor I. My friend's plans were somewhat indeterminate."

"I am glad it worked out for us. We are beginning to recover from the unpleasantness of the murder, but the more cheerful people we can gather, the better."

"I agree," Ellen smiled at him. "It would help if the murder could be resolved. But for this evening I think I shall take advantage of the fresh sole. When I smelled the sea today, I said to myself I should think of this as a seaside visit. Then I saw you downtown and hoped you had been to the fishmonger." She paused. "I am very glad to be back, in spite of a bad start my first day."

Rick's brow was furrowed. For the first time Ellen thought he looked his age. "It is very important that I help people feel this is not only a pleasant hotel but a safe one. And on top of the foot and mouth, it is clear that this summer will be difficult."

He poured her a glass of wine from the bottle she had brought earlier for her stay. As he went toward the kitchen with the orders, Ellen suddenly felt her loneliness. She was the only person alone at a table, as the others began to chat among themselves. She began to write again in her little notebook.

Question 1. When did you first know Miss Deschamps was murdered?

Question 2. Where were you when you heard the scream?

Question 3. Did you notice anything when you were in the lounge during the evening? Either about her behavior or concerning anyone else relating to her?

Question 4. Where was your room in relation to where she was killed?

Question 5. Had you ever seen her before that evening?

Question 6. Did you see anyone come in during the evening who was not here at dinner?

That was all she could think of. Ellen unfolded her napkin and placed it on her lap. It was discouraging. She knew the police had already asked those questions, but perhaps the people would tell her more or drop some detail that they had only just remembered.

How in the world, she asked herself, *did the Willapark murder relate to the Oxford murder? Were both women in the ring of thieves that stole rare books?* Perhaps it was time for her to start talking about her own work at the Bodleian. After all, she was setting herself up in some way to serve as a decoy. Surely someone would approach other than the small man on the way to town this afternoon. *Being a detective takes patience*, she told herself.

Dinner was delicious as usual. How Rick managed to have a first-rank chef in such a small place she did not know. Especially since his son, the original chef, had gone to New Zealand. But the food was the best she had found in England. Some French sauces, and beautiful fresh vegetables from the hotel kitchen garden. She decided not to linger for the savoury, much as she loved cheese. She went instead into the lounge with the bar to get a wingback chair near the center of the room. That way she could be assured of seeing the people she wanted to talk to about the murder.

Lisa was already at the bar. "Let me treat you to an after-dinner drink," she said after they had exchanged greetings.

"I need a clear head tonight. I am trying to get some answers about the night of the murder. Chief Inspector McInery asked me to see if anybody who was here that night remembered anything more. So I'll have tonic water, no gin, please." She kept her voice down. "Don't say anything about it, though. Maybe people will talk to me more freely than they would the police." Lisa nodded briskly and poured the tonic over two cubes of ice.

"Could I have a couple more ice cubes? It's my American habit, you know."

As Ellen sat down, the doorbell rang twice, and Lisa went to answer it. By now the outer door was locked for the night. If people went out for the evening, they had to ring when they came in. She heard some muttering in the hall, and Rick came out of the kitchen to take luggage upstairs. As Lisa came back to the bar, she said, "Just someone from Exeter who came in and wants an early night before walking tomorrow morning."

Suddenly chilled, Ellen wished she had seen who it was. Then she shook her head, as if to blow away the cobwebs. She could not spend all her energies on fear.

Her cell phone rang in her purse. She walked out into the hall to answer it. It must be Douglas. No, he couldn't make it; he was still with the Devon constabulary and would come by in the morning to see her and find out what she had learned. "And I have a little news about the man who put the note in your purse" was the last thing he said. She wished he had told her what he had found out, but perhaps he was using a phone where there were other people around.

The dark velvet chair felt very comfortable when she returned. For a moment she closed her eyes, full of the heavy meal and happy and tired from the day. She opened them quickly, however, as she heard Mark's voice nearby, ordering a brandy. He picked the glass up from the bar and headed towards her.

"Most of them are still having coffee in the dining room, but it gives us a chance to chat. Welcome back to the scene of the crime," he smiled wryly.

"And you," she said. "I should think you would be afraid to walk home over the meadow these dark nights."

"We can't let fear control our lives. At my age, I might have a heart attack when I walk out the door."

"What worries me most," said Ellen, "is that we have no idea who the murderer was. Surely it was not one of us, and yet how did anyone get in and out of the hotel after murdering that woman? I take it you had left before it happened?"

"Oh, yes, I was sound asleep. Brandy and the long walk home, plus the charming evening telling stories, had pretty much done for me."

"I don't suppose you saw anyone around the hotel when you left? No, it would be too easy if someone were lurking by the front door when you went out."

"Too bad it wasn't that easy, but no. The police asked me that. The only people I noticed were a dark-haired man and a very short woman who had gone out for dinner in Boscastle. They were just pulling into the parking lot when I left. The lot is very well lit, you know. If anyone had been hanging around and was not actually hiding in a car, I would have seen him—or her. But I did notice a strange car. Coming every evening for dinner (I spoil myself that way since my wife died), I notice the cars. This one was an old Rover."

"It could have belonged to someone who came too late for dinner," she said slowly, but this was surely a clue, however slight.

Four or five people came in from the dining room then, and their conversation about the evening of the murder was interrupted. Ellen decided to wait until breakfast to talk to the two couples, but just as she got up to go to her room upstairs, Ann came up to her.

"I don't know whether you will see that distinguished chief inspector, but if you do, I wish you would tell him I thought of a detail he might be interested in."

Ellen nodded. "As a matter of fact, he has some information for me, and he is coming by in the morning. We might meet here in the lounge after breakfast if you have a few moments before you go off sightseeing."

"I'll say good night, then," said Ann, and walked back to her husband on the large sofa. Ellen turned to the small group. "Good night, everyone. I need an early one, or I turn into a pumpkin." A murmur went round as she walked to the door and moved towards the stairs. Her room again this time was at the top of the steps, the first on the hall.

As she pulled back the duvet and crawled between fresh sheets in the pale rose and aqua room, she gave a sigh of satisfaction. The color softened by shadows pleased her as she turned out the light and began to sink towards sleep. "Ah, to sleep," she smiled to herself.

* * *

Some time later she sat up in bed, breathing hard. Was it a bad dream? The dread rose in her throat, and she reached for the bedside light, almost turning it over with the suddenness of her movement. Her eyes went to the door. Perhaps she was reenacting the night of the murder when the scream had awakened her, but the silence was almost palpable. Then she saw him, a dim figure beside the door.

Chapter Fifteen

"Get dressed," Ackman said. "Just pull your clothes over those pajamas. We are going somewhere special, but not dressy." He chuckled softly.

Ellen could not see the face of the dark man standing beside the door, but she remembered it from the other time: hard eyes and a mouth that barely moved when he smiled. She could hardly breathe. Perhaps if she screamed, everyone would come running. But she could see well enough to notice the knife that gleamed in his hand.

"Don't think about calling out to anyone," the tall man said, as if reading her mind. "I should be on you with this knife in a minute, and I would be out of here before the hotel owner could burst out of his apartment door. I have already checked out everything. No!" He raised his hand in warning, perhaps at an inadvertent movement. "You will dress in about three minutes and walk softly down these stairs to the front door—and out. I will be holding your arm, don't forget. And you are too small to run fast enough to get away."

Ellen put the thought of screaming out of her mind. Perhaps she could pull away outside and hide in the dark, when he let go of her to get in his car. She was breathing rapidly now, but she took two deep slow breaths, trying to calm herself and her shaking fingers as she reached for the jeans and blue sweat shirt. Thank God the chest was just across from the bed. Why was Ackman here? She had hoped never to see him again after the London incident. What did she know or have that was valuable to the ring of rare book and manuscript thieves? They had her husband's manuscript.

A few heart-stopping minutes later, the two of them were walking down the stairs, Ellen hanging on to the banister for balance while her left arm was held in a viselike grip by the man beside her. When they exited the front door, she wondered if anyone heard the odd noise it made when it opened. He closed it with his other hand and half-dragged her across to his small red Peugeot. He was so tall that she was almost running. There seemed not to be a moment between his pushing her into the front seat and getting in himself. By the time she sat up, he had leapt in, locked both doors, and was starting the engine. She could only hope that someone would hear the noise and come in pursuit, but the hotel remained silent and dark.

"Where are we going?" she asked.

"Just keep quiet—you will know soon enough. If you bother me, I'll put a tape on your mouth."

Ellen thought of waking up in the London room with the gag and her hands bound behind her. She determined not to say another word. Perhaps they would go to meet someone else—maybe the comparatively friendly man from the art group, Desmond Boyer, with whom she had spoken after the last kidnapping. She tried to figure out what road they were on, but there were few clues at night on the country roads of Cornwall. She imagined the walls on the side with the vines that covered them. She was imprisoned now—speeding up and down the dark ribbon of the road in the chrysalis of an old car with a man who was the enemy.

Perhaps Douglas would find her. No, he was too old to be dashing in pursuit, but perhaps he could get back-up from Devon or even Scotland Yard. It would surely be morning before she was missed. She refused to think about what might happen before then, but she knew that Ackman was not very high in the organization—there must be someone else who would question her.

"What is your first name?" she said softly. Perhaps she could charm him into being a little less distant and professional. The car crunched to a stop on a pebbled space, the sound piercing the chill night air. Ellen was conscious of being on a hill, but she could only see a few yards beyond the car. Ackman took out a silk scarf and tied it in a blindfold over her eyes.

"Forget my first name—you couldn't pronounce it anyway." As he bent over her, she smelled the citrus shave lotion he wore. *Why bother with such refinements when you are kidnapping someone?* she thought. "You English don't do languages," Ackman said softly. "Abdullah, though, if you care. This blindfold will keep you from telling anyone where you are—not that you will have a chance."

As he helped her out of the car, she almost stumbled on the stones she felt through her sneakers, but again he had her arm firmly held and she righted herself, pulling back in aversion as she brushed his hip. She heard him opening a wrought iron gate as they walked onto a softer earth, probably grassed over. A few yards later she heard a key thrust into a keyhole, then a heavy door opening slowly.

"Move it," said Ackman, pushing her ahead.

"How can I? I'm afraid I'll fall. I don't know where to walk."

Ackman removed the scarf. "This is it, Madame, your new place of residence. Look around."

Ellen still saw nothing but an empty hall. "Where am I?"

"This is an old church. Why not pray to your god or prophet?"

"Yes, I will," said Ellen quietly. "I have visited the old churches in the Tintagel area. Some have been here since 1100," she added, knowing he would not care. The local tourist information had had a package of brochures that mapped a walk of eight churches in that area of Cornwall. Two years ago she had actually tried to follow the maps, arranging with John the taxi driver to pick her up each day at the farthest one late in the afternoon. She searched her mind. Which one could this be? Not the one where the poet and novelist Thomas Hardy came when he was an architect in his early life. In the early 1880's, renovation was badly needed, as the church had not been repaired since the 1600's, and she had actually seen Hardy's drawings of the pew carvings on the back wall. *This is a different one*, Ellen thought. Obviously she was not in the narthex or the chancel, perhaps in the basement.

"Where I come from, there are buildings from the fifth century." Ackman sounded superior. "In those days, you Brits were painted blue."

"Not really." Ellen bristled, though she was American. "The fifth century was the height of the Celtic civilization—even Christianized and flourishing in Ireland. And Cornwall was important then too."

Ackman opened another door at the end of the hall, and Ellen realized as she saw a window that they were still on the main level of the church, not in a basement. They must have entered through a side entrance. The room he pushed her into was small, almost filled by a small altar and a kneeler, on which a large book lay open. In the corner was a small wooden chair. "I thought this was a good place for you," Ackman laughed slyly. "This is the place where people come for private prayer requests. Don't worry. The church is closed now to repair the front entrance. No one will disturb your prayers for rescue. I'll leave you now." Ackman started for the door.

"Aren't you going to leave me water or food? Just tell me why I am here."

"I'll be back with water and breakfast," he said. "But it is not up to me to tell you anything."

Ellen wanted to sit in the chair and get her breath, but first she knelt. She realized to her relief that she had actually been here on her walking tour. Ackman must have driven around Tintagel to keep her from knowing that he was staying so close to Willapark. *Then perhaps*, she imagined, *he in a roundabout way had headed for St. Materiana, just down the hill from the main street that led to the Castle Hotel.* That was the only church she had visited that had this room off the chancel. She looked at the book that lay open on the wooden frame in front of her and realized that she recognized it also. It was filled with prayers, often futile attempts to communicate with the dead.

Sad little notes, many not prayers at all: "I am sorry I did not go with you that last night to the store—maybe both of us would have died together or perhaps we would have not gone by the hill road, where that big truck was barreling over the top." Her anxiety with her own situation resonated with the sorrow in that slanted cursive statement, and Ellen's eyes filled.

That was one near the beginning. Another one two pages before the end: "My darling, I miss you more as the days go by. I can't believe you have been gone for almost a year now. I still wear your old robe." So much grief over losses.

Occasionally a prayer of desperate need: "Please, Lord, help me to go on. The children need me, and I need your strength." Many prayers were demands of God. She could not help remembering the dark silence of the Lord in Bergman's 1962 film *Winter Light*. The movie had threatened her faith in the early years of her marriage.

Then she turned to her own entry of two years ago. "Oh God, thank you that the death of James brought me a measure of closure, even forgiveness of his weakness."

She noticed that her page was still only a few leaves from the blank page the book lay open to now. Not many came here with their prayers. The mystery of it all was too much to figure out, but she would not lose her faith just when she needed it so much. Some priest had said once in a sermon she had heard—and she had remembered it at dark moments—"Foxhole faith is designed for foxhole times." God seems closer then.

She looked up at the altar then, but the stylized wooden Christ seemed rigid and far away. Surely that crucifix was a late addition, going back to the High

Church Movement in nineteenth-century Anglicanism. Keble and Cardinal Newman, that group in Anglicanism. It had at first been a disappointment to her to see how much had crept into the church decoration since the early days. The building and the tower were 1100, but services, she remembered, had been held in this place since 600. Most of the church decoration was much later, something she had begun to accept as part of a live parish, where the religious life was still being carried on. People continued to need to honor their dead with memorials—to make their churches culturally relevant. When she thought back over her earlier tour, that had been what she loved most: visiting churches still in use, not mere museums from the dead past. Contrary to her initial impressions, the nineteenth-century traces of that period had been most immediately vivid.

She wondered at her thinking so much about the church when her situation was this desperate. Perhaps it was a defense against her helplessness. Better to think about Thomas Hardy and the church he helped to renovate. That he had been an architect before he was a great novelist and a poet she had not known until she went to the church where he had met his wife, sister of the Rector there. Later, Ellen had read poems he had written after his wife's death, poems filled with sadness over a marriage that was not happy. Like her own with James, she realized, tears welling again. She must stop; she could not afford weakness in this situation. Only God knew the balance of the fault between two people.

But still the church was a place that held evidences of its history and that of the local people, a preservation of memory that she missed in America. She closed her eyes then, trying to pray, but she heard footsteps in the hall. Ackman with breakfast, she hoped. The key in the lock grated, and she looked up. Yes, only Abdullah. She practiced the pronunciation of his first name in her head, the last syllable somewhat more clear than the usual English or American *schwa*.

"Welcome, Abdullah." She tried to take a friendly tone. "I am starving!" She smiled up at him, using her best Miss Congeniality look.

He seemed impassive to her charm. She knew already he thought her too old for flirtation or indeed anything else in a sexual line. Thank God. But she needed nevertheless to establish some kind of relationship if she were going to come out of this alive.

Ackman said nothing, however, just passed her a plastic cup with hot coffee, no cream. She hoped there was at least sugar. Then he handed her a breakfast roll.

"Did you bring sugar?"

The dark man shook his head and turned towards the door.

"Don't go," she said, racking her brain for something to keep him there. "I've thought of something we might discuss. Money."

"You bitch. You don't think you can bribe me, do you?"

"We all need money, and you are necessary to the operation. You can cover it up. The rest of them can't do what you do—they are too close to institutions and the art establishment. I'm American, after all. I could take some out of my retirement account."

"You have no idea what would make it worthwhile." Ackman grinned.

"That is why I am suggesting we talk. I have a certain amount available that I brought with me to deposit in my account in Britain." Ellen tried to keep the amount vague. "I come here often enough to have an account at Lloyd's Bank. But if it isn't enough, perhaps I could arrange to raid my retirement at home. It would be a little more complex, of course, and take more time." Thank God James had given her that idea. That might be best. In the meantime, she could work with McInery and perhaps evade the payment. But she knew that would be difficult and even more dangerous than her current situation.

Abdullah sipped his own coffee, his dark eyes calculating as he looked at her. "Even American academics don't make much."

"That depends." Ellen felt her spirits lift.

"And how could I be assured you would pay?"

"Perhaps I could take a manuscript, and you could pass that up the line."

"What good would that do? I would only get the courier fee."

"Oh, that's the way it works." Then she could have bitten her tongue. She needed him to think she knew nothing. Otherwise, her life was even more in danger. Quickly, she hoped to cover: "I mean, I could do that for you; and then when I delivered, I could slip you the extra, in exchange for putting me on the plane for home. We could set up the schedule now, and I could go back to the hotel."

"Sorry, the Big Guy is on his way now to talk to you."

"What 'Big Guy'?"

"I'll let him tell you what he wants you to know. But after he talks, he probably will let you go for now—even though you did not go home, as we told you to the last time. All that depends, of course, on how cooperative you are this time."

Ellen shivered. What if she weren't cooperative? But of course she would play for time. Ackman left the room then, locking her in. *This time I will pray*, she told herself. She needed strength from somewhere.

Her knees began to ache as she knelt again on the large kneeler. She said a short prayer, mostly "God help me," like the prayer of Rick as he tried to rescue his son from the Cornish sea. Suddenly she felt overwhelmed by the need for sleep. She took off the hooded sweatshirt over her head and laid it on the floor. Hard as it was, she would try to sleep—only ten minutes would refresh her, she knew, as she stretched out, bundling the soft material into a pillow for her head and neck. It was monstrously uncomfortable, but sleep would come now. The caffeine in the coffee had had no effect.

* * *

Perhaps a half hour later, Ellen opened her eyes. Mark Johily was standing over her, and she swam up into consciousness confused. He was not a tall man, but he stood as if at attention, his Navy experience embedded in his muscular frame, even in his seventies. His white hair was combed straight back, but one lock broke free over his brown eyes. What was this? Had he come to rescue her? Or had he just stopped in the church to pray, this man who had seemed so sad over the loss of his wife? After all, she knew he had moved to Cornwall to recover from her long illness and painful death from cancer, and for years now had been retired from the Royal Navy.

"I'll give you a hand," he said, helping her get up from the floor. Ellen tried not to lean too heavily on the older person. After all, at forty-nine she should be able to manage to rise from the awkward position in which she found herself. Nevertheless, it was difficult, almost comic, for both of them, but after some effort she managed to stand. There was no place really for both of them in the small prayer room.

"Let's walk into the graveyard outside," Mark invited with a smile. "You must be surprised to see me here."

Ellen was still trying to recover from her nap and the sudden appearance of someone unexpected. "Yes," she admitted. Then she was silent. And where did he come into the situation? Surely not a compatriot with Ackman, and yet—here they were walking down the hall of St. Materiana and out the side entrance.

"Let's perch here and talk," Mark suggested as he sat down on a nearby gravestone.

"Perhaps we should not sit on the graves," Ellen said.

"Oh, the owners of these are long gone!" Mark laughed. "No sacrilege intended. I hope Ackman did not overextend his orders. Sometimes he seems like a gangster. We try to be civilized."

Her last fragile hope disappeared with the way he put himself with Ackman and the thieves. For a moment Ellen wanted to scream at him, *Civilized—is it civilized to kidnap someone in the middle of the night, to threaten a gag, to tie a blindfold over her eyes so that she could not see where she was?* But she stopped herself. "Oh no, it was better than the last time in London. But perhaps you don't know about that. Anyway, this morning he even brought me coffee and a bun. Now you tell me why I was spirited away in the night." She stood up from the gravestone. She wanted to hear this standing up.

Mark remained seated, running his hand through his hair awkwardly.

"Why?" Ellen's voice rose insistently.

Chapter Sixteen

"How much do you know?" Mark looked at her quizzically, as if he had not made up his mind how much to say; then he stood up as well. "Let's just walk around while I catch you up."

Ellen felt more at ease on the graveyard path. There were no trees. Indeed the whole area was open, and her anxiety about what might happen to her if she did not cooperate was beginning to dissipate. Despite her intuition not to trust him when they had walked to the falls together, surely Mark was not dangerous, and she didn't see Ackman lurking anywhere. But then he always appeared out of nowhere. She paused by a seventeenth-century marble tomb—she had recognized the emblematic style of the cherubim carved on the top—obviously holding one of the few really wealthy scions from the past. Probably one of the earliest memorials in the churchyard. Most of the stones surrounding were simple rectangles, and many were from the late nineteenth century and even the twentieth. She remembered from some of her study of earlier centuries that most of the poor were buried in simpler ways, sometimes even mass graves. Though that was more common during plague years. A few elaborate eighteenth-century tombstones were grouped nearer the church.

Mark had paused with her. He laid a hand on her sleeve, and she tried not to shrink back, covering her confusion with a burst of anger and staring directly into his bright eyes. "Tell me, please, what is going on. Don't I deserve a little information? Snatched out of my room in the middle of the night, brought to this strange church...." She would not let on that she knew where they were.

"Why not go back to the Willapark, where we can sit in the lounge and be comfortable while we talk?"

Mark laughed. "I hate to tell you, Mrs. Adams, but you can't go back to the hotel now that this has happened and I have been seen to be involved. Don't worry." He clearly saw her look of horror. "You won't be hurt, but you will have to be removed from Cornwall and ultimately sent home."

"Like the lost sheep from foot and mouth," she said sadly.

"Don't sentimentalize," he warned, his voice rising slightly.

That gave her a hint that he did not like the criminal edge of the situation either, but who knew? Perhaps he was a murderer, not the nice older man he seemed to be. She was learning not to judge people by their faces. All those serial killers on the tellie who looked like good-looking athletes.

"I don't. It's more a question of seeing the world as it is. The last time I was here, my husband was murdered [*Forgive me, God, for stretching it a little*]. Now I can't seem to get free of the ring of manuscript thieves he had become part of. Maybe I should join you and get some of the rewards." She looked up at him with large eyes. After all, for his age she was a young thing, it occurred to her, not as ancient as Ackman had clearly let her know she was for him.

"Oh come now, we are not the usual thieves. We just work for people of taste." Ellen noticed his voice was softer, as if he were including her among the more sophisticated. He went on: "It is a kind of distribution of beauty to those who appreciate it. Why should beautiful and precious books or manuscripts be in the hands of uneducated librarians? When there are those who value them for what they are."

"Yes, whenever I handle those beautiful books in the Bodleian or the New British Library, my very hands treasure them, as if I might connect to those early printers or even the monks who spent a lifetime making those manuscripts."

Ellen felt herself suddenly too sympathetic with the thieves and changed direction: "Still, collectors are often not people who really know the things they collect. It is mostly market with them. And scholars can have access to those books and manuscripts as long as they remain in libraries." Ellen knew she should not argue but could not accept the rationalization that Mark was protecting himself with.

"All right, all right...." Mark drew back from her when she changed her tack. He was clearly exasperated. "Let us not argue about this. You are not going to change things. Back to the beginning. You know that James was involved with us. What did he tell you?"

"Not much—that he had stolen a manuscript. That he owed you for an advance and needed money from our retirement. I couldn't really believe it all. I was more concerned about his infidelities but was utterly shocked to hear he had violated all the ethics of the academic profession." That was pretty much all she had known until this trip and what Douglas had filled in recently.

"And what happened in London to you?"

"You surely know about that. I had brought a small *Book of Hours* from Pennsylvania that I found among James's things. I was going to turn it over to Scotland Yard, but someone lifted my bag at the airport as I entered the country. In an effort to get it back, I met with the woman I thought had taken it and was drugged in a taxi and taken away—by Ackman, by the way—and questioned by a French curator. Then they let me go and told me to go home."

"But why didn't you?" Mark shook his head reprovingly. "That would have saved us all a lot of trouble. What are you thinking, still lurking around with that retired Scotland Yard chief inspector?"

"What do you mean? I just wanted to finish my vacation. I would have had to pay extra to change my flight home. And what do you mean: 'lurking around with' Chief Inspector McInery? I came back to Cornwall because I thought the London people would not reach this far."

"And why would you think that? What about the murder at Willapark?"

"Surely a coincidence. Nobody has seen a connection," she lied, hoping she could make him feel safer about what she knew.

"We are not taking chances on you. Give me the key to your room, and I will go and collect your things from Willapark. I'll tell Rick you have decided you must go back to Oxford. Your friend there has suddenly been taken ill.

"But the real script is that you can stay at Neftan's Falls for a couple of days, and then I or someone will take you to Oxford to the Bodleian, where you will get what we need. Perhaps then you can take it through France to Italy to our contact there. We'll talk about that later. Don't worry, and don't start making plans to sneak away, because we will be with you all the time. We let you go free last time, and look what happened."

"Just let me go pack my own things and say goodbye to Rick and Lisa. They will think this is too strange, and when the chief inspector comes, he will notify the police, I am sure."

Mark shook his head slowly. "You must send him a nice little handwritten note then, and ditto for Rick and Lisa. By the time you and I go on the Normandy Ferry from Plymouth to France, Scotland Yard may be looking in Oxford or even London, but not in Plymouth."

Ellen wished she had not said anything. Perhaps the notes would reassure them all. Possibly she could embed a hint or two in the notes themselves. She began to rack her brain for some way to encode messages. False name for her friend in Oxford? What else? She began to chew her nails as she thought.

Then she saw Mark looking at her shrewdly. She would have to be careful to throw him off the scent. "Don't you think you should go now before they wonder about my not being at breakfast? I have never been known to miss a meal." She looked at her small gold Seiko. It was already nine o'clock. Perhaps Douglas would be there already. He had said he was coming at ten. Ellen looked up at the leaden sky, still, in spite of the clouds, lighter than in Oxford except in the late afternoon when she took her nap on the second floor of the Victorian house. One of the reasons she loved Oxford was that experience. At the end of the May days, big puffy clouds blew by with the island winds and showed blue sky in between. For a few moments, feelings washed over her for this ancient place, whatever the miseries of her current situation. The contrast between the beauty of the place and the muddle of her life. What a contradiction—she had always thought of this place as a peaceful getaway.

Such feelings pulled her back into her own tendency to think the best. How mysterious it was that the human mind was mostly optimistic, believing in an order that did not exist in the human situation. If she had learned anything with age, it was that the world was not what she had expected as a young woman. Throughout her life, she had said to herself from time to time: *It is not what I expected, not what I thought—human beings, friendship, marriage, the world in general.*

Still her own positive thinking sometimes had helped her move on from difficult times. She must use her optimism to trick this deceptive man. She must somehow make him think of her as a charming woman, no matter what. Perhaps that would protect her if she were going to be in his company.

* * *

Ellen found herself a half hour later in a small room in the rundown house near Neftan's Falls. Mark had handed her into his silver BMW and driven from St. Materiana down the main road past the farm that was the entry to Rocky Valley to the trail that led to the Falls. As they passed the road into Willapark with its elegant palms, Ellen sighed inadvertently but futilely.

They pulled up and stopped suddenly in the parking lot across the road from the trail. Then they walked across and hiked along the beautiful creek to the stairs where tourists climbed up to buy tickets to the entrance. Mark walked briskly, and she was at pains to keep up. Conversation had been minimal as they hurried along, though Ellen could not help noticing the many birdsongs she heard from the trees in the woods along the way. She knew he was eager to get to Willapark before she was missed.

She was sitting now at a rickety desk beside a small window that looked out the back at a stand of pin oaks. The tourists who came mounted stairs at the front of the house, so there was no chance for her to call out to anyone, she realized as she tried to write her notes to Rick and then to Doug in some way that gave clues to her situation.

In front of her was a blank piece of stationery. Mark put his head in. "You have ten minutes, and then I will leave, even if you haven't finished. Maybe that would be better anyway." He looked at her as if he suspected something.

"If you do, you may find Scotland Yard following you from the hotel," she warned.

"Okay, okay," he said sharply. "Just get on with it."

Ellen wrote slowly on the page, allowing her handwriting to slope slightly. She didn't want to be too obvious.

> *Dear Rick:*
> I am sorry I had to leave without saying goodbye. I got a call on my cell last night from Prue, and she is ill. It may be the cancer is back, and she needs me to come as soon as possible. In case of surgery, which may not be necessary. I'll be in touch. Thanks for your hospitality.
> Here are included pounds for the rest of my bill.
> Regards,
> *Ellen*

She chewed on her pen, trying for something to give Doug a clue. At least Rick would know that she had already paid the full bill. He would then try to get in touch. She had not dared put a phone number in it, partly because she did not know where they would take her, surely not Prue's. But for Douglas she needed something more precise. She thought of his blue eyes, so concerned as he stood by the mantel in the Savoy when she had found her way back there in London after the first time they let her go. She wanted him to know she was all right so far—but also that she would pursue their investigation and fulfill his trust in her abilities. A new beginning. Whatever the dangers, this was a new beginning. Perhaps she still had a chance.

Ellen bent over the desk:

Dear Douglas:

I am sorry not to make our appointment this morning. Ann of Dick and Ann from Portsmouth (I forget their last name) in the hotel wants to see you, so your visit won't be a complete waste of your time. I hope the investigation goes well, even if you are no longer involved. It was always a foolish idea for me to risk it all trying to get back the manuscript James took. I have decided to go home and stay out of everything.

I am still thinking about our brief but lovely visit to the National Gallery. That painting by Bellini with the strange Madonna and child in the desert—the surreal space—is something I shall always remember. What church was that in the background?

Thanks for everything. Sorry not to say goodbye.
Ellen

Ellen folded the notes and then on second thought left them on the desk. She knew Mark would read them before taking them to Willapark. Just then she heard the key turn. He was right on time.

Mark walked quickly to the desk. "I'd better take them now. You were right about timing being important." He scanned the letters. "They look all right, just right for a polite American lady, somewhat impulsive." He put them into the envelopes and handed them to her. "You forgot to put the names on the envelopes."

Ellen picked up the pen again, scrawled the appropriate names and handed the envelopes to Mark. "Hurry back," she said softly, a wry note in her voice. "This is not the most beautiful room in Cornwall. If I am in your power, we should probably keep moving."

"I am not sure yet when we will leave. Perhaps I'll just send you with Ackman, but I don't entirely trust him with what we want you to pick up."

"Come along for the fun," she flirted outrageously then, holding her hands up, palms outward to reveal her shapely upper body and deliberately widening her large eyes. At the same time, she was conscious she needed to put on her makeup, refresh her lipstick to look her best. Oh well, perhaps his vision was not perfect.

A flash of response that Mark quickly covered as he turned to walk out. At the door he paused and looked back at her. "Don't get ideas, my American friend. I am not so old I don't recognize manipulation. I'll be back and let you know what we'll do. Just remember who is in charge."

Ellen smiled her sweetest smile. The arrow had hit, however he resisted. The door closed and she walked to the small bed up against the wall and lay down, suddenly drained. Adrenalin had kept her going, but she knew she needed at least another nap to make up for the broken night's rest. As she closed her eyes, her thoughts went to the visit to the National Gallery with Douglas that she had tried to use in her note. Almost an atmosphere of dream surrounding her, she saw them walking in the large exhibition room of Italian religious paintings just outside the small transition room with the four Veroneses on each wall. The Bellini and the Breughel, both representative of the strange darkness of the world, she had never been able to understand. Did anyone? Perhaps Iris Murdoch before her Alzheimer's took over her brilliant mind—a mind always searching for that simple truth that could only emerge from the tangled net of good and evil that confronts us daily. Both paintings had a Christ child at the center in the arms of the mother who is the emblem of God's deepest compassion. But the world in each was quite differently portrayed, the symbolism of each layered and complex.

Ellen felt herself falling, falling, closer to sleep, but the images in her mind held her somehow. She needed to think about them; new insights were hovering. Perhaps she was already asleep, not just on the edge of dream, as she had felt herself. The Mary of the Bellini seemed to be growing larger, larger and larger, as if expanding on a giant television screen, now beginning to speak. Her mouth did not move, but the soft and musical voice clearly came from the image. "Desert is the nature of the world," she said, gesturing to the background of the painting where she sat. "Galilee is in the desert. Jesus came out of the desert. He went into it every time he needed to pray."

That was all that was said, and then the scene shifted suddenly to the stable scene of the Breughel. Surrounding the child and his mother, the four kings focused their gaze on the child. Had there also been a soldier or two? Every eye was on the child, but the horror of it was the nature of evil and hostility reflected in every face. The world not ready for the message shone there so clearly in the painting called the *Adoration of the Kings* by Pieter Breughel the Elder. All the Christmas scenes in art, all the devotional scenes with humanity at the foot of the promise of the Christ child—all somehow erased by this vision, the human atavistic need to kill writ large on the faces. It foreshadowed the future beyond this Christmas scene, the Crucifixion to come. Yes, the soldiers that seemed out of place were pointing forward to that moment in thirty-some years as well as showing the envy of the kings for this new king they had traveled so far to see. The image loomed dark in Ellen's dream.

Though she did not wake immediately, she moaned in her sleep, and her head moved back and forth upon the pillow as if she were trying to break free of this vision of reality. When she woke a half hour later, she knew she had been dreaming, but she could not help sensing the dark reality of her own situation mirrored in this dream.

Too much of life does not involve free will, she thought, however she blessed Milton and his explanation of evil as the necessary dark side of free choice. The representations here were simply emblems of the darkness and bestiality of human nature, worse than lost sheep. Perhaps the Calvinists in the seventeenth century were right: even those who tried to find the path of goodness were sometimes caught in the toils of those who had chosen the darkness.

Neo-Orthodoxy, that is what Reinhold Niebuhr and some of the modern theologians in the middle of the twentieth century had called it: trying to face the truth of the holocaust and the evil behind it. *You are letting yourself think too much*, Ellen warned herself. She needed to be alert for when Mark and Ackman returned from Willapark. But she was in danger of being overwhelmed by the dream. Not education, not the arts, however advanced in the German state, had been able to change the basic sinfulness, the core selfishness, of mankind. New political structures of check and balance were the only hope for containment, and even they had a slim chance.

She ran a comb through her hair quickly and glanced in the only mirror, a small one over the desk. A little lipstick. No time for more makeup, even though she knew her face shone. She tried to remember that her situation involved mainly collectors. They were simply people who had become obsessed with beauty and rarity in books and art, not vicious. *Evil, yes*, That was evil when it coldly set aside the laws of civilization and remained insensitive to suffering. Worse perhaps the paths that deception led to. But initially, at least, there was no malice involved—not envy, hatred, murderous motives. Surely those people did not realize the line that had been crossed with the murders.

That was the trouble—there were no small sins. The boundaries were passed before one knew it. Perhaps they did know briefly, but their own survival instincts had taken over, at least among the leadership. She could not figure it out, perhaps because the only one she really knew was James. What had driven him to it after all? And had he known of murders? Probably not. She would think about that later. A combination of lust and greed perhaps, but how had it taken him over?

Chapter Seventeen

About thirty minutes later, Ellen once again found herself blindfolded, hands tied behind her (a silken cord, not a rope), and bumping along in a car somewhere in Cornwall—or that is what she thought. The drive was not been long enough for the London or Oxford destination. She still could not figure out why the two men, Mark and Ackman, had stormed in at her door and dragged her off in such a hurry, refusing to answer questions. They remained silent with each other in the front seat. She had parted from Mark on reasonably cordial terms when he went back to the Willapark. The only thing that might be possible was that either Rick or Douglas had picked up something from her note and begun to probe. What could it have been?

Certainly Rick would think it strange she did not say goodbye and that Mark was coming for her things—and of course he knew she had already paid her full bill for the week. Even more specifically, Douglas also would have known that she would not just change her mind about the case and decide to go home, but he in turn would be subtle enough not to let the two men know he was suspicious. Perhaps that was why they were moving her quickly; they must have sensed the questions of Rick and Douglas even if they had not been voiced.

Just then Ellen felt rough hands virtually lifting her out of the back seat of the car. She could see beneath her feet more pebbles. Was it another church she was being stashed in? But she heard a heavy door opening and a dignified English voice: "Welcome, Mr. Mark. Sir John is waiting in the study."

Obviously someone a bit further up the structure of the group. New character appears. Ackman again took off the blindfold and untied the cord on her hands, grasping her arm firmly. *Ouch*, she thought but did not say.

"Welcome," said an elegant English voice, and she saw a slender man in a blue blazer coming out of the library on the left. "In here," he gestured, holding the door open. She looked up into a rather pink English face with vivid blue eyes as she passed into the room.

Ellen found herself seated before a fire with books reaching the ceiling on both sides of the airy room. A fire was unusual for the mild May weather, but she was glad to be warm for a change, and Sir John seemed of an age that needed more heat than most English houses allowed for with their high ceilings and spacious rooms.

"My dear Mrs. Adams," Sir John addressed her then directly, "we meet under unfortunate circumstances. You should have taken the advice given you in London and gone home. But what is done is done. I should like to ask you a favor now that I have you here."

Ellen tried to nod encouragingly, thinking she knew what was coming. After all, she knew nearly as much as James about rare book rooms where sixteenth-century books and even manuscripts might be spirited away.

"You are thinking I want you to permanently borrow a book," he said, giving her a shrewd look. "Yes, there is a manuscript I want, but in addition what I really want you to take is a painting. If you take both, you will confuse the authorities because we usually use different people for the two tasks. But I can only have you do this on certain conditions."

Ellen could not contain a slight gasp—a painting, that was much more difficult than a book or even manuscript. She knew the ways of rare book librarians, having visited a number of such places either for herself or in helping James in his research. But she knew nothing about the security of art galleries or museums. Success would require a team of thieves working together, she mused. She could not afford to reject it all out of hand, however. She must play for time. She opened her eyes and deliberately brightened her expression, trying to look interested. "Yes, that is a brilliant notion," she leapt in boldly.

"This house you see, this glorious fire—with a Labor government and British taxes what they are, I must supplement my income." Sir John looked pained. "What I inherited has not lasted into my advanced years. But you will not be interested in my problems." She noticed that he looked up at the crown molding, thinking it was in need of paint.

"You have enough problems of your own, and now that you are retired or close to it, and your husband is dead, you would perhaps be glad of some supplemental income yourself. Several of us have discussed your general situation. One of the conditions is that you would choose to share in the profit. That is the only way we could trust you."

Ellen tried to clear her head of the rather fuzzy sense she had of fear, confusion, and hunger. Yes, she had begun to retire too early. Fifty did not allow a pension. "I've had almost no food today. It is hard for me to concentrate and understand what you want of me—even to make decisions." Perhaps she could delay her answer somewhat.

"Of course, I understand. Let's talk after you have a hot bath and some food. I'll send up your bags and a tray. Shall we say four o'clock?"

* * *

At four o'clock Ellen was back in the library, clean, brushed, and refreshed by a large roast beef sandwich. She had lain down for about twenty minutes after her shower, but the minute she closed her eyes she felt as if she were in a nightmare landscape, almost her earlier dream. A weight lay on her chest. She was already embroiled in too many lies. Although she had finally told Douglas the details of James's death, it was almost as if she were developing another deceptive personality for the people who had captured her. Why had she agreed to become involved as a detective? It was another name for a deceiver, a role-player and a liar. No wonder some people slipped into being double agents. It was more like posing as a spy but becoming inevitably more and more a part of the elaborate ring of thieves. If you pretended hard enough, the mask grew into your face. She knew that from acting when she was young. One actually became the parts one played for awhile. One must tell the truth from one's center or one lost oneself.

But her safety depended now—and she shuddered at the thought—on being able to remember all the deceptions she was trying to trick them with. How could she even remember the ways she was going to lie? She had always prided herself on telling the truth in the smallest thing. When she was younger, Iris Murdoch had convinced her that even social lies build a network that chokes the truth and made the world a non-navigable road. She had read one Murdoch book a long time ago where one character among the many was the truth-teller, and whatever the immediate consequences of telling it—and there were many and devastating ones—truth was the only way ultimately to order and light in the world. But she had no time now to think about Platonism and how it might change the world that had disappointed her so much. Only after James had lied so frequently and in so many layers had she begun to realize fully how destructive deception was. Earlier in her life it was an intellectual position she had given assent to, but now she felt it in her bones.

Ellen dressed quickly then to silence her thoughts, and she went downstairs just a few minutes before four. Across from where she became settled in the library sat a man she had not seen before, dressed in clothes vintage 1906: pleated gray tux and a silk striped school tie of some sort knotted through the loops of his belt. His shirt was white, worn with an open neck, and he had a tweed jacket slung around his shoulders. His lank blond hair turned slightly at his shoulders in what she had once thought of as a long bob, with a heavy bang or fringe falling over his right eye.

"Hello. Michael Dougherty here, Mrs. Adams."—He almost winked in his exaggerated friendliness, putting out his hand to her.

"Hello." Ellen suppressed her reaction to what struck her as eccentricity and found her hand gripped in a firm shake. She shook herself slightly and took on the pose of sophisticated older woman that she believed would convince them to trust her as both a manuscript thief and an art thief.

Sir John smiled from the large leather wingback. "You must be surprised to see someone else. We are quite a network. Obviously you will not see everybody, but we needed to reassure you that, if you do the art part of the job, there will be experts helping."

"Dear Lady," said Michael with a surge of Irish charm, "I am an expert on alarm systems—in Ireland we have learned how to come and go without detection," his accent flavoring his speech.

Ellen looked at him with some curiosity. "How did you get involved?"

"Money, of course, and the pleasure of dealing with perfectly lovely persons, not the brash criminals one usually encounters. You are an example."

She tried to live up to his compliment, smiling suddenly and sitting up straighter so that her auburn hair swung on her shoulders. Was this the lying she feared or was it a kind of play-acting—drama in a good cause? She needed to believe the latter for the present. She was practical enough to do this for a short time. For a short time only and then she could return to her real self. Perhaps even James had thought that at one time.

"Money," she almost purred. "I need money too. I am a little weary of living on half retirement. Do you think I could just do this one time and go back to my old life with a little more comfort?"

The men in the room all looked at her as if they were trying to read the change. Could they trust her? She knew they were thinking she would not be able to break away once she began. They seemed not to be able to imagine attitudes beyond their own experience. "I know what you mean about how the most beautiful things in the world often are in the hands of Philistines. Perhaps we can correct that just for once. What is the painting you want me to take? And how can you manage the alarm system so that I don't get caught?"

Sir John got up from his chair and walked to the French windows. He slowly packed his pipe and looked out into the misty afternoon and the long line of cedars along the road that led to the estate. The richness of the surrounding room, its leather-bound books and beautiful soft green walls around the double mahogany doors suddenly helped her see why he was working so hard to keep his inheritance. The French chairs with their oval upholstered backs were placed gracefully with more comfortable leather wingbacks in between.

"You sound reliable, Mrs. Adams, almost as if you can be trusted, but we have to set this up so that all of us are confident. Perhaps it is better not to let you know which painting until closer to the theft. But I will give you a hint—it will be a sixteenth-century religious painting that you will know something about, a painting in the National Gallery in London. Perhaps that will whet your appetite, since you have done research in that period."

Ellen frowned. "Either I am trusted or I am not. Why should I risk everything if I am to be treated like a hired thief?" She got up from her chair and walked over to the window where Sir John was standing. "I am not a young woman—not a child. I have certain skills you need." Almost unconsciously she jutted out her small chin and drew herself up to her full height.

Sir John looked down at her, a faint condescending smile on his face. "I do believe the challenge appeals to you. Or at least—"

Ellen interrupted, "Let's get this straight now. I am a partner in this. Or nothing. Do your worst." She was trembling, but she put both hands behind her back to hide it.

"What do you think?" Sir John turned to Mark, barely glancing at the Irishman.

"In for a penny, in for a pound." The Englishman nodded, his expression serious.

"The painting is the Breughel Nativity—Breughel the Elder, *The Adoration of the Kings*. It has been an important part of the Christmas season audio tour that the Director himself recorded this year. The exhibit brings together all the paintings in the Gallery (or the best of them) that show the figure of Christ—from his birth to his Resurrection. The only modern ones are Dali and Spenser. From an artistic point of view, the most interesting point that is made is the growth of realism by which Christ becomes increasingly human in form and face.

"This one does not focus so much on Christ himself as those who have come to view the divine birth. The unusual element is the almost super realism of the faces of those who are usually shown as adoring and transformed. In this painting Breughel paints the realistic faces of a corrupt world. The collector claims that it is the most radically modern and the most true painting of a sacred subject that has ever existed. Most people who see the exhibit are both horrified and struck by the startling images."

"I have seen it." Ellen thought of her quick view of the exhibit with Douglas. "It would be missed quickly, and that is a problem."

Mark chimed in, "If it is taken at night, by ten in the morning the alarm will go out. If you take it, you will have to be out of the country by then. But after all, it is a religious painting, and these days most collectors want impressionist paintings or post-impressionist ones that have no religious symbolism. So it is probably not as valuable monetarily as many lesser pieces."

"Surely Scotland Yard would pursue such a piece." Ellen paled at the thought.

"Oh, yes." Dougherty smiled at her. "It is part of the National Treasure, if only worth a million or two. Brits do not take kindly to losing their heritage."

"But this is Flemish, isn't it?"

"Yes, but for a long time part of the collection at the National Gallery. Don't you think they would pursue the Elgin Marbles even if some Greek took them from the British Museum, as they have been threatening to do for years?"

"Just tell me the plan," said Ellen, suddenly weary of theorizing. She was hoping that, before she had to take the painting, Douglas would find her.

"All right. Here is the scheme." Mark took a sheet from his inside pocket and unfolded it, then handed it to her. "This is only your part. Everyone has his own part and his own instructions. It fits together like a puzzle. Then if anyone gets caught, the police don't necessarily know how to get the others." He reached down and patted her shoulder, and Ellen had to grit her teeth not to shrink from his touch.

"That makes sense," she said coolly, looking first at Mark, then at Sir John and Dougherty. "I suppose you will all be involved?"

"Not all at the Gallery. I shall meet you at the ferry in Portsmouth. But look first and be sure you understand your instructions."

"And what about the manuscript of the *Book of Hours*? How does that fit in?"

"Read your instructions," snapped Dougherty, and she saw the temper beneath the Irish charm.

"All right, all right." Ellen looked down at the sheet in her lap. There were only seven items in a list:

1. Get the ms. from the Bodleian on Monday morning.

2. Take a coach to London. They leave every twenty minutes from the Bodleian.

3. Get off at Hyde Park and take a taxi to the National Gallery. It will be slow in the afternoon, but you will probably arrive at the Gallery by three-thirty.

4. Walk up to the second level and head toward the new section of the building where the gift shop and the restaurant are located.

5. You have a map of the rooms that shows where the exhibit is being held. Pay for your entrance ticket and start walking through. Don't take the audio this time; just follow the instructed path.

6. When you arrive at the painting, you will discover that it is off the wall, and someone on a ladder is doing something with the light. Wait until he hands you the wrapped painting. It will be rolled like a print. Walk deliberately out of the building through the gift shop so that what you are carrying will be less noticeable.

7. A taxi will pick you up at the entrance and drive you directly through the city to Portsmouth and the Brittany ferry. Ackman will be driving.

Ellen looked up. "And then what?"

"If you make it, you will see," Mark smiled at her.

Chapter Eighteen

Ellen walked into the National Gallery, past the entrance desk, and up the marble steps to the ground level. Across the street a crowd was gathering in Trafalgar Square. Perhaps another demonstration against the killing of all the sheep, even those not shown to be infected. Just yesterday a woman in Wales had brought her six sheep into the house and insisted that they were her pets. Farm people were protective of their stock, perhaps spending so much time with animals that they unconsciously identified with them.

Turning left at the top of the stairs towards the new Sainsbury Building, Ellen strolled in the direction of the exhibition of the religious paintings that had been the centerpiece of the Gallery since before Christmas. It was approaching closing time, but she moved along slowly, hoping no one would notice her. She did not want to run into anyone she knew from Oxford or even a visiting academic. She had been told already, however, that there were a number of cameras in the building, probably at least one in each room that held a small exhibit of individual artists or styles in the rabbit warren that was the National Gallery.

The special exhibit of the religious paintings had already been extended once, as it was so popular during the long Christmas season. She knew she would have to go down eventually to the basement level below the Museum Shop to be at her destination. Beneath the surface of the practical actions she was taking, she recalled how the exhibit itself had shown through the arrangement of paintings a gradual focus on the way the artistic representation of Christ changed through the centuries from the symbolic style of early Christian art. Ultimately one saw as art moved from the early centuries through the symbolism of the Middle Ages and finally to the early Renaissance the face of a deeply human Christ—in an increasingly realistic style. The twentieth century surreal and abstract paintings, however, did not fit into the historical movement, of course, but there were only two representations, one a resurrection with the tomb at the center, another surreal and yet expressionistic.

No art historian herself, she nevertheless had noticed that the Christ of the Orthodox tradition after the church had divided into East and West was not so much personalized and realistic as representative of a profoundly human man, even a simple man of the people, dark, bearded, and strong with the masculinity of a carpenter. She loved that image in contrast to the pale and languishing Jesus of the nineteenth century, however sensitive his features and attitudes towards children and the poor. Not that any of this mattered in the light of the painting she had contracted to steal with its major emphasis not on the baby Christ himself but on the surrounding human worshippers. Their faces, however, pointed forward to the developing realism in style, perfectly individualized and expressive.

After she had become aware of James's theft of the manuscripts, she had researched the black market of rare books and works of art. The police always said when anything of that sort was stolen that dishonest collectors had been behind it, hiring professional thieves and coordinating efforts in England and Europe. Recent research denied that interpretation, but it seemed to be true in this case, from what she had been able to find out. Sir John had suggested strongly that he had a buyer in Monaco. Clearly this theft was not the solitary desperate drug addict, who thinks it is an easy go to cut a picture out of a frame when the guard has turned his back or gone to the toilet. Nor was it apparently a glamorous thief trying to pull off an exciting caper. No, it was a well organized group with representatives in Europe, England, and probably America, who kept in touch with unscrupulous collectors. Which meant, of course, that particular works of art were targeted. The easy jobs were in small museums with small works that could be easily transported. Or with libraries that dealt mainly with carefully screened scholars. But Ellen was not in charge of an easy target. It still puzzled her that they wanted her to take something so high profile. Perhaps they wanted her to be caught, it occurred to her. But why?

Ellen felt her flesh crawl to think she was in a museum that obviously had considerable protection for the art. Brits were not slouches when it came to police work and the new advances in technology that went along with it. Perhaps the group she was working with had been originally responsible for the story the police still seemed to believe, though many of the recent thefts had been by solitary thieves. Only ten per cent of the paintings stolen had been returned to their original museums. Perhaps only the solitary thieves had been caught. After all, if they had to look for buyers; in contrast to such a ring of thieves as this, they would inevitably leave more clues as they explored contacts.

Or so Ellen mused as she looked around her at the rooms she passed by on the way to the exhibit. She smiled to herself, beginning to think more like a thief than a detective. She almost found herself not wanting to be caught, but that was because she wanted to find out more evidence to lead to the leaders of the group in Europe. Scotland Yard and Douglas (she did not deceive herself about how much his opinion mattered to her) would be profoundly grateful, and they would look at her with new eyes, unbesmirched by knowing she had not told the whole truth about James's death. She knew that on a psychological level she herself would not be free of James's guilt and her own guilt for not caring enough when he died until she had made something of an atonement.

"Can you tell me where the ladies' cloakroom is?" An aging woman in a white wool suit touched her arm. As usual, Ellen thought, she was being mistaken for a native. She had dressed like an Englishwoman for years.

"Near the restaurant in the Sainsbury Wing," she smiled, gesturing in the direction she was going, and the woman hurried on with a muttered thanks.

At the Baroque room Ellen paused. She wanted to take a look at the Rembrandt painting of Paul writing his epistles. Surely she had time, and it would calm her nerves. She felt like a real thief, though she had told herself she was actually protecting the collection in the long run, trying to get these people caught. But so far she had not heard from Douglas. She had managed to post him a cryptic note to let him know she was all right and had convinced some of the ring of thieves that she was willing to work for them. Still she kept hoping that he was tracking her. Perhaps he was clever enough in his methods that they were not aware of his doing so. She stood for a moment or two in front of the Rembrandt. Once a cashier in the café of the British Museum had told her that she must see the Prodigal Son at the Hermitage—to him, an art student, the greatest painting ever painted.

"Why?" she had asked. She had known, of course, that the subject matter was influential, but the cashier had said, more importantly, that it was the light on the hands of the father, the compassion of those hands as they grasped the shoulders of the kneeling son. That laying on of hands expressing absolute forgiveness, love that transformed and redeemed souls.

No, thieves should not be allowed to break in and greedily seize these sacred works of art. St. Paul in person writing the epistles was the key to the preservation of Christianity. She had always felt that without those letters being read among Christians all over the world in small gatherings, there would have been no early Church that could survive and be transferred to all the cultures of the ancient world. Not that she had been all that religious most of her life, but she believed that the great Christian ideals were deep in the best of culture. This painting showed art doing something human beings don't live long enough to do. As Rembrandt's vision of the writing, this painting showed for generations Paul bringing to the great story of the gospel a probing of meaning that was still read in churches and seminaries and history courses throughout the world.

Ellen noted the irony. She would prevent the erasure of the artistic past, at least in some small measure, by infiltrating the forces of evil. Of course the others did not think of it that way. Their rationalization was that they were bringing art to those who loved it most, taking it out of the hands of uncaring institutions, ambitious curators, and thieving governments set on their own prestige. Even dear England still kept the Elgin Marbles, though they strove to return art stolen by the Nazis to Jewish families who had owned it. Maybe they had a case for Lord Elgin, but lies and robbery were not the answer. Ellen herself believed in art being available to a wide number of people through museums and education. The values around such institutions must be protected. That was partly why she had been so angry at James. They had both spent their lives trying to fight death by passing on the wisdom of the human experience. The art was so great a part of that, along with precious books and learning. Wasn't that what education was all about?

But down to practical things. She must hurry a little now. She needed to go to the cloakroom before she went into the exhibit so that the camera would catch a different image from the one the other cameras had. It was easy for a woman to change her looks, and her captors had been willing to pay for the "props" she told them she would need to accomplish the theft. She had tucked a black wig in the waist of her long skirt, and in her purse was a chiffon overblouse with green flowers and bat sleeves that would cover her black jersey. With some extra makeup she would look like a different person. A few minutes later she stood before the mirror in the restroom stroking on a black eye liner and adding mascara to her normally pale lashes. She finished off the makeup with vivid red lipstick. She stared back at the image she had created, liking it, even if it did suggest the demi-monde of Paris and the posters of Toulouse-Lautrec.

Too little time. She had taken too much time in getting here, though when they had let her out at the King's Cross tube station, they had told her to come as near closing as she could manage. She took the lift down to the exhibit, worrying that they might not let her in forty minutes before closing.

"Oh yes, it is all right," said the woman at the desk. "You can probably make it all the way through, but if closing comes while you are in there, I shall give you a rain check."

"I come often," said Ellen in a lowered speaking voice. "That will be fine. But I have been to this exhibit once before. There are just a few paintings I want to see again." She smiled in a friendly way. "When is the exhibit closing? There don't seem to be many people here today."

"Next week is the last week. It was extended, you know, after Christmas."

"I know. Well, I am on my way," she added as a sort of goodbye, knowing the woman would remember her and describe her dark hair and eyes and the bold print that folded into almost handkerchief size.

About a third of the way through the exhibit Ellen came to the Breughel painting, but she did not see the promised repair man on a ladder. What had happened, and what would Plan B be? She looked around for the guard but saw no one. If she acted quickly, she could perhaps still get the painting, but the absence of the other member of the team was perhaps a signal that it wasn't on for today, whatever the reason. She had included a small knife among her preparation purchases, arguing that it would provide her at least a minimum amount of defense in case it was needed, but she had not cleared her Plan B with the others. The decision must be made quickly. She tried to foresee the consequences, but there was too little information.

She looked at the face of the soldier in the foreground of the painting. Evil and aggression were clearly and boldly focused in his expression, even as he gazed towards the holy light that bathed the Christ child. Yes, she was engaged herself in a battle against such an enemy as he represented, and this way she would seize the upper hand with the others if she could get away with it. Even if she were caught, Douglas would come to her rescue. Or was her faith in Scotland Yard too naïve? She took a deep breath and pulled out the small sharp boning knife James had taught her to use on one of the few fishing trips they had been on together.

"Madam," said a cockney voice from the door, "only thirty minutes until closing."

She almost jumped at the sound, trying to conceal the knife in her hand. "Oh yes, I just wanted to look at this Breughel a few more minutes."

The man in uniform had passed on, to make the announcement to others still in the exhibit, she concluded.

Ellen breathed a sigh then reached up quickly to the painting, cutting around the edge of the canvas. Thank God, no alarm went off. Had it been disabled earlier as promised? The knife was very sharp and cut smoothly until just in the right corner where she had to struggle a little to pierce the painted canvas. She rolled it up and tried to put it in her large purse, but it stuck at the end so that one end of the rolled painting protruded. Perhaps she could cover that with her hand, she thought, and buy a poster that she could place beside it to conceal the other protuberance.

Walking slowly and deliberately, she went out the exit area of the exhibit. Not the same woman, of course, at the desk at the end. She saw an umbrella stand filled with posters of the Dali painting and took one to the counter. "Thank you, Madam," the woman said, handing her three pounds change from the ten-pound note. Ellen walked, more quickly now, to the lift up to ground, passing the large gift shop on her way out the Sainsbury Wing.

Out the door now. Quickly. She half expected some buzz or alarm, such as that most of the department stores had if you exited with something not paid for. But nothing, no sound. Would the taxi be waiting at the curb, driven by Ackman? At last she was on the sidewalk. Smooth as glass.

No one was there. Just the normal dense traffic. Perhaps he was caught in it, not able to get near the curb. She hoped she would not have to wait long. She would not—no, she would hail the first taxi. But if he were not driving, what should she do? A train to the ferry in Portsmouth? But she had no address in Paris. Perhaps, however, they would have someone on the ferry to direct her. That was probably the safest bet.

Or she could opt out now and call Scotland Yard at the number Douglas had made her write under Mother in her address book. She was sorely tempted. But so far, no hullabaloo. Perhaps she could continue and lead the police to the whole net or at least some of the leaders. Last night in the B&B where they had put her for the night, with Ackman on guard, of course, they had come in briefly to be sure she had her instructions straight.

Again, she had reminded them that she had agreed on the basis of being a partner—or nothing. They had ostensibly assented, but she could tell they did not trust her. The more she saw of Mark, the more she found a dark edge. The kindly old man who had told the story of Rick's rescue of his son from the cave—all those loving human brave values—had been only a surface. The real Mark was much more calculating.

"Taxi, Madam?" One of the black cabs drew up beside her. The graying driver looked too distinguished for such a competitive job.

"Yes, if you can take me to the next train to Portsmouth."

"I don't have the time table, but I'll take you to the station from which it leaves."

"Done." Ellen climbed in gracefully, her smallness for once an advantage.

What a long day it had been. Too long. Yesterday she had been in the Bodleian in Oxford, where taking the small medieval manuscript had proved to be easy. She knew their system well. Almost anyone who was allowed in Duke Humphrey's would be incapable of violating the privilege, the trust by which they were allowed to study there. Except her own husband. And now herself.

She had once published a small edition of George Herbert's poems, which had given her insights into their security that would keep all decent academics from slipping beyond the boundaries of civilized behavior. *Not James*, she thought bitterly. She still did not know him, though she had tried to forgive his weaknesses.

Chapter Nineteen

Two hours later Ellen was at the dock for *The Duke of Normandy* ferry. She had walked directly to the taxi rank when she arrived from London at the Portsmouth train station. On the short ride to the dock, she hoped all along the way that she would meet one of the members of the group as soon as she got out of the taxi. But she found herself pulling her small bag along the concrete. It was not until she was inching up the gangplank among a crowd of people that she heard a soft voice beside her. "Here I am," said Mark, jostling her slightly. "Did you think I was lost? We tried a little test on you."

"Why would you do that?" Her voice rose in irritation. "I had no idea what I was supposed to do. By the way, I have never seen such a mob. Why are all these people going to France? I've never been on the ferry before."

"That is the way most Brits go, but back to your question—it was an important test," he said. "If you had bolted, we should have known we could not trust you. Of course, I knew you would not, having gone so far. Do you have the painting?"

"Of course I do." She remained silent, angry at how well Mark seemed to read her character. Though it was an odd risk for them. Was the painting not important? Perhaps they did not have a buyer yet. She thought about the little research she had done on art theft. She could not remember the statistics on how often thieves had buyers before they took the paintings. Much of what she had read suggested that the paintings were often chosen on the basis of how easily they could be stolen. Could the men with her be doing a little work on the side that the organization did not know about?

"Yes, we had done the prep so that you could take it. Wires cut, no alarm at the door out through the Sainsbury Wing. What is your cabin number? The journey is overnight."

Ellen looked at him. "I know it is overnight. I bought my own ticket. Why do you want to know? Surely I have proved myself as a partner now." She lifted her shoulders—she felt like a genuine undercover agent. Douglas would be proud. But why had she had no word from him? Still, she trusted him completely, and she knew that Scotland Yard was the best police force in the world. She did not want to think about some of the things she had read about art theft, how ninety percent of paintings stolen were never found. That Isabel Gardiner Museum in Boston—just a small museum with several really precious paintings—no one had ever recovered the postage-sized self-portrait of Rembrandt or the rare Vermeer. But that was a small museum with nothing like the security of the National Gallery. Douglas was surely only a few steps behind, she comforted herself. Even the London metro cops on the beat were known for their skill in keeping order. And usually without violence, even in the face of IRA threats.

"Where do we go from here?" Ellen asked as they reached the top of the gangplank.

The lines around Mark's eyes crinkled as he smiled. "Now the fun part. We shall just enjoy ourselves on the ferry tonight. French food, you know. You won't be able to know you are not at Willapark with the French chef."

"But then what? Do you want to come to my cabin and see the painting?"

"Of course I want to see your etchings," he laughed at the old joke, "but I shall do that later when we have our meeting before we go our separate ways—you and Ackman and I. That is, you and I will go one way and Ackman another. And there is also a new person boarding now that I want you to meet."

Mark guided her to the left with the crowd at the top of the gangplank, but naturally neither tried to stand along the upper deck to wave to well-wishers left behind. As she brushed by a large woman with multiple bundles, an unpleasant odor of female perspiration assailed her. The mingled smells of people in crowds always bothered her, often more pungent to her in England or Europe than when she was at home—both more perspiration and more French perfume, along with the smells here on the ship of sea and wood and damp. Although sometimes unpleasant, it added to the sense of adventure, with an edge of anxiety.

Why anxiety? she wondered. The obvious, of course: traveling with criminals she could not trust. Here she was with a strange thief, about to leave the familiar shores of Britain, almost a home to her, for the exotic French mainland. They would land in a small town in Normandy; she had forgotten its name already, but she began to be nervous again. She would be increasingly far from Cornwall and perhaps from Douglas, who was fast becoming almost a heroic figure to her—a personal rescuer.

She knew so little about what was going to happen next. That was part of their plan, of course. If she had bolted, she would only be able to alert the police to the *Normandy* ferry. She knew that in complicated sting operations often the tasks and the knowledge of details was divided among the actors in the hope that, if anyone were caught, he would not be able to give the police enough information to catch the others. By now she and Mark had reached the set of elevators or lifts on the deck. She walked in and said over her shoulder: "Cabin 4C, C deck."

Ellen watched him take note of the numbers as he stood outside the elevator door. "I'll meet you for some dinner in the alternative restaurant. I think they call it the Casablanca Room," Mark said. "Isn't that romantic? There is no formal setting on these ferries, anyway." He grinned. "This is not the glamorous way."

She nodded and pushed the button for C deck. Was this the way sophisticated thieves behaved? She found herself a little disappointed. It did not seem much like the movies. *Why not room service where we could talk? But after all, this is only a ferry, not an ocean liner,* Ellen reminded herself. Also, it was possible that Mark was not very far up the line of the hierarchy. Certainly not as important as Sir John at the country house, and perhaps not as deep into the action as the French curator she had met in London when they kidnapped her. After all, the people who did the dirty work, the actual thieving or kidnapping, were low on the scale of things. The head people wanted to pretend this was simply redistribution of valuable art objects—to people who really deserved to have them. People of taste and judgment. Ultimate snobbery, of course.

About two hours later the three men came to her cabin. She and Mark had already met and eaten French onion soup and a fish salad in the bistro—not her idea of a real meal, but adequate. The other two had not been there. She was glad she had brought some health bars in her luggage. The small cabin now was crowded with the four people. She was the one being treated. The others would sit up overnight in the large lounge. Two of the men sat on the lower bunk, and Ellen perched on the only small chair. Mark stood, leaning against the built-in bureau, twirling a short string with a key. Ellen looked around at the men, trying not to stare or smile. She felt as if she were in an old Alec Guinness movie with a rag-tag group of thieves. She associated herself with the professor, while the other three were a disparate group: Mark, the oldest man, lean and hard still from his life in the British Navy but now with a shock of white hair falling over his face and his gray suit somewhat worn and rumpled; Ackman, handsome and dark but somehow showing in his face the brutality he was capable of. The third man was unusually slight, about five three with long thin arms dangling from an oversized t-shirt with Tower of London stamped on it, a pathetic version of Peter Lorre. And she, though she had washed her face carefully, still with traces of the eye makeup that made her look exotic. She scratched her head briefly, happy to be free of the black wig.

"Where next?" said Mark. "I am sure we are all eager to know our assignments."

Ellen nodded, suddenly afraid. Now she was in the midst of it all, one of the gang of thieves. Where was Douglas? Would she ever get back to normal life, or was she so trapped in the spider web of deception, already guilty of stealing the manuscript and the painting, that she would wind up dead or in prison? Perhaps if she lived through it all and the police caught them and took them back to England, no one would believe her when she said she was working for Scotland Yard. If anything had happened to Douglas, perhaps no one else really knew what she was doing.

"I have a special task for you two," said Mark. "You must meet me at a farmhouse in Provence outside of Arles. We'll talk about it later." He nodded to Ackman and McLaughlin to leave. She smiled, thinking in the gangster speech of her childhood movies: "Get lost, guys." They both muttered a goodbye, looking at her curiously as they let themselves out the cabin door.

Ellen already had figured out she was not going to be informed of the plans for the two men. Perhaps it was just as well, but if things came to a head somewhere soon, she wanted the information for Douglas. Did she dare ask? *Not yet*, she told herself, though she knew that these two were carrying on the criminal, possibly brutal, activities that had become necessary or might become necessary if there were difficulties at some stage.

"As for you, Madam, now that you are a seasoned partner, let us see the painting. Is the door locked?"

Ellen nodded, even as she walked over and tried it. Then she reached into the large bag on the floor of the small closet and pulled out the rolled up canvas. She spread it out carefully on the bureau and felt a shock all through her body at the sight of the face of that evil king among the onlookers. Human greed, human aggression. An emblem of the group surrounding her. *Cutting it out of the frame must have lowered the value of the painting itself,* she worried, hoping it could be restored when returned. *It would be returned,* she tried to reassure herself.

"You will be glad to know that you are going with me to the buyer. He lives in partial retreat in the south of France. We are making a somewhat roundabout journey from the North, but when we reach Paris, we shall take the fast luxury train to Aix-en-Provence. We want to make it difficult for anyone to follow us. The buyer lives just outside Aix. We'll spend one night in Mont-St.Michel, as if we were legitimate tourists, in case anyone is tracking us, then on to Paris to catch the train for Aix. We may also spend one night if we don't make the train."

"I've never been anywhere in France except Paris." She was almost excited by the idea of Provence. Aix was the major small city in the South, which she had never explored. Real artists had come from there: Cezanne, for instance. Wasn't it also where Van Gogh had been in an institution? No, that was in a small town nearby, she remembered. She had read somewhere he had done most of his best paintings there, where a doctor had been particularly helpful. The doctor had given the artist freedom from confinement in a small room to go out into the grounds and paint outside.

"And you, Mark. Have you been there often? Do you do this kind of caper often? Every six months or so? Did you know my husband James?" She tried to keep her voice from rising.

Mark walked towards her, slightly smiling. "As a matter of fact, Ellen, I did. I helped him take at least three manuscripts to the buyers in Europe."

"But I thought Ackman was ordinarily the courier."

Mark's expression was serious. "Where did you hear that?"

Ellen shrugged. "I don't know. I must have picked it up from him."

"I doubt that." He looked at her calculatingly. "Perhaps one of your Scotland Yard friends," his voice rose towards a question. He held the painting up to the light. "I hope you did not take a great deal away from the value by cutting the painting out of the frame. I admire the skill Breughel showed in portraying this king; his expression is so real. The baby is totally expressionless. Christianity is so much more bland than human nature."

"It is always easier to portray the darkness in the world," Ellen could not resist saying as he handed her the canvas.

Mark seemed to soften. "Let's go to the bar for a nightcap, and I'll fill you in on my dark past—not all of it, but a sketch."

"All right—I admit I am curious." Ellen picked up her stole and purse, but first she rolled up the painting again and put it in the small closet. Mark opened the door and stood there. *After all*, she thought, *it is only about nine, and I might learn something useful.* Not that anything was useful about James now, but she must garner as much as she could for Douglas and Scotland Yard.

As they took the elevator and then walked along the outer deck to the Lighthouse Bar, she felt his hand under her arm and wondered. The wind from the North Atlantic was cold, and Ellen pulled her woolen stole closer. She wondered if she and Mark were becoming in some sense intimate in this common enterprise? Minutes later, at the small table in the dim room, she saw him looking at her with something like interest—not just the calculation she had seen before. She smoothed her hair automatically and then mentally chastised herself. The habit of a lifetime, part of the animal nature to preen before the male of the species. She had always been a watcher of birds and recognized the behavior in herself. More dangerous was listening to his story and becoming interested in him as a person—this man who belonged to a ring of international thieves. She looked up to see the waitress approaching.

"A glass of white wine with ice." She knew she needed to keep her wits about her with some form of spritzer.

"A small brandy," said Mark to the middle-aged barmaid. "I am more careful of drinking too much since I have lived alone, but it is a pleasure to have someone to be with for a nightcap." He smiled warmly.

Ellen nodded. "I know what you mean." No French restaurant worthy of its name would have waitresses instead of waiters. Did the same apply to the bar on a ferry? Ellen was not sure, never having traveled this way before.

"You know of course about the loss of my wife. I am known in Tintagel for my long period of mourning. And of course I miss her—Alice. She was a lovely woman who kept the home fires burning all those years when I spent most of my time at sea, first in the Royal Navy and later when I fished with the two skippers in local waters. I went in about the beginning of World War II. I was only about fifteen. We were students together and married when we reached nineteen. And we were as happy as people can be who don't have children, a real family. She was always loyal, and I was most of the time. But no, I was not overwhelmed by grief when she died after a long illness. I was glad she was out of pain, and I was happy to be free for something like this job. A bit of adventure.

"The stories I told around town about my loneliness were only partly true and in the last three years have become something of a cover that allows me to come and go between Oxford, London, and Bosinney whenever there are jobs to do. They are not regular, you know, and small town people always see you going and coming. With me, they think I am so unhappy that I have run up to town for a show or shopping just to have a change."

"Aren't you blowing your cover now with me?" Ellen asked.

"As you say, you are now a partner. I know things about you just as damaging—more so. I have not actually committed a theft of a major art work. Besides I know you will go back home after this. We will see to that."

The waitress put their drinks before them. "Anything else?" she inquired. Mark shook his head, and she moved away.

Ellen wondered why he was telling her about his wife, probably to clear the ground for seduction. She needed to protect herself from that. Or perhaps he just needed to tell the truth for a change. He was an attractive man. She knew she would have liked him if she had not known he was involved in criminal activity.

"Tell me a bit what you did in the Navy and how you became interested in art theft—or theft of rare books." She smiled and softened her own voice, trying not to show her judgmental side.

"I was always interested in the tales the sailors told in the various ports about smuggling. I never did any myself, but I stored some of the information that came my way, and then after my retirement I celebrated by drinking a little too much in the Morse Bar at the Memorial Hotel in Oxford. From that evening I date my involvement."

"I don't understand."

"I met your husband and admired his adventurous nature. He was alone, and we spent several hours talking about his life—even you, and how you would never understand what he was doing. Perhaps he did not know your love of adventure." He gazed at her shrewdly. "Later a young woman joined us, a student—perhaps he was having a brief fling with her—probably not." Mark's expression changed as he looked at Ellen. She felt her smile freeze at the mention of her husband's disloyalty. She watched him as he tried to backtrack from what he had said.

The conversation went well enough after that, skirting the surface of things as they sat there, but they left the subject of James.

"Why did you do it, though?" she pressed him. "I too feel the lure of adventure, but the risk is terrible. Prison at your age—even at mine—is so scary."

"I guess I don't feel that it is violent crime, in some sense less criminal than most businesses indulge in. Even those huge corporations we read about. Only a few CEOs get caught and sent to some fancy prison for a few years, after piling up money in off-shore accounts. In this business, the buyers are really people of taste and quality—not nearly so vulgar. I know a man in Manhattan who runs an antiquarian business and sells old maps. He gets far more than we do for old books, and he remains a respectable businessman."

"What do you mean? He doesn't steal the maps, does he?"

"I think he does. In fact, he told me once how he managed it at the Beinecke."

"So it does not seem morally wrong to you—more like a clever way of distinguishing yourself from the stodgy community?"

"No, I would not go that far, but I don't really see how anyone gets hurt by it. And I of course benefit from my independent use of intelligence."

"Yes," she said softly, "I am beginning to feel that way myself."

"No, it will be different for you—just one caper, and you will be home free. But I gather you have a life, a profession still and a daughter at home."

"Yes, that is true," she said, wondering if she were lying.

Chapter Twenty

Ellen woke at two-thirty. The dial on the bedside table shone in the dark. Then she heard the knock again. It was not loud, but it set her heart beating. Could it be Ackman again? She shivered at the memory of tape binding her mouth. She had not let herself relive that particular small horror. No, surely not now. She pushed back the warm duvet.

Perhaps it was Mark. He had seemed to be flirting with her in the bar. What did they call that now? Coming on to her—whatever that meant. But surely he would not until after the delivery of the materials. Ellen admitted to herself that she found him attractive in spite of his age. His experience traveling the world gave him a surface, perhaps an ironic edge that she had not glimpsed in men other than James. She calmed herself as she picked up her robe from the foot of the bed.

But no, he would not jeopardize the project. She sensed a firmness at his center, a hierarchy of values that in some odd way she was beginning to trust, even if he were a member of a gang of thieves. It was too important not to disturb the plan at this point. Maybe it was the police at the door, and she would be out of this situation that seemed beyond her control. She groped for her slippers, but when she realized they had slipped under the bed, she moved towards the door.

"Who is it?" she asked, warning herself not to open the door until she knew.

"Your friend," said a familiar Scottish voice.

"Thank God," she breathed, taking off the chain and unlocking the lower lock.

Douglas edged in, bending his head slightly at the small door. She had forgotten how tall he was. He hugged her then, suddenly kissing her on both cheeks, like an Italian. She never know quite how to get her nose out of the way during this salutation Brits had recently seemed to adopt. But she was too glad to see him to mind feeling like a clumsy teenager.

"It's about time!" She tried to cover her emotion with irritation.

"That is a fine welcome, Lass, after all the trouble I have had finding you."

"I sent a message to the answer phone number you left. About the ferry, you know."

"There must have been some lag in the recording. I didn't get the message until almost ferry time, and I drove like a madman to make it to Portsmouth. They have missed the painting at the National, of course, though not the manuscript at the Bodleian."

"No, I did not check it out, just removed it from shelves over the working desks; so if someone hasn't asked for it, it should not be missed until they do a formal check of the shelf. How often they do that, I don't know. So what now?" Ellen suddenly felt herself relax. Now that Douglas was here, perhaps she could stop carrying the anxiety of this role.

"Hold on a bit. I wish I could say let's just fly away, preferably together, but since we have gone this far—or you have—the Metropolitan Police want me to ask if you might go farther. Even see if you can identify some contacts in the den of thieves in Europe. I should of course shadow you as long as it works—and dash to the rescue if it doesn't."

She didn't remind him that he had been absent when she was taken in a car with tape over her mouth to meet the Lord of the Manor. "Yes, I expected this," she said knowing that risk was the name of the game. Now they knew hardly more than when they had started. The others were not even responsible for the thefts so far. She was, and the abductions were only her word against theirs. She would have to uncover more about the identity of the Europeans involved to atone for what James had done. Or even her own guilt in covering up how he died.

But somehow she had an uneasy feeling. Something was not right. For instance, how could Douglas follow them after they arrived in northern France?

"All I know is that we are going to Mont-St.-Michel and then to Paris—to catch a fast train South. To Aix-en-Provence, I think."

"Don't worry." Douglas put his hand on her shoulder. "I'll be just a few steps behind, and you can use the little phone if necessary. Just don't lose it, as they can possibly find the calls you have made. Trust me, I've been a policeman all my life." He did not mention the other consequence of losing the phone, that without it she would have no way of contacting him if she were in danger.

"After all this is over, we shall have some time for ourselves." He smiled, then sighed. "But for now…."

She knew what he meant and steeled herself. "Then I won't see you for a while?" She looked up at him, almost willing him to stay.

"No, it is too dangerous for me even to be here, but I thought you needed to know I was near. By the way, why not give me the painting for safekeeping?"

"No, I can't. I don't dare. Mark might want to see it again, or even to take it himself."

"Yes," Douglas said slowly, "I can see that. Then goodbye." He kissed her again lightly, on one cheek this time.

As she lay in bed, unable to sleep after he had gone, Ellen saw in herself a mixture of feelings. Of course, she was reassured that Douglas had come at last. But somehow she had not really understood where he was all this time. Perhaps they had simply not had enough time to talk. And just how would they meet again? She could not help wondering, even fearing, what would happen to her. Perhaps a shot in the head—she remembered what she had read about the efficiency of assassins. She turned over in the narrow bed, her legs aching a little from the cramped position.

The next thing she saw was a green meadow. She realized even while observing it that she was dreaming. How could she see a meadow when the channel lapped outside her cabin? But no, it was a vast green meadow with a river running through the middle. She remembered her Greek epics—reading about the underworld as she glimpsed Charon poling a large boat down the middle. She waited on the shore until he approached. Was she going to be allowed, like Odysseus and later Aeneas, to journey into the land of the dead?

Perhaps she would even see James and have a chance to walk away, as Dido had shunned Aeneas for his desertion of her. But somehow she sensed that the dream would not stick to the past, that it might hold new information for the terrible situation in which she found herself. The next moment opened almost in a movie frame.

Charon (that was his name—she had never known how to pronounce it, just that he was the ghostly ferryman) approached, his eyes staring like the figures of the dead in horror movies she had occasionally seen. She heard herself moan from a distance as she slept.

"Step into the boat," he said in a perfectly normal voice, and she knew she could not argue. For once, she did not stumble or need help. She simply stepped in, feeling as if her movements were even graceful. *There is something to be said for the dream world*, she told herself even in her sleep. Then the boat glided smoothly along the vast river. Occasionally she heard the sounds of birds, some flying high over them, some singing elaborate bird songs from the shore. Were there animals in the underworld? Certainly they were there in her dream now.

In moments the boat pulled up to a dock. Dream time is not real time—Ellen knew that even then.

"Off here," said the boatman laconically, and she climbed up a few stairs and out. Then she saw him, James. He looked as he had looked when they were married, fresh and young, and she found herself wondering if her own wrinkles were still there, the ones she had noticed around her mouth in the bathroom mirror.

"Oh, Ellen," James frowned at her, "are you dead too?"

"No, I am just dreaming. It is all those times I taught the underworld in the *Odyssey* and the *Aeneid*. "No, I am not dead—not yet." She knew she sounded a little superior.

"Have you forgiven me yet?"

She looked at him then. She was not sure. She was not sure she knew what forgiveness meant. It always had seemed a partial thing. He was certainly handsome with the good looks of youth, though his eyes had dark shadows around them. It was not how he looked, she thought, that was the problem. Nor his charm. He could always turn it on. "How do you feel about your life?"

"It is different here," he said, looking down at his hands, which seemed transparent to her. "Not much time to think. And I can hardly remember the years of teaching dullards."

"I didn't know you felt that way about your students." She looked at him, trying to see beneath the surface.

"Well, it is different here," he repeated. "I've met people I like to talk to."

"Just what do you talk to them about? And by the way, why did you get involved with manuscript thieves?"

Ellen awoke then, before she got an answer. She turned in the bed and sat up. Awake now, she stared out into the dark room. Where had this dream come from? Surely it was all anxiety from the theft and working with the men she did not trust. But now she wondered it she were not still trying to understand what had moved James to his actions—actions from which she was still suffering the consequences. She knew she would never be content until she knew more about how and why he had seemed to change his fundamental nature. She had thought often that he was too rigid, almost too literal in his values. *The branch that does not bend may break.* Perhaps that was what had happened. But how? She wondered still. She could not see how he had rationalized such a crime against the academic community.

Perhaps he had not thought he had lived up to his earlier hopes for success. He was not at Harvard or Yale, after all—not even Madison or the University of Michigan, even with his brilliant brain. A small liberal arts college had not fulfilled his ambition. He would inevitably blame the system. Her mind ran on. She could not get comfortable enough to sleep in the narrow bed. It occurred to her as she tried to straighten the twisted covers that perhaps when James began to deceive her, his own wife, with affairs, he came to feel that there was nothing wrong with deception. Shouldn't she have known?

She had heard teenagers say that it was a lesser thing to steal from institutions than from individuals. She moved her head in irritation at the fallacy involved. She would still try to probe these issues in her conversations with Mark. He must have the whole set of attitudes fresh in mind. But, after all, he was a Navy man, not someone who had spent his whole life identifying with schools and libraries.

She tried to count sheep, then waves that she heard lap against the ferry, then finally the swells she felt as the ship moved across the channel. Ellen was not used to riding the sea like this. She would be happy to arrive on dry land, even in the land of Normandy, not her familiar England nor her American home. Perhaps she was a little homesick. She pushed back the covers then and went to the tiny bathroom to take some Advil. She would need to be alert tomorrow.

"Ellen." She was almost asleep when she heard the knock on the door and the muffled voice. "Ellen, let me in. There's a problem."

"Who is it?" she asked, snatching up her robe.

"It's Mark. Ackman, it's Ackman."

"Mark or Ackman," she asked, standing at the door, "which is it?'

"It's me, Mark. Let me in."

Ellen turned the key, and Mark squeezed in. "Ackman is dead," he said, his dark eyes blazing.

"Ackman dead?" Ellen repeated. Strange. Something was wrong. She sank down on the bed. "Did you two quarrel about something?"

"Of course not!" Mark looked astonished. "Why should we? Our plans were all set."

Ellen sat on the bed, her knees shaking. She should have gone with Douglas, no matter what. This caper was going to be too risky for a woman who was primarily a teacher, a reader of mystery novels, not a professional detective—always too naïve about the dark side of people and the world. How had she imagined she could deceive a group of thieves and trap them for Scotland Yard? But it was too late for regrets now. *I must respond to the situation*, she thought, looking up at Mark's lined and expressive face. She had been through enough in her life to know when she must stiffen her spine and go on. She could see from Mark's expression that he meant what he had said. No, he was genuinely surprised at Ackman's death.

"What now? What do we do?" She deliberately put herself in the same boat with Mark. He was all she had to rely on.

But she was taken back by his answer. "I'm afraid, Ellen, that I must ask you to help me move the body. I have stowed it in my closet for now, but we should carry it to the nearest rail and push it over into the channel. It's wrapped in a blanket."

"Why not the other man, Harry? Why can't he help?"

"I am not sure whether or not he is the murderer." Mark put his hand on her shoulder. "I should not ask if there were any other choice. I know neither you nor I counted on murder. I don't even see why or how it could have happened. His face is smashed in."

Shocked, Ellen stared up at him. "I am not sure I believe it is a necessity, but all right. Wait outside the door for a moment, and I'll dress and come with you. I am not strong, but perhaps we can carry the body in a blanket, if you will let me stop and rest from time to time."

Chapter Twenty-One

Ackman proved to be heavier than they had expected. Of course, they had never wondered what it would be like to carry him. She tried not to think about what she was really doing, helping to carry a corpse. Alive, he had been tall, a little rangy, almost handsome in his dark way. Mark was wiry, however, and strong; and the two of them managed, with frequent rests—every few steps from the cabin to the deck—while Ellen caught her breath. At about four a.m. the two of them struggled to lift the body in the blanket high enough on the rail to push it over. Ellen looked around quickly when the splash sounded down below. They had not met anyone on the way, as the rail was on the deck just outside Mark's cabin.

A few hours later, at about eight, before the landing was announced, the two sat in the bar drinking coffee. Neither had had any sleep, and conversation was desultory. Ellen had a nagging feeling that Douglas might have somehow been involved, but how she could not imagine. Perhaps she should have pretended she had a heart condition that prevented her helping with the body, but she knew that if she were going to penetrate the secrets of the group she had to become closer to Mark.

"Any instructions before we land?" She made an effort to smile and be animated.

"Meet at the foot of the gangway," said Mark quickly. "I'll get a taxi then, and we can dash to the train for Mont-St.-Michel. If we miss the ten o'clock there won't be another until late afternoon."

"Okay. I am packed. I had better go back to the cabin. By the way, any more ideas about Ackman? I noticed the single hole in his temple—very little blood." She dropped her voice at the last sentence.

"Yes, it seemed to be a very professional killing—not that I know much about such things. But who did it, I don't know. It could have been someone not at all involved with us—our group. He was hired because he himself was capable of violence, unlike the rest of us." Mark seemed to study his fingers spread out on the table. "Of course I have known that such things happen from time to time in this process—as in the case of the woman at Willapark, but seeing it first hand makes it too real. There were also rumors of a murder in Oxford that no one has solved. Perhaps I should get out when you do."

Ellen was surprised at the revelation of feeling as she looked at Mark's face, the lines pulling down into an expression of deep sadness. It must be the shock of the death: the dead body itself—having to touch it, to dispose of it. She shuddered at the thought of the wound she had seen, but perhaps more, she suspected, at the feel of the body in the blanket, so heavy, so lifeless. She looked at Mark with something like sympathy. For the first time, he was not simply the Other. Perhaps he had deceived himself long enough about the genteel nature of the crime in which he was involved.

"Maybe you should think about that. Greed can be a powerful motive. But I must go now, or I won't be there for the taxi." Ellen saw him look up at her, then turned and walked away quickly from the small table in the bar. She mustn't get too sympathetic with the thieves. But her thoughts had moved to Ackman. She needed to know more about him. Certainly he had been capable of violence. She had sensed that immediately in the way he had gagged her, maneuvered her body out of her room and later into the car going to the manor house. And did Mark mean he had killed the woman at the hotel? Or someone else in Oxford? Then she remembered Douglas mentioning the Oxford murder. She wished she had asked him more about it.

Maybe she should call Douglas and let him know the latest development. *I will do it from my hotel tonight*, she decided.

* * *

About twenty minutes later she was being handed into a taxi near the foot of the gangplank. Mark had the manners of his generation. The drivers seemed to have a rank there almost too close to the large ship, but it was convenient for the luggage that had been piled near the foot of the gangplank by the ship's stewards. Ellen glanced around as Mark got into the car beside her. She knew she would not see Douglas, but she could not help hoping she might glimpse him nearby. Of course she did not.

The taxi went directly to the train station, and almost before she could grasp the change in scenery from Cornwall, Oxford, or London and react to the Frenchness of the town, they were en route to Mont-St.-Michel. The train was speeding through the countryside, which seemed to her only subtly different from England. Perhaps all of Northern Europe shared flora and fauna. But she knew that the colder country of Normandy must make some differences that she was not seeing this time of year.

Mark was dozing beside her. She could get off the train now and go straight back to Cornwall, but she knew she would not. No, she was in too deep, and besides she wanted to know what would happen. It was almost as if she were coming to life again. She had been nearly frozen for a long time, and now she was beginning to thaw, as she had a special job to do. Since she was betrayed and abandoned by James, she had felt as if she had little purpose. Even the teaching had not been what it once was.

She looked over at Mark and saw that his mouth was open. She still did not know all the details about Ackman. *Only children are beautiful when asleep*, she thought, and then a tug of what she might have termed tenderness pulled at her. She straightened the overcoat that lay over him, sat back and closed her own eyes. It would be at least an hour before they could arrive at the station in the small town across from Mont-St.-Michel.

Almost immediately she opened her eyes again, still a little too excited to sleep. Or perhaps the door of the compartment opening quietly alerted her. Douglas's head was visible now, with a finger across his lips. She got up and went out the door as silently as she could into the aisle outside. The train had gathered speed and was rocking along the rails. She braced against the inner wall.

"Come down nearer the door between the cars," Douglas said softly.

She followed him, looking back now and then to see if Mark were behind her, but the aisle was comfortably clear so far. When they reached the door that led out into the space between the cars, Douglas held the door for her, and they both stepped out onto the sheltered space. The noise of the train was almost deafening there. Douglas gestured for her to go ahead into the next car.

"Why are you taking this chance?" she asked.

"Because I know about Ackman." He looked down at her.

"Yes, I did not bargain for being involved in a murder. Tell me about the

Oxford murder—was he involved? I am an accessory now, since I helped dump the body over the rail of the ferry."

Douglas grasped her shoulder gently. "I know. Don't worry. We shall get you clear of it all when it is over."

"I should go back now in case he wakes up."

"Yes, but I shall contact you in Paris. Unless you want to leave now and just take a flight back to the States? Anyone would understand."

"No." She looked at his worried blue eyes. "I'll go through this as far as I can get. I owe it to libraries where I have done research."

"I know you feel that way, but you are not responsible for your irresponsible husband." Douglas shook his head, impatient at James even now.

"Right. I'll try to talk myself out of it. Just think I am doing it for England, my adopted country." She moved then quickly—to go back to the compartment before she changed her mind.

As she entered the small door, Mark stirred and opened his eyes. "Where have you been?"

"To wash up," she said delicately. "Did you have a good nap?"

"Oh yes," he said, "though I dreamed about Ackman."

"Did you learn anything from your dream?"

"Yes, I think so. I think I know who killed him. It was one of your people, that inspector you know."

Ellen almost laughed. "How absurd," she said. "He isn't even around. How was he in your dream?"

"All I know is that I have seen him recently, on the ferry, perhaps also at the dock. His face was there in my dream, incredibly distorted by anger."

"Did you meet him at the hotel when he was investigating the murder?"

"Yes, he questioned me, as did that woman they sent down from London." Mark rubbed his face. "I am so tired. Last night's caper took it out of me. As I said, maybe I shall stop with this one." He looked down at his watch. "I think we get into Mont-St.-Michel soon. About twenty minutes. I still can't imagine who killed Ackman, unless it was someone on the other side."

Ellen looked at Mark shrewdly. "It could have been you," she said, knowing it was foolish to reveal her thoughts to him.

Mark opened his eyes wide. "Why would I do that, presuming I was capable of it? I needed him, if for nothing else to keep you in line or to take you places we want you to go without arguing." He chuckled.

"You've got my number. I do argue a lot." She brushed back her bangs and sat up straighter.

Just then the porter came by and put his head in the compartment. "Mont-St.-Michel soon—four minutes." She could manage that much French.

"Thank you," said Ellen, standing to get down her small rolling bag.

"I'll do that." Mark got up. "I am old school, you know." He lifted down both bags, hers and his from the rack over his seat. Then he smiled down at her warmly.

"I know you are too smart not to begin asking yourself questions about Ackman. I'll tell you a little about him. It can't matter now that he is dead. As far as I know, this is the story of Ackman. But let's wait until we get to the hotel and have a drink in the bar."

"Okay." Ellen was curious, but she would wait.

* * *

Mark and Ellen sat across from each other in the bar of the hotel. It turned out to be across from Mont-St.-Michel itself, and the tide had already come in for the evening, water surrounding the causeway. They decided to wait until morning for a quick trip over to the church and the village that had been built at the foot of it; they would not really have time to sightsee, but they both wanted a glimpse of the famous place. Once she had seen a good film about it.

"Now for Ackman," said Mark.

"Yes, you promised me his story. I am a teacher after all. Stories are important to me. They are the way I approach life."

"I don't really understand that, but as I get older I find myself more interested in biography. Ackman has a particularly indicative biography. You know, of course, that he was from Iraq, trained by Saddam's special forces. But he got into trouble with a colonel in his division and was about to be demoted, maybe even executed, and he had met one of the members of our group, who smuggled him out of the Middle East into Italy."

"No, I did not know that, though he looked Middle Eastern, and I noticed he wore an Islamic symbol on his ID bracelet."

"Yes, he was a serious Muslim, I suppose, though he did not pray five times a day facing Mecca the way my Turkish friend does. Anyway, we recruited him, as I told you, for his special skills—military skills or police skills that would help him take someone like you prisoner or even shoot our way out of some attempt by the police to capture us or our stolen goods.

"But obviously that was not a frequent occurrence—neither situation, so we gave him a courier job for his day job, so to speak. He was not especially happy with the arrangement, I gather. He even said to me once that he resented not getting paid as much as those who lifted the art works, but I reminded him that he had not had the education or the class training to get by with the thefts."

"I am sure it did not make him happy to hear that."

"No." Mark rubbed his hand lightly over his face, remembering the discussion. "He almost hit me when I mentioned those things. Sore point, I suppose."

"I should imagine he might get a bonus if he had to do anything dangerous or violent?"

Mark looked at her, raised his eyebrow. "Do you mean like killing the woman in the Willapark? Or kidnapping you? I am not sure really. I do not handle the payroll. Sir John would know. I think Ackman always felt like an outsider, but he and I had a few conversations late at night. That is how I heard at least part of his story."

"But do you know why he was killed?" Ellen leaned forward.

"Not really, but I can speculate. I think it really started about three years ago when he came to me about James. I remember it vividly. He stood at the Morse Bar in Oxford. James had just left. I don't know why—perhaps I heard him say he was meeting someone. But Ackman was full of admiration for the American professor. He turned to me suddenly and said, 'We need more like him in our group.' He never called us a gang or any word that would suggest we were outside the law. He was careful that way."

"Why did he admire him?" I was puzzled. "The two men seemed so different to me. Perhaps that was the attraction."

"Yes, that was partly it. But on a deeper level, your husband was both elegant and kind to those on a lesser social level. Englishmen tend to be snobs, even the most liberal ones politically."

"But I thought they were much less racist than Americans tend to be—"

"Oh, yes, but class is more important to Brits, and Ackman was after all largely uneducated except for the military skills he had. But James treated him like a colleague."

"I see," said Ellen, thinking more kindly of her husband, in spite of the many flaws he had revealed before his death.

"Ackman had a terrible time within the group, both in England and in parts of Europe, because he was in most ways so crude and also because most of us did not want to face the more brutal and violent side of what we were doing. Just let me tell you a story that illustrates why he was so delighted—even changed—when James took him up, almost as a friend."

"Okay, though I need to go to bed soon if we are to take a quick trip to the mountain in the morning. Would you like another brandy? My treat."

"No, I have had enough. And the story is not long." Mark smiled at her. "You look lovely this evening in that deep blue."

Chapter Twenty-Two

Mark took off his glasses and rubbed his eyes. "I too am tired, but about Ackman. When he first came to us, he barely knew English. Perhaps that explains in some sense why most of our people condescended to him. But he was bright enough, and he seemed to have a feel for the job, for people who were collectors. He knew what it was to really want things. He grew up in straightened circumstances, like most Iraqi. Though of course most of our collectors have everything from his point of view, they are really obsessed with a few beautiful things—or perhaps even with the glamorous value of them."

"I have often wondered about their motivation—even James, wanting to make money that particular way. But of course, like most people, making more money was hard. He had more or less reached the top of his salary scale."

"Anyway, we all knew the first time he had to kill someone for the group. It was a case where he was supposed to meet someone outside a museum who was stealing a really valuable manuscript. One of the guards had come in pursuit, and Ackman was waiting outside the door. He simply took out a gun and shot him three times in the face. Then he took the frightened thief to a hiding place near the docks in London and called me to meet them there."

"That made you an accessory, I suppose, from a legal point of view."

"Yes. Somehow I did not think about it at the time, but you are right. If I ever get caught by the police, I shall have to face that."

Nothing was ever as simple as she had thought growing up, but this group of thieves was especially complex. She could not really think of Mark as a murderer, but he had tolerated it all for the sake of the exciting business of stealing books and art, things that were rare and valuable; and her own husband must have known more about it all than just his theft of rare books and manuscripts. Perhaps if she remained part of the group for long enough, her own clear morality would erode. After all, she had already stolen a painting and helped cover up the murder of Ackman.

Mark rubbed his eyes. "We'll talk tomorrow," he said. "Perhaps you will see how Ackman got himself in trouble with some rough characters from other groups who were interested in the same things we are. I think his murder was a crime of vengeance from some people he was friends with as a courier but whom he managed to move in on later when he was solid with us. Perhaps it had to do with that guard he killed or even the woman in the Willapark."

A few minutes later she was in her room in the small hotel. From her postage-stamp balcony she could see the lights of Mont-St.-Michel across the causeway. A few cars were still coming across, and in the moonlight she could see the dark water that was everywhere except for the narrow causeway. How many tourists and even pilgrims had come this way in all these years? She would have to find out more about the history. She would get a guidebook when they took their walk in the morning. Just now, for her, the mountain that rose in front of her seemed an emblem of human beings reaching up towards the truth, perhaps never reaching far enough. Mostly like sheep, they bunched together in herds, often unable to recognize their true shepherds. She knew that there was a gold statue of St. Michael on top, the chief warrior against Satan. Warfare seemed a curious out-of-date symbol for the way to discovery. Her own adventure seemed somehow part of that.

Ellen shivered slightly as she went back into the room from the outside. It was cooler than she had realized. She was uncomfortable about what tomorrow would bring. She could not help wanting to get on with it—to take the painting to the buyer as soon as possible. She slipped off the long dress she had worn to the bar, feeling its red silk with pleasure as she hung it in the small wardrobe. Then, as she turned around in her bra and panties, reaching for her nightgown, she had an odd feeling that she was being watched. Ellen shook her head slightly, as if to slough off the feeling. She felt sure she had locked the door, but could someone have slipped in before she returned from her drink with Mark? And who could it be?

As if in answer to her unspoken question, a deep voice said, "It's me, Ellen. Don't be afraid." And she recognized the slight Scottish burr. She picked up the navy satin robe that lay beside the gown.

"Thank goodness, Douglas. I felt there was someone here. How did you get here? How did you get in the room?"

Douglas laughed, his voice slurred, "I was on the train—remember? The same way you got here. I told the hotel maid who was outside with her cleaning cart that I was your husband. Actually I had a nice nap on your bed. I hope you don't mind."

"Of course not." She felt calmer now. "Why didn't you speak to me when I first came in?"

"Perhaps because I liked watching you." He walked over to her, and she could smell the scotch. "You know, don't you, that I am already a little in love with you?"

For some reason Ellen felt uncomfortable, although she had already explored some of her own feelings for the man. They had agreed at one point to leave anything personal until the situation was different. Douglas had had too much to drink. He reached out with both hands and held her face between them, and she was conscious of freezing slightly. Then he moved his right hand down slowly and undid the satin loop of the belt of her robe, and the warmth spread through her as her eyes closed and she felt his lips move down to hers. *What the hell*, she mused. She knew well enough that life was short.

* * *

She woke with the first light, and she was alone in her bed. The sheets were thrown back on the other side, as if Douglas had sprung up in the night and left. She stretched her legs, her body warm and comfortable after love. She felt a little foolish, as she had known she would. She had been married for so many years that she had never had a really casual affair. She had grown up before girls like herself would do such things, or maybe it was because of the community she came from. And what did she really know about Douglas? When she was young, she had needed to know someone for a long time before he became her lover.

When she rose to bathe and dress, she looked in the closet to check the bag in which she had secreted the painting. It was not there. Sudden adrenalin, and she searched frantically. No, it was not there. *Naiveté again*, she thought. She had believed she had learned her lesson with James, but obviously not, unless there was some emergency for which Douglas had taken the painting. But why had he not told her, if that was the situation?

Sudden tears of anger filled her eyes. Not again. Trust undermining intelligence. What would she tell Mark? Perhaps she should wait until Aix-en-Provence to reveal that the painting was missing. But that was risky, of course.

Ellen went into the bathroom. And what did this mean? How was Douglas involved? Did he perhaps plan to take the painting to the National Gallery and have her picked up by the international police? Or did he have a buyer—perhaps in the group that had killed Ackman? She decided to give herself a little time. It was just barely possible that he had taken the painting to protect her—especially to protect her from deeper involvement with the workings of the gang

By ten o'clock, Mark and Ellen had made a quick trip to Mont-St.-Michel and were heading for the train to Paris. They really only saw some of the village at the bottom of the mountain, as they needed to hurry back across the causeway. She had wanted to go to the chapel near the top, to see some of the religious paintings there, but their schedule limited them to what was largely commercial, except for a breathtaking few moments when they were able to walk out and see the view from about one-third of the way up the mountain. From there they had seen the town across the causeway, the causeway itself, and even though it was morning some of the water lay in pools and suggested what it looked like at night, when all that mysterious tide had come in to surround the mountain, making it once again an old fortress with golden St. Michael guarding it from the top.

Another train trip—the daily train that left at 11:00 from the small village for Paris. This was the beginning of getting the painting to the buyer and undoubtedly involved meeting other members of the gang. For a moment, fear and excitement mingled in her sense of anticipation. Mark left her in the back of the taxi with their bags while he ran into the station house for tickets. She had stopped smoking years ago, but suddenly the stress made her want to light a cigarette.

Think of something else, she told herself. *Try imagining one of your favorite places of retreat or renewal.* She rather liked that technique of pop psychology. She heard him before she saw him. Douglas was reaching into the taxi.

"Come with me right now. No, leave your stuff in the taxi." Douglas took her arm and almost pulled her out of the car. "We have to hurry. Someone dangerous has spotted us."

They were running towards town as Mark came out of the train station. Ellen had a moment of regret as she thought of him finding the cab empty and their luggage still sitting there. She recognized that she had come to feel that he was almost a friend. Her adventure was starting a new phase, she knew, and perhaps it was better to be with Douglas, but at the back of her mind her questions about the painting were nagging her. Something had changed about her feelings for Douglas. She was torn between feeling that possibly the sleeping together had drawn them closer and her worries about the missing painting. There had been something missing from the lovemaking, perhaps love itself.

Douglas opened the door of a Rover there on the little street outside the pharmacy. "Get in. I rented this for us, and we shall drive back to the ferry dock on the French side. I hope we can lose the man I am sure was Ackman's killer."

"I want to hear that story. How did you know him?" She rubbed her forehead, knowing she must learn the answers to other questions first. "But for now, what about the buyer for the manuscript and the painting? Information will dry up if we don't continue with the agreed-upon plan. We'll get no further with trying to break the ring of thieves."

"Some chances are not worth taking." Douglas glanced at her out of the corner of his eye as he drove. "I could never forgive myself if I got you killed."

"I was not sure you cared when I discovered you had taken the painting." Ellen knew she had to be honest with him at this point.

"I know. I started to wake you, but I thought it was safer for you that it should just disappear. I needed to get it back to the National Gallery as soon as possible. The upper brass had begun to worry; not everyone had thought we should stage such a coup."

Who were the "brass," and who had objected to the original plan? The explanation seemed a little lame. Why could he not have confided in her? But she would say nothing now. Perhaps they could talk on the ferry back.

The car was stopped at a crossroads, and the silence was uncomfortable, at least for Ellen. "What time does the ferry leave?" she asked.

"Nine tonight. We shall make it if nothing delays us. Of course, it takes longer by car. I am hoping the guy who is following us is trailing after Mark now."

"What do you think Mark will do after finding me gone?" Ellen rubbed her eyes. She seemed allergic to much of the France she had seen. She was glad to be going back to England, almost sorry not to be heading for home.

* * *

At ten o'clock that night the ferry had sailed, and she and Douglas were in their separate cabins, both exhausted from the tense travel by car. As if by common consent, whatever romance had existed between them was to be postponed. There had been no sign of the man who was following them. Who could he be? What had been his connection with Ackman? That was the last thought Ellen had before sleeping. Sleep was what she needed.

But not the dream that came. This dreaming was getting to be a habit, and she knew even in her dream state that she would wake up tired and anxious. She saw herself in green, the whole scene suffused in light and dark greens, perhaps the symbolic tones suggesting how happy she was to be going back to the lushness of the English countryside. But during the dream, she just caught her breath at the wonderful shades of green. Then she realized she was walking in a patch of woods. At first she did not know whether it was Cornwall or Oxford. Then a stranger came along who said, "Hey, lady, this is Wytham Woods. From the top of the path you will see all of Oxford." He pointed sweepingly towards the top of the hill, his peculiar shirt with pointed sleeves almost like that of a medieval jester. When she reached the top of the hill, however, and the beginning of the Pilgrim's Way where centuries ago pilgrims had journeyed, instead of Oxford stretching out beneath, all the branches of the old trees joined as in a dense canopy and blocked out sky and view—so much so that she stumbled. When she looked down, she saw she had stumbled on a palette knife covered with blood.

She woke up suddenly, her nightgown twisted. She was frightened for a moment as she looked around the dim room. Although she struggled to separate dream from waking, something of the fear remained. Ellen felt her heart beat more rapidly in her chest, as if she had been running or climbing the hill of her dream. *Breathe more deeply,* she told herself, *and concentrate on thinking, not just reacting to the dream.*

The day had been more than she could easily absorb, and there were still loose ends. She told herself that, when morning came and she met Douglas for breakfast, she needed to get some things straight. She tried to order the scenario. Like a film director, she wanted to have the stories of what had happened to her in the last week in an orderly sequence. *As an English teacher,* she reminded herself, *I am a story teller; and now, for almost the first time in my life, I have lived an intensely concentrated adventure directly—no looking on or looking back. No telling a tale from a distance.* She had been smack in the middle.

Starting where? she asked herself. It calmed her somewhat to plan the questions she must ask Douglas. Maybe she needed to write them down, like a lecture outline, so that she would remember to stay on track. She had not realized how timid she was, how used to an orderly rational existence based on familiar values, even familiar experiences. She was a grownup in her research and teaching, but she had been incredibly passive in her personal life. How could she think she could metamorphose into a double agent, a Scotland Yard detective and a clever thief, overnight? The shock of James, his betrayal, his secrets, his death—all those things had changed her. They had made her realize that she was an old-fashioned dependent woman. She had not been able to ask the rational questions about their relationship. Denial, that is what some would call it.

People were right: most teachers were protected. Teachers were different animals from detectives or double agents, even though her highly developed imagination had helped her enter both those worlds. As she thought about it, she felt a little disappointed she would not get to see Provence—at least Aix-en-Provence, where Cezanne had grown up. And what had happened to her idea that she was starting a whole new career? She would have to rethink. Clearly.

Perhaps she had been wrong to get involved. She had not been able to prevent any crimes, that was certain. She herself had been kidnapped. She had stolen a manuscript and a painting. She had foolishly thought of herself as Scotland Yard. And why? Only upon the word of Douglas. Since then, she had been kidnapped twice and committed a major crime herself. She was shocked to realize that she had not even asked to talk to anyone else in the official world.

Then she heard the door handle turn. She looked through half-closed eyes at the shadow standing in the door. She feigned sleep and also tried to recognize the face, but there was no light on it. Remembering the knife in her dream, she almost held her breath, hoping he would simply close the door and leave.

Chapter Twenty-Three

In the eternal moment of the door opening in that silent and ominous way, Ellen breathed lightly. She had an odd sensation that many things were rushing through her mind in mere seconds. The sense of movement ended in a revelation that she did not know enough to figure out what to do now. All her life as a teacher she had been a researcher, but now she knew that in this particular set of circumstances she had not asked the right questions. That was why her thinking had remained unfocused and her heart was beating so rapidly. The newness of the situations in which she found herself had caused her to postpone too many questions. Unfortunately. Now perhaps it was too late, but she promised herself that, if she lived through the next few minutes, she would be more systematic. She must submerge her shyness, even her womanhood. Like Poirot, she must use the considerable gray cells that were hers.

The shadow at the door moved in quietly and shut the door behind himself. Yes, it seemed to be a man in a long trenchcoat. But perhaps not. Ellen tried to lie as still as possible, to breathe as if she were in a deep sleep. She was glad she had not confronted the visitor when she heard him go to the closet, put something inside, and move quickly back to the door and out again. The risk had been that he might have walked to the bed and killed her. She shuddered as she thought of bloody knives or even a swift bullet to the brain.

For a few seconds she listened for returning steps, then rose from the bed and went to the closet. As it was too dark to see, she doubled back to the bedside table and turned on the small amethyst-colored lamp. When her eyes adjusted, she saw into the closet from the door she had left open a moment before. There was a small plastic bag on the floor inside the closet. She picked it up gingerly, always leery of bacteria. Her mother had done too good a job when Ellen was little with all those hand-washing warnings.

When she pulled open the plastic bag, the smell wafted out in an aggressive stench. Blood, stale blood. Ellen peered into the bag then closed it. Was it the dagger of her dream? No, but it was a small bloody hammer. Why would someone put it in her closet? Someone must be trying to frame her. Who could it have been? She slid the extra dead bolt on her door. She had forgotten that previously. Ordinarily, she would have gone to Douglas's room and shared the frightening information, but somehow she knew she wanted to keep it to herself until she figured some things out. She hid the little bag in the secret pocket of her suitcase. But Douglas…. "Douglas"—she spoke his name aloud. He was not what he had seemed. He still had not even told her where they would go when they landed in England.

* * *

The next night she sat in the Willapark in the bar after a sumptuous dinner of roast lamb and tiny potatoes with a rich brown sauce. Even the vegetables were elegant—the usual peas, but more interestingly, fresh small asparagus perfectly cooked, still keeping its shape. It was almost as if she had been transported back to her first night in Cornwall. Except, of course, there were different people sitting there now, and Mark was not among them. When the ferry landed, both she and Douglas had gone to London, where he put her on the train for Bodmin Parkway and Cornwall. John the Cornish taxi driver met her, to drive her to Bosinney. He asked her if she had enjoyed her time in Oxford and her trip to France.

She saw that there would be no awkward questions. Douglas had passed the story around earlier of her unexpected travel. She would find out the details later, but so far she did not think there would be any need for elaborate explanation on her part. She was covered. Now she looked around the bar. She did not know anyone there well enough to have to explain. Yes, there were two or three people from the time she had been there earlier. She searched her mind for the information she had gathered after the woman was murdered. There had indeed been at least two couples who were staying longer than the usual two or three nights—one from Devon, the Loftons, she remembered vaguely. The other couple's name she was still groping for.

Rick came up to her with a small glass of Benedictine. "This is a welcome-back drink," he smiled, his dark moustache turning up slightly.

"Telephone—you have a call, Mrs. Adams," Lisa, his wife, interrupted. "You can take it at Rick's desk in the hall if you wish."

Ellen got up from the soft green wingback, putting down her untouched drink.

"It's me, Mark." The deep voice was unmistakable on the telephone. "We need to talk."

"I thought you would be here for dinner tonight," Ellen said coolly, as she wondered what she should do to stall him until Douglas came. And all the questions about where she was and what she should be doing at this point crowded into her mind.

"You don't know what you have done—we'll talk about it later, but I can't understand why you disappeared from the taxi. You passed that first test when we did not pick you up outside the Gallery, but you failed this one. I had tickets to Paris."

"Just come over now, and we shall find a place to talk."

"No, we had better meet somewhere else. How about the pub in Tintagel? The Cock-of-the-Walk, next to the tourist information. You can take a walk there without suspicion. But don't leave now. Maybe morning for coffee would be less conspicuous." He seemed curiously indecisive. She agreed that they would meet at ten the next morning.

In minutes, Ellen was back in the bar, and no one really seemed to notice. She wished Douglas would come before morning but doubted that he would. She perked up suddenly as she heard the conversation. People had circled round to the Willapark murder. Who was the woman?

Ellen broke in, "Do they know any more about the woman than they did right after it happened?"

Several people turned towards her, but the Wiley woman with her take-charge manner answered first: "We don't know everything, but we know a bit more. The woman's name was Helene Deschamps."

"The name she gave to us that night before it happened was Marie Deschamps." Ellen frowned. She was puzzled.

"Yes, I know, but no one was sure for a while what was her real name."

"Where did she come from? She seemed ordinary, if beautiful."

"We know she was French. Like her name, though her English was perfect. Someone said her mother was English and she had a sister Marie who married a rich banker."

Ellen shook her head. "But why would anyone murder her? Was it someone in her family? Or did she do something that involved her with criminals?" She hoped to discover if anyone here knew more information about the ring of thieves.

"I am bored with the murder. We never get any further with the subject," a small man who was drinking a large glass of brandy commented slowly. "Let's talk about another subject. How about how Englishmen hate sex?" No one picked up on what he said, so he went back to his drink.

Lisa, perhaps trying to do a hostess change of subject, came out from behind the bar with her sweet sherry. "So what else is new?"

Ellen had an overwhelming desire to tell the story of her adventures. What would they say if they knew she had stolen the Breughel? She smiled to herself, for the first time enjoying the irony of having entered the world of cutthroats and thieves, and said sweetly, courting the notion of herself as a somewhat retiring teacher of middle age, "One of the things I like about England and Cornwall is that not much happens. Or rather, the pace of what happens is slow. What is the recent news on the foot and mouth disease?" Images of dead sheep haunted her. She hoped the international group of scientists had come up with some vaccine or cure.

"The scientists only reinforced the massive killing of sheep that Cornish farmers were resisting. One woman brought her six sheep inside the house to claim them as pets. They were almost human to her. Sheep have been associated with humans since Biblical times, you know."

Ellen envisioned the sad face of the farm woman. Yes, animals were companions to those who spent most of their time feeding them and caring for them. *It is a maternal thing*, she thought, remembering all those years when her daughter was young, almost as if there were a strong ligament—even an umbilical cord—that bound them together even when the child was separate from her body. She never had felt that way about an animal, not even her favorite dog, but she could remember when she had been conscious of where her daughter was all through the day—perhaps not when she was holding forth in the classroom, but always when she was in her office. Or when she remembered that it was nearing mealtime, or when she told herself she had to pick her up at soccer at three and then come back to school for the late afternoon meeting. No wonder the Cornish men had been so threatening about the government ruling that wherever there was a single infection in a group, all the animals had to be brought to various central places throughout Cornwall and Wales to be killed.

It seemed for a few moments as if everyone felt the same way, a kind of grief that sat on their chests and made them silent. *Do we empathize with sheep because we too stray or at best wander around, not knowing our direction?* she wondered.

"Sheep is not a good subject either," said Ellen. "Perhaps it is my bedtime."

She got up and looked around. About eight were gathered there still in the warm room Rick had made into a bar, but she only looked at the dark-haired woman who had seemed so bossy. "Thanks for the evening," Ellen said vaguely as she headed for the stairs. She did not want to go up by herself. Associations with the murder of the French woman were crowding in as she held to the walnut banister. She shook her head slightly. What was it Dylan Thomas had said about blowing the fumes away? He was talking about pipe smoke, she recalled, and a happy Christmas walk in Wales, but she was thinking of the shadows in her own mind, the memories of events that floated around the hotel—the difficulty of getting at truth when there was so much deception.

In spite of those dark thoughts, as she walked up the broad steps to her small room with the rose and aqua wallpaper, Ellen felt as if she had come home in some mysterious way. Maybe she should retire here eventually and spend her old age walking the coast path. Perhaps Rick would rent her a room on a permanent basis. If things continued to go well with Douglas—but she did not want to jump ahead. The sound of the waves was the sound of time passing, time past, blending with the present and the future. What was the future of an undercover agent for Scotland Yard? Perhaps death or ignominy; perhaps a lifetime of hiding out. *But it was a new way*, she told herself. She did not know the possibilities yet. There was something about time as a continuum that created a whole out of all the fragments and disparate experiences, a human sense of continuity.

That wholeness was what she missed in her own life since James had let her know he had gone long ago. For years she had had delusions of connections that did not exist. Now she could hardly believe she was connected to anyone. Her life as a mother was over, only vague connections left as a grandmother.

She walked into the cool rose and aqua room and closed the door, taking care to lock it twice behind her as she shot the extra bolt. Was that new since she had been here last?

Probably, but suppose Douglas came in the middle of the night? He would knock, she knew. She would not take her chances on the murderer. Anyone might have pass keys, but she would think about that tomorrow. And yet she felt as if she had made a conscious decision when she woke again in the middle of the night. The clock glowed 3:30, and someone was knocking softly on the door. She got up, pulling on her robe, but paused before she moved the bolt. "Who is it?" she said softly, longing to crawl back under the duvet.

"It is me, Douglas," he almost whispered. "Get up. We are going to my house." Ellen opened the door then, peering out into the dim hall.

"I'll go into the bathroom while you slip on some clothes, but hurry."

"This is getting to be a habit, waking me in the middle of the night," she said sleepily as she managed to open the drawer and pull out a warm jump suit. It seemed to her it did not matter any more that he would see her in her clingy silk gown, but he went dutifully into the bathroom, and she pulled it over her head and stepped into panties and the velour walking suit, putting an extra sweater around her shoulders. It would be cold out this time of night.

A few minutes later they were in his old gray Rover convertible, the car he kept in Tintagel for his use when he was there. He usually was in Oxford now that he had retired, but he liked to come here whenever he needed to get away. And she believed he felt about the Cornish countryside as she did, that it was a place of peace and retreat.

She jumped as a voice rose from the back seat. "Hello, there, Ellen." Mark laughed a little as he spoke. "You don't get forgiven quickly for dumping me and absconding with the picture."

Ellen looked at Douglas and then away quickly. Apparently he had not said anything to Mark about the painting that he had taken out of her closet on the ferry. She thought quickly; what was Mark doing in the car anyway? "It all happened so fast, Mark. Douglas came up to the car and told me that a very suspicious thug—perhaps someone involved in Ackman's murder—had been spotted following us."

"Yes, Douglas told me that later when he came to Tintagel, but you two could have taken me along. I had a helluva time getting to the ferry when I finally realized you had not just gone in to wash up at the station. The train had left by then, and I had to pay the taxi to race it to the next station."

Something was fishy. Ellen felt it. Surely Douglas and Mark were not linked somehow in this? She vaguely remembered Mark mentioning that he saw an old Rover in the car lot the night of the murder. Could that have been Douglas's Rover? Confused, she decided that she would not say anything else. She did not want to spoil Douglas's game. Let Douglas dig his own grave. But she could not resist asking, "We did not see you on the ferry. Why not?"

"No, I waited until the next day. I had to contact someone."

More mystery. "Where are we going now?"

"To my house—I told you," Douglas answered irritably.

"All right," Ellen said meekly. She would simply be silent until she knew what was going on. The old car sped through the darkness, turning several times until they pulled up before an ungainly frame house. Ellen could not have retraced the path, she worried, uneasy in spite of herself. They all got out of the car. The morning air was chill. The two men together. What was going on?

Douglas unlocked the large front door and gestured to her to enter. Ellen walked into the oak-lined hall, glad that the lights had been left on. At the next door she hesitated. "You should lead the way." She touched Douglas on his upper forearm.

"Just go straight ahead," he answered briskly. He was behaving as if they had never come together in any romantic way. Perhaps he was covering up for Mark's sake. Ellen was almost afraid to speak; she might give away her position as the undercover woman of Scotland Yard—her new profession that she fit so badly. Her euphoria about a new adventure seemed to have evaporated.

Minutes later no one had said anything, but Douglas had gone into an inner study to get drinks. She looked at Mark but said nothing. He was for the moment deep in thought. Ellen looked around the room. Of course the house was not a mansion like Sir John's, but she was pleased to see that the room was both cozy and warm in its décor. A small but bright fire glowed beneath the Adam mantelpiece. Ellen suddenly coveted the green Chinese vase that stood between two silver candlesticks. You would not know from just looking around this room that there was no woman in the house now.

The thought made Ellen flush as fantasy took over her imagination. She put her hand up to her cheek, inwardly chastising herself as Douglas came back into the room and handed drinks around: Scotch for the men, something that looked like lemonade for her. *Learn to act your age*, she reprimanded herself.

"It's time to talk." Douglas looked down into his glass and paused, almost portentously. "This may be something of a shock, but I have a ticket home for you. It all has become too dangerous. Mark has come over to our side, by the way. You will probably be glad to hear that he has furnished information on the network in exchange for immunity. The dumping of Ackman's body, after all, made the two of you accomplices to a murder."

Ellen stood up and walked to the window, looking out into the darkness, playing for time before she answered. Her heart had begun to beat more rapidly at the words. Obviously the personal meant little to Douglas. He was absorbed in the case, so long drawn out and so complex. *That must be it, but perhaps I could come back in six months,* she tried to tell herself. She had underestimated the degree of his seriousness about it. Yes, Mark must have given him all he needed to track down major members of the European group. They would be slowed down anyway with the death of their major courier.

"So you have the painting?"

"Of course. I returned it immediately, but the recovery has not hit the press yet. The upper brass was already distinctly uncomfortable. Pieter Breughel the Elder is too valuable to be stashed in a tube and moved through several countries by public transportation—no insult intended. I am not an art person; I did not think of all the ramifications. Of course, I knew you would try to take the best care possible of the canvas."

"It has survived pretty well for hundreds of years." She spoke dryly, thinking of how important it had seemed to stop the ring of thieves that might be successful in many more robberies of precious stuff. Ellen accepted the sop of praise, but her mind was racing ahead. Why had they approved the theft to begin with? Why had he not consulted them earlier? What was her particular value to the Metropolitan police as an untrained agent? It must have been the connection with James that was a last resort when the group was tightly unified.

Now that Mark had come over... she almost comforted herself that she had had something to do with the change, but probably the main motivation had come from confronting the physical facts of Ackman's murder. Surely originally—even from what he had told her—Mark had deceived himself that the operation of the group was largely a genteel scam, distributing the wealth and beauty of the world.

Ellen turned away from the window, knowing that her rumpled suit and untidy hair were not really pleasing images. She could not use feminine wiles at this point, though she felt the undivided attention of both men: Douglas's eyes bright upon her, Mark's softer brown ones concerned.

"Yes, if you are waiting for my answer. I will go home, but what about my things?"

"I'll take you back to the hotel for them." Douglas smiled at her broadly then. "I knew you would understand—perhaps even be relieved."

"Not really." Ellen looked at him. "I'm a romantic. I thought I was on a new adventure. You made me think I was embarked on a new profession. And I wanted to see Aix-en-Provence and search out Cezanne's childhood. I read somewhere that they have laid stones—you can follow in his steps to school.

"But yes, I am old enough to see when I am not useful. When does the plane leave from Heathrow? Will you drive me or should I call John?" To her surprise her voice was cool.

"Mark and I will drive you. We need to return to London anyway to talk with the police." Douglas smiled then, but without much ease. He too was obviously uncomfortable with the way things had turned out.

"About the painting—has it been re-hung?"

"Not yet; they have sent it to the experts to be sure there is no damage."

The image of the king's face from the painting—evil portrayed so brilliantly in a few lines on that face—loomed into her mind. The three kings of the epiphany. She remembered from the old story that they had gone to Herod to find out where the child was. Somehow that led, she knew, to what Biblical scholars spoke of as the Slaughter of the Innocents. She would like to look at the painting one more time. Perhaps when she came to England next she would go to the National Gallery and really absorb the contents. It was an emblem, after all, of the world and its strange mixture. The painting was meant for leisurely reflection, perhaps meditation, not just the passing glance as one walked through an exhibit.

The vividness of the contrast, the holy babe at the center with the light shining down versus the human faces. The two groups in one space, but the only real intersection the stare of the human at the divine presence. From the most positive point of view, Ellen thought, the wonder of the divine entering the darkness. Once she would have fixed on that as the message, the Incarnation and its miracle. But what was it to become human? The sacrifice of the divine in the mingling was a mystery. The artist showed the human in the visit of the kings—if she were looking at it from the best point of view, perhaps the need of the human, the need of the darkness for the light. But her past ten years had brought her to a more ironic vision: the power of evil, lust, and greed dominated in the world of history.

It would take more faith than she had to think that the light could change it all. And even the embittered Breughel must have felt that the icon pointed forward to the crucifixion. A necessary event perhaps—the human darkness organizing itself to expel the light. Ellen could not move forward from that. Not now when all her plans had failed and she was headed home under mysterious circumstances. "Who did the two murders?" she asked. "And why?"

Douglas looked at her. "Ackman, of course. I am not sure why, though he stole the money intended for the woman in Oxford. It must have had something to do with his sense that he was underpaid and underappreciated as a courier.

As for the woman in the Willowpark, she was sister to your woman on the plane. She had the manuscript you were returning. Ackman was commissioned to get it back and went too far."

Ellen wanted to know more detail, but she would wait, she decided. She watched the men finishing their drinks quickly as they compared notes on the fastest route to Heathrow—almost to London and then a cutoff. They would probably have to go through Exeter, but that was the only big city, and surely the M-whatever had some loop around the city. When Ellen rose to go to the car, a slight dizziness made her sway. Her lemonade had probably had gin or vodka, and she was not used to alcohol, especially this early in the morning.

"I love Cornwall," Mark said as the three walked outside. "It's the pace of life here. I'll be glad to give up these anxious travels without going to prison."

Neither Douglas nor Ellen replied. She did not want to speak of the money that would now not be coming in to supplement his naval retirement. She told herself that Cornwall was a cheap place to live.

As they sped through town in the early morning darkness, Ellen glanced to the side at Douglas's profile. Then she realized he had not turned toward the main road between Bosinney and Tintagel. No, they were headed out of town. Just as she started to ask, they turned into the long driveway and pulled up at the front of Sir John's manor house.

"Why are we stopping?" she asked, feeling the anxiety in her voice.

"Just a brief errand," said Douglas, "but let's all get out. It will be too cold in the car to wait."

Vaguely fearful, Ellen walked ahead of the men. She wondered how Douglas would cover her presence here. The elegant valet answered the door and gestured to them to go into the study, not the drawing room she had been in the last time. The walls were lined with books, and comfortably worn leather chairs were scattered about the room. A sofa was pulled up near the fire and a kneehole desk stood in front of the one window, with various papers stacked on top. Sir John was obviously not fanatically neat. But it was all a comfortable setting she thought, perhaps worth shady dealings to preserve from the tax man.

Sir John came into the room, his dressing gown over pajamas. "To what do I owe this early morning visit?" His voice was scratchy, his courtesy obviously strained.

"I understood you wanted to deal with this undercover agent," Douglas said, steel in his voice.

Ellen felt the blood drain from her face. Here it was, the something wrong she had sensed earlier. Perhaps she would faint, it occurred to her; but somehow consciousness won out, and her mind began to race with the discovery. Douglas—how could it be? He was clearly linked to the ring of thieves. He had killed Ackman—why? *And maybe Helene Deschamps too*, she thought, remembering the old Rover in the car lot. She remembered she had never spoken with anyone else from Scotland Yard. How could she have been so naïve? Well, at least there was nothing to fear. They were simply sending her home. She would think about the deception and betrayal involved later.

"What do you mean?" Ellen interrupted, her voice loud in the silence.

"Dear lady," said Sir John, a contemptuous note in his voice, "surely you did not think you could trick us this way. Our group has survived more sophisticated police work than yours."

"And where exactly do you stand?" She turned towards Douglas, still somehow hoping he would reverse the obvious situation.

"My retirement too seemed very skimpy," he said, looking at her almost regretfully. Then more crisply: "Surely you had your doubts."

Sir John interrupted. "Let's cut this short—I need to get back to bed for a couple more hours' sleep. You should not have brought her here. Take care of it yourself." The lack of specificity was ominous.

Before she could move, Douglas had her by the arm and was almost pulling her towards the front door. In his other hand was a small revolver. Mark was following, and Sir John had sat down in one of the chairs. "Take her into the garden," he said. "There is no one around. You miss Ackman now, don't you? You should never have killed him."

Ellen turned her head towards Douglas. "You are hurting me. But I guess that hardly matters."

His eyes met hers, but they were cold now, perhaps a little desperate, she thought. So Mark had been right; perhaps he had known already about Douglas. They must have worked together before. He was known to him as a fellow thief, not a retired policeman. Yes, of course, a retired policeman, as he himself was a retired Naval officer. But she had not been entirely stupid. He was retired Scotland Yard, but a public servant gone bad. There it was, greed in the world, deception practiced like a profession. She had been right to wonder about what it did to people to tell lies, even in the face of a good ending. Means justified? Not really.

She was almost running now, her small frame struggling to keep up with his long strides.

"Are you going to say anything to me before you kill me?" Ellen played for time. She could not imagine how she could get out of this, but even a few more moments of life seemed worth it. "Don't I deserve to hear the story?"

"I suppose you do," Douglas said, gesturing to her to sit on the stone bench in the garden. "Yes, as you have guessed, I have been in on this all along. But we had not stolen a painting before this, much more valuable and much more difficult to do. When the murder happened at Willapark, we had found the perfect person to try it. We thought we could sacrifice you if you could not do it. If you had been caught, I simply would have denied any connection, whatever you said, and your history—your husband's thefts and death, would have made you suspect—especially once I told them you had been present when he drowned. But you were amazingly successful, and then we had to figure out how to proceed. You know the rest. I have the painting now, and Mark and I are heading for Aix."

"Did you have to pretend you were attracted to me?" Ellen asked angrily.

Douglas did not answer—only raised the gun towards her. "You were very sweet. Any other last words?" he said deliberately.

"Yes, just look at the painting, the image of the wicked king looking towards the child. You are that person, caught in deception and greed, creature of the darkness after a decent life. Is it worth it?" A note of pleading crept into Ellen's voice. She heard herself and stopped. At least she could die with dignity. She closed her eyes.

Then she heard a shot and opened them. She touched her head and then her breast, to reassure herself that she was still alive, and saw that Douglas was falling to the ground in slow motion. Mark was holding both hands and pulling her up then, and they were running to the car.

"I could not stand there and let it happen," he said. "I had my own pistol with me. And what you said about deception helped me know that we can use the truth to face the consequences of all this violence. But quick now. I saw earlier that Douglas had left the keys in the car for a fast getaway."

They clambered in and almost immediately were roaring down the road into the estate, thinking that they had a few minutes before Sir John coped with the body or sent his valet to do it. There were many places to bury a body on the huge estate, much of it virgin forest that now lined the drive on either side.

"I have the airline ticket for you, but I would prefer if you would come with me to Scotland Yard."

"I owe you my life. Of course I will. I shall even plead for you to get off in exchange for information you can give them. But I want you to tell me what you knew about Douglas, too."

Mark looked at her then as the car settled down to the speed limit on the Bodmin road. "You are quite a woman—part of my change of heart," he said wryly. "I wish I had met you a year after my wife died. I should never have gone this direction."

"You almost convince me that human nature has possibilities. When I realized about Douglas, I had lost hope."

"It is surely a dark mixture—human nature, that is," he said as they made their way towards London, the hedgerows almost blocking the morning light.

"I began to feel that I was getting some strange message from the universe in that Breughel painting. It was so insistent in the evil it portrayed. The Christ in the center almost abstract, the emphasis so clearly on what is wrong with the world. Particularly human beings. The appearance of worship, the truth of evil."

Mark looked at her quickly. "You have been hurt by the deception you have known. First James, then Douglas. Only two men, however. The world is full of good people as well."

"Perhaps." Ellen wanted to believe it, but she felt herself changed. More aware of darkness. Still, she knew the feel of sun on her shoulder. Perhaps nature could heal. "And now the day is beginning to break," she said, as they drove over the hill to Bodmin. A few sheep were scattered in the field, perhaps due to go to slaughter that day. Or perhaps not. She would come to terms with all she had experienced later, after she got some rest. But now to London. She was curious about what would happen.

Printed in the United States
97784LV00005B/160-162/A